SURPRISE

Homer thought he heard the whisper of feet behind him, although he knew it wasn't possible—hell, he was hidden up on a roof and no one had seen him climb up that pile of wooden crates at a back corner. He glanced over his shoulder, merely to satisfy himself that it was his imagination.

What he saw made his blood run cold. A towering giant of a man loomed above him, a bloody Arkansas Toothpick in one hand and a pistol in the other.

"Let me guess," Smoke Jensen said, his voice like a horseshoer's rasp across an anvil, grating. "You came up here with that rifle to go bird hunting. I've heard it's a good time of year for whitewing doves."

Homer's heart stopped beating altogether for a moment or two as he heard the deadly tone behind the wisecrack.

"I . . . I was gonna fix a leak in this roof," Homer explained with his voice breaking. "Honest, I was . . ."

In a blinding movement Smoke Jensen's blade penetrated Homer's belly. White-hot pain raced through his chest and abdomen when the blade twisted. Something popped inside him, and it hurt like hell.

"I never met a man who fixed leaky roofs with a rifle an' a bottle of whiskey," the same voice said, as Homer felt himself slipping into a black void.

His eyes closed. Then Homer Suggins began the long sleep.

BOOK YOUR PLACE ON OUR WEBSITE AND MAKE THE READING CONNECTION!

We've created a customized website just for our very special readers, where you can get the inside scoop on everything that's going on with Zebra, Pinnacle and Kensington books.

When you come online, you'll have the exciting opportunity to:

- View covers of upcoming books
- Read sample chapters
- Learn about our future publishing schedule (listed by publication month *and author*)
- Find out when your favorite authors will be visiting a city near you
- Search for and order backlist books from our online catalog
- Check out author bios and background information
- Send e-mail to your favorite authors
- Meet the Kensington staff online
- Join us in weekly chats with authors, readers and other guests
- Get writing guidelines
- AND MUCH MORE!

**Visit our website at
http://www.zebrabooks.com**

PRIDE OF THE MOUNTAIN MAN

William W. Johnstone

Zebra Books
Kensington Publishing Corp.

http://www.zebrabooks.com

ZEBRA BOOKS are published by

Kensington Publishing Corp.
850 Third Avenue
New York, NY 10022

First Printing: December, 1998
10 9 8 7 6 5 4 3 2 1

Printed in the United States of America

Chapter 1

Bill Anderson picked a piece of stringy beef from between his yellowed, broken teeth with the tip of a bowie knife. He sat by a fire on the Kansas Territory prairie, surrounded by his men. These were not ordinary men; travelers, cowhands, or drummers in search of a buyer for their wares. In flickering firelight from a shallow pit dug into flinty soil between endless miles of rolling hills, twenty-nine hard faces watched Anderson as he laid out his plans for a forthcoming raid. These same men had been with him since the end of the war, trusted members of a gang he selected with care, with a purpose. After the collapse of the Confederacy and Lee's surrender at Gettysburg, remnants of a band known across the middle of America as Quantrill's Raiders were left without a cause, without an excuse or a reason for their black deeds, other than simple greed and bloodlust. Bill Anderson had become widely known as "Bloody Bill" for his penchant to draw blood from victims, even those who were utterly defenseless. A trail of bodies marked Bloody Bill Anderson's passage across the states of Missouri and southern Illinois, and territories such as Kansas and Nebraska. Looting, robbing, and taking a terrible toll in human lives, the remaining members of Quantrill's Raiders roamed free as they had during the war, taking whatever they wanted by violence long after the Confederate States of America had ceased to exist, running from the law now and then, a small force of United States Marshals charged with policing vast, empty stretches of the western frontier.

"There's two banks in Dodge City," Bill said, his thick voice commanding the full attention of those around him. "Both're full of cattlemen's money, accordin' to what I've heard. We hit 'em both, hard an' fast, right after they open. Divide up in two parties. Kill every sumbitch we see ridin' in, so folks don't get no crazy ideas 'bout shootin' back if they's got guns. They've got 'em a young City Marshal. Last name's Earp. He's got two or three part-time deputies, mostly farm boys who won't know which end of a gun shoots lead. We strike fast an' hard. Make examples out of them that tries to fight back. Gun 'em down like ducks comin' off a pond . . . turn them dirt streets red an' we won't have no trouble to speak of."

"I hear Dodge can be a tough town, Bill," a voice said from a dark spot beyond the circle of firelight. "Maybe you hadn't oughta figure it'll be that easy."

Bill's pale gray eyes searched for the owner of the voice among the faces he could see. "There ain't no room in this here outfit fer a man who ain't got backbone." Anderson stood up slowly, his gaunt, six-foot frame outlined by what was left of his Confederate uniform, a pair of low-slung pistols tied around his slender waist. "Was that you, Curly? You the one who said that?"

Men backed out of the way until Bill could see Curly Boyd standing by himself at the rear of the group. Curly was from Missouri, a seasoned veteran of dozens of raids despite his youth and poor eyesight requiring spectacles.

"All I said was, it might not be so easy," Curly replied to Bill's question, sensing the danger he'd put himself in with a casual remark.

Bill's lips drew back across his teeth, a twisted grin with no mirth behind it. "You done turned yellow-dog on us, Curly. I got no use for a damn coward . . ." As he spoke, Bill drew one Colt .44 with characteristic speed, a quickness that put fear in the hearts of brave men. "You ain't left me no choice, Curly. I gotta make an example outa you." He aimed for Boyd's head, and for a brief moment some members of the gang wondered if this were only a ploy. Would Bloody Bill actually shoot a member of his own gang?

"You ain't . . . gonna . . . shoot me, Bill?" Curly stammered as the click of a pistol hammer ended a few seconds of silence. "We been together since the war . . ."

The explosion of a .44 slug ripped through the night quiet, Bloody Bill's only answer to Curly Boyd's question.

Curly's head snapped back. The right lens in his wire-rimmed spectacles shattered. His hat flew off, swirling into the night as the force of impact made him stagger backward. Those who were standing close to Curly saw a plug of his curly black hair erupt from the rear of his skull, spiraling like a child's top toward the ground. A spray of dark crimson blood followed the twist of hair and bone fragments away from the back of his head, squirting across his sagging shoulders, running down the back of his shirt, falling like red rain on flinty soil behind him.

"Jesus, Bill," someone muttered softly.

Curly's knees buckled. He sank to the ground as though he meant to pray, blood pumping from the back of his skull, pieces of glass still clinging to the wire loop in front of his right eye socket. Curly remained on his knees a moment, staring up at Bill with his one remaining eyeball.

"How come you got to shoot Curly like that, Bill?" another voice asked from across the fire. "All he said was, Dodge had a real bad reputation as a tough town . . ."

Bill ignored Curly to glance across at the speaker, a tall, whipcord-thin gunman named Tom Hicks, a former artilleryman from Boonesboro, Tennessee.

Bill fired point-blank into Tom's open mouth. The crack of lead striking teeth sounded like snapping green kindling wood in the fleeting aftermath of Anderson's blasting pistol shot.

Hicks fell over on his back, feet kicking, reaching for his mouth with both hands.

"Son of a bitch!" a husky voice said. "Lookee there! Tom's front teeth come plumb out the back of his neck. Two of 'em's layin' there underneath his skullbone. Look, Shorty! Them's two of Tom's busted teeth, sure as snuff makes spit."

"I see 'em," a stocky gunman replied, standing a few feet from Hicks. "I reckon he shoulda kept his mouth shut."

The acrid scent of gunsmoke swept across the fire-pit, a blue cloud carried away by the wind.

"Any more of you sons of bitches got anythin' to say?" Bill asked, sweeping the assembled men with an icy stare. "We's gonna rob them Dodge City banks just like I said. Any man in this here bunch who wants out can saddle his horse an' ride, or he can say what's on his mind an' wind up like Curly an' Tom."

Curly Boyd fell over on his face, groaning once. His boots began to shake with death throes. Everyone could see a large hole in the rear of his head where a tiny fountain of blood was spurting forth in regular bursts, keeping time with the slowing beat of his heart.

Across the fire, Tom Hicks made soft choking sounds as blood filled his neck and lungs. The rest of the gang stood silently, looking from one dying man to the other.

"I ain't heard nobody else complainin'," Bill said, with a final glare passing across faces illuminated by the fire's yellow glow. "Dodge City," he said again, almost a challenge. "We're gonna empty them vaults. Kill a bunch of folks, so everybody'll remember not to tangle with Bill Anderson an' his boys. We'll show 'em."

"We could hang that City Marshal. String him up by his neck to a tree some place so people in these parts'll know we ain't just foolin' around," said a gunman with heavy black beard stubble hitching his thumbs in his gunbelt.

Bill nodded. "We'll put folks in this Territory on notice we mean business. I like your idea, Roy. We'll hang that Earp feller right on Main Street."

"Sounds good to me," a kid by the name of Carruthers said as Tom Hicks began whimpering softly.

"We could burn down some of the town," another said from a spot near Curly Boyd.

"It'd make a pretty fire," a gunslick from Missouri by the name of Sammy McCoy announced, his smile easy to see since he stood close to the fire. "Light up half the damn sky in Kansas Territory."

"A fire sounds good to me," Bill replied, holstering his Colt when it became clear that no one else would challenge him. "It would be a reminder to them Kansas farmers an' cattlemen who come up from Texas that we ain't just foolin' around."

"I like fires," Sammy said, grinning. He had eyes that were badly crossed, so it appeared he was continually staring at the end of his nose. "We could burn the whole damn place plumb to the ground."

"Shut up, Sammy," his brother Claude said. "Every man in this outfit knows you ain't right in the head. Shut up so's we can listen to Bill."

"Them banks are gonna be stuffed plumb full of money this time of year," Bill said. "Cattle buyers are havin' money sent so they can buy herds early in the spring. This one's gonna make us rich, boys."

Tom Hicks called out for his mother in a blood- and phlegm-choked voice. "Help me, Momma! Please help me! It hurts so bad, Momma!"

Heads turned toward the dying man's prone form.

"Somebody shut him up," Bill snapped. "I'm tired of hearin' him complain."

"How we gonna do that?" Sammy asked. "How we gonna shut him up when he's damn near dead anyways?"

"Smother him with your saddle blanket," Claude replied in a dry, emotionless voice, "or find a big rock an' put it in his mouth so he can't say nothin'."

"But he ain't got no teeth in front, Claudie," Sammy said. "How the hell's a rock gonna stay there?"

"Why don't both of you shut up?" a booming voice said from the shadows beyond the fire.

Faces turned toward the speaker . . . everyone knew the sound of Jack Starr's voice. Starr was a remorseless killer, a man who took pride in the number of victims he had claimed over a lifetime.

Starr ambled over to Tom Hicks. "I'll take care of it," he said, pulling a Dance Colt conversion from a cross-pull holster tied to his waist.

He cocked his pistol, aiming down for Tom's forehead. "He never did have no gumption," Starr said. "Now he's layin' here cryin' for his mama like a sugar-tit baby." Starr fired, and the explosion echoed from the silent prairie around them.

Tom's body stiffened. Bill Anderson grinned when he saw Tom's muscles contract, then relax. A final, bubbling breath of air escaped Tom's bloody mouth, then he went still.

"Nice shootin', Jack," Bill said, still smiling, "only it ain't gonna win you no prize money on account of you was standin' so close."

"Got tired of listenin' to him," Starr replied, glancing across the fire at Curly Boyd. "If Curly makes one more noise I'm gonna do the same to him."

"Curly wasn't no bad feller," Sammy offered. "He just had trouble seein' things on account of them spectacles."

"He turned yellow on us," Bill snarled, reading the faces he could see in the firelight. "Any sumbitch who turns yellow on me is gonna die just like these two."

Boyd had the misfortune to groan right then, putting a deep scowl on Jack Starr's face. Starr walked around the firepit with his pistol dangling from his fist.

"Are you gonna shoot Curly, too?" Sammy asked, like he couldn't quite believe it.

Starr looked over his shoulder. "I'm gonna shoot him, an' you besides, if you don't shut up, Sammy," he said, cocking his Dance again. "How the hell are we gonna sleep tonight with them two makin' all that noise?"

Sammy fell silent. Starr aimed down at the back of Boyd's head and calmly pulled the trigger.

As the noise from the gunshot faded, Bill Anderson addressed his men. "Get some sleep, boys. Come the next week or so we're gonna rob us a couple of banks an' spill a little blood. I want everybody rested. Let's turn in . . ."

Chapter 2

Smoke Jensen took his wife in his arms. "I love you, Sally. We won't be gone long, maybe four or five weeks. These Hereford crosses don't trail as well as a longhorn. It's those short legs that slow 'em down. Dodge City ain't all that far, and it's the closest place to sell these crossbreds to eastern cattle buyers. Let's just hope short legs won't keep us from makin' it that far."

Sally smiled up at his rugged face in the glow of an early morning sunrise peeking across the mountains. "Those short legs carry more beef," she said, an undeniable fact. Crossing their longhorn cows with Hereford bulls had been her idea. "I told you so."

"Can't remember a time when you didn't claim to be right," he said, grinning into her beautiful eyes, seeing his reflection in them as if they were liquid pools.

"I *am* always right," she said, widening her smile.

He cast a glance down at the meadow where more than three hundred long-yearling steers, fattened and ready for market, grazed peacefully under Pearlie's watchful eye while Cal saddled a young horse at the barn. An early fall had painted the grasses with frost, and as the sun rose, a silvery mist lifted from the meadow. "Right pretty sight, ain't it?" he asked, reluctant to let go of the woman he loved, the woman who had changed his life so dramatically from a gunfighter to a peaceful rancher high in the Rockies, helping him build a ranch they had named Sugarloaf.

"It is a pretty sight," she told him quietly. "Just make sure you get back here in one piece to see it with me for the rest of our lives."

"Can't hardly see how there'd be any trouble. Nothin' much between the Dodge City railheads and here besides open country and a few hills."

"You seem to have a knack for findin' trouble almost any place," Sally reminded him, her smile fading, worry replacing it in her face.

"That was before, when my past wouldn't leave us alone. I figure all that's over now."

Doubt lingered in Sally's eyes. "Promise me you'll avoid it, Smoke. I worry every time you're away."

"Then stop worryin' this time, woman," he said, a mock note of reproach in his voice. "This is gonna be the most peaceful cattle drive in history. That's why I'm only takin' Pearlie and Cal along, 'cause we've only got three hundred steers to worry about, and it's empty country. I'm leavin' Johnny to help you keep an eye on the place while we're gone, an' to lend a hand with chores."

"Just promise me you'll swing wide of trouble," she said again.

He gazed down at her lovingly. "You've got my word on it, Sally."

A ruckus at the barn distracted them. Cal, too young to fully understand the nature of a green horse on a chilly morning by noticing a hump in its back, swung his leg over the saddle cinched to the back of a bay three-year-old colt. The bay gave a snort and downed its head, beginning to buck as hard as it knew how away from the barns and corrals.

Cal wasn't ready for the suddenness of it, his reins held too loosely to pull the colt's head up. All he could do was hold onto the saddlehorn for all he was worth while letting out a yelp like a scalded puppy, trying to fit his right boot in a free-swinging stirrup to help him keep his balance.

Rocking back and forth, losing his hat, his face as white as winter snow, Cal tried desperately to hang on as the bay sunfished and crow-hopped, lunging several feet into the air to rid its back of an unwanted load.

A roar of laughter echoed from the meadow when Pearlie saw Cal's dilemma. "Ride 'em, cowboy!" Pearlie cried between spasms of laughter, suddenly gripping his sides.

Cal managed to survive eight or nine jumps aboard the colt's back before he went sailing over the bay's head, his arms outstretched to break his fall in the frost-laden grass.

"Lookee yonder!" Pearlie exclaimed, pointing to Cal's quick departure from the saddle. "I'd nearly swear that boy's done gone an' sprouted hisself a pair of wings!" He broke into another fit of heehaws.

Cal landed on his chest with a grunt, skidding along on the slippery grass, looking about as helpless as a newborn lamb until he slid to a stop, sprawled flat on his face.

Sally stifled a giggle. "I hope he's okay, Smoke."

"He's fine. That grass is near 'bout as soft as a feather mattress. It'll teach him a thing or two."

Cal raised his head, noticing that Smoke and Sally were watching from the porch of the ranch house. And he couldn't help but hear Pearlie's endless laughing from a spot near the edge of the herd.

Cal spit out a mouthful of frosted grass. His face was red with embarrassment. He spoke to Smoke. "Sorry, boss. I reckon I pulled that cinch too tight first thing this mornin' on a half-broke bronc."

"It wasn't the colt's fault, son," Smoke said, trying to contain his own chuckle. "He gave you every warnin' he's got. There was a hump in his back a mile high. One of these days you're gonna learn to notice these things."

Cal pushed himself up to his hands and knees, giving Pearlie a scowl downslope for continuing to laugh. "It ain't all that damn funny!" he shouted, until he remembered Sally was there. He gave her a bow of apology. "Sorry for the language, Miz Jensen, but Pearlie hadn't oughta laugh so hard at a man's difficulties on a cold mornin' like this."

The colt, a gentle-natured animal, stopped bucking to look down at Cal. Most good young horses resisted being broken to a saddle and bridle right at first, a way of showing they were bred with spirit.

Pearlie let out a final guffaw and then pointed to the bay. "See yonder, Cal? That colt's plumb ready to apologize for what he done, turnin' you into a sparrow on the fly when you's all dressed up to be a cowhand. He's sayin' he's sorry by the way he's holdin' his head down like that. Why, it even looks like he's got tears in his eyes.''

Cal stood up angrily to retrieve his fallen hat. ''If Miz Jensen wasn't listenin' I'd give you a piece of my mind, Pearlie. No need to poke so much fun at an honest mistake.''

''Mistakes can git a man killed,'' Pearlie said, seriously. ''That young horse is tryin' to teach you a few things about how to stay alive.''

''I'm afraid Pearlie's right,'' Smoke said, watching Cal dust off his Stetson before approaching the colt to grab its loose reins. ''A man who wants to stay above ground in this wild part of the country had better learn to look for the little things, the warnings nature and animals give you. That colt was tellin' you plain as day he wasn't ready for a rider. I've shown you how to lead a young horse off a few steps firsthand, so it gets used to the feel of a cinch. Some of 'em will crow-hop a time or two, just to let you know they ain't happy about the idea of carryin' a rider.''

''I remember you showin' me that, boss. I reckon I plumb forgot this mornin'.''

Smoke watched Cal lead the bay away from the barn, and to the boy's credit he was paying close attention to the colt's back.

He turned back to Sally and bent down to kiss her gently. ''You know I'll miss you,'' he admitted, before he released her from his embrace.

''I'll miss you too, Smoke. Please remember what I said. If you can, let other men settle their own disputes.''

''I'll do it,'' he promised, starting down the porch steps to mount his Palouse stud, ''just so long as they don't wind up involvin' me or my friends or these Hereford yearlings. We've worked hard for two years to get this breedin' program started and this'll be our first crop to sell. I've got a good feelin' about it . . . that we're gonna be makin' some money on these calves.''

He stepped aboard the stud and reined toward the meadow with frosty breath curling from his nose and mouth when he turned in the saddle to say, "Goodbye, Sally. If you need anything, send Johnny to town, and Louis Longmont will do whatever's necessary to see that you get it, includin' helpin' if anybody shows up who don't belong.''

Sally nodded. "We can take care of ourselves out here, in case you haven't noticed before. But if I need anything I'll send for Louis.''

Smoke knew it was more than just an empty statement to make him feel better. Sally was every bit as good with a gun as she was in the kitchen with a frying pan or a baking tin. Tied behind his saddle, he carried over a dozen warm biscuits she'd made that morning, and almost as many sugary bearclaws. His mouth watered as he thought about them.

"Let's move 'em out," he said, riding up to Pearlie.

Pearlie aimed a thumb at the barn. "Better make sure that young 'un don't git airborne again afore we leave, boss. His feathers wasn't tested all that good a while ago.''

Smoke chuckled, looking back to watch Cal mount the bay very carefully with a much shorter grip on the reins. The bay let out a snort, then its back settled, and it responded to the pressure from Cal's heels, moving off toward the herd at an easy walk.

"He's learning," Smoke told Pearlie, casting a glance across the backs of their steers spread over the meadow. "A man can't learn it all at once. Takes time.''

Pearlie shrugged. "I'd never let him hear me say it, but he's makin' one helluva fine cowboy. Works hard at everythin' he does an' don't mind long hours or rough conditions, don't matter how cold or hot or muddy it gits. He's a good kid, makin' a man outa hisself in reasonable good time. He still ain't much shakes with a gun, mind you."

"Most men are better off not knowing about guns," Smoke offered as they rode wide to send the herd eastward. "There's some things that just aren't necessary."

Pearlie gave him a puzzled expression. "That's mighty strange advice, comin' from you, Smoke."

"It wasn't my idea to learn how to kill another man. It was circumstances that forced it on me, and Preacher was there to teach me what I needed to know."

"You sound like a feller who's got regrets, boss."

"I've got some, I reckon. Times were different back then. A man did what he had to do to stay alive."

"Can't see how things have changed all that much," Pearlie said. "There's parts of this country still full of bad men who take what they want with a gun."

Smoke sighed. It wasn't really a topic he cared to discuss at the moment. "That's where men like me can come in handy, if there's a need."

Pearlie looked toward the sunrise as Cal rode up. "I sure hope the need don't arise on this trip," he said offhandedly. "I got used to it bein' real peaceful this past summer."

Smoke swung his horse away to sweep some of the steers into a bunch. "No reason to believe we'll have anything different on this ride," he said, wondering. Louis had told him a few tales about some shootings in Dodge City and Abilene that spring, but this was information Smoke had kept from Sally and the others.

Cal was dusting off the front of his mackinaw. "If this here bay colt is any indication of what's in store for us," he said, "we're in for a mighty tough drive. When a man sets out to go some place, an' the first thing happens is he gits bucked off real hard, I don't see it as no good sign."

Pearlie couldn't stifle a chuckle. "If that same feller who got bucked off knowed a thing or two 'bout horses, he wouldn't be tastin' frosty grass first thing in the mornin' for his breakfast."

Cal ignored Pearlie's remark to eye the burlap bag behind Smoke's saddle. "Since it was Pearlie who first brought up the subject of breakfast, how 'bout we eat some of them bearclaws Sally made?"

Pearlie wagged his head like he was disgusted. "She made 'em fer the trail, son. Hell, we ain't hardly more 'n a few hundred yards from the ranch house yet."

"Don't keep me from wantin' one or two," Cal replied, on the defensive.

"I reckon you're gonna tell us gettin' throwed off is such hard work it gave you an appetite," Pearlie said, chuckling again.

"You look fer the worst way to put things, don't you?" Cal asked, turning his colt toward a yearling steer that was reluctant to stop grazing long enough to join the herd.

Smoke grinned. This sort of banter would continue for days, and at night around the campfire. It was Cal and Pearlie's way of showing closeness. They were good men, different as night and day, but men he could count on, and that was what made them so valuable to the Sugarloaf brand.

"Ride point until we get 'em across the valley," Smoke said to Pearlie. "Me and Cal will gather up all the stragglers and be right behind you."

Without a reply Pearlie spurred his sorrel toward the front of the herd to guide the cattle across a winding valley. Smoke was satisfied. The trail drive to Dodge City had begun.

Chapter 3

Dave Cobbs saw them on the horizon. They came from the east beneath a cloud of dust, too many horsemen to be out in an empty stretch of Kansas prairie without purpose. Dave was sweeping the narrow front porch of his trading post, a little store by a creek without a proper name, calling it simply Cobbs's Trading Post at the Creek, which he had built out of logs and clay mud with his own hands, and with Myra's help. It had been a profitable trading season, the best in eight years of strenuous toil to establish a spot east of Dodge City where cattlemen and farmers could purchase or trade for staples. He had even painted a sign for the roof out front, although the paint had faded some after several winters full of snow and sleet and heavy rains.

He turned to the open doorway and spoke to his wife. "We got riders comin', Myra. A big bunch. Maybe twenty or thirty. They'll probably be wantin'

whiskey. Dust off them bottles of corn squeeze an'
give the countertop a swipe or two. Wouldn't want
to create no bad impression.''

There was something about the horsemen, even
from a distance of half a mile or more, that made
Dave vaguely uneasy. "They don't look like drovers,''
he added over his shoulder. "Wonder who the heck
they could be.''

"Just so they've got money to spend,'' his wife
replied from the log building. "We can't pick an'
choose who comes this way. I'll get the children in
the back, so they won't be no distraction. Darlene
can watch over the little ones . . . give the baby a sugar
lump to keep him quiet.''

Dave thought about his thirteen-year-old daughter.
Darlene was becoming a woman . . . *budding*, it was
sometimes called. Men had begun to notice her. "It
sure is hard to figure why there's so many of 'em,''
he said, sweeping faster to rid the hand-cut planks of
dust and dirt, one eye on the approaching riders.

"I'll put out the Arbuckles coffee so's they can see
it real plain,'' Myra said. "A bunch that big's liable
to need three or four pounds of good coffee. Be sure
an' tell 'em these beans are fresh off the wagon from
St. Louis.''

"I'll mention it,'' Dave agreed, squinting to keep
the sun's glare from his eyes as he finished his sweeping along the porch steps. "From the looks of 'em,
I'll bet they're after whiskey. Nearly all of 'em are
carryin' guns, rifles booted to their saddles. Maybe
they're hide hunters, or somethin' like that. I can't
quite figure why they'd be carryin' so many guns
otherwise. Hunters is what they'll turn out to be.''

"Let's just hope they turn out to have some hard
money to spend,'' Myra called out from the back of

the store. "Seems like it's too early for buffalo hunters. Buffalo haven't put on their winter hair yet,
accordin' to Mose."

Dave recalled what Mose Baker had said a few weeks
back, that this would be a bad year for buffalo hunters
because the herds had been thinned by the previous
year's hunt to such an extent there were few big
bunches wandering the Kansas hills. It was hard to
ride in any direction without coming across huge
piles of sun-bleached buffalo bones.

"You keep the baby quiet while we got customers,"
he heard Myra tell Darlene. "Shut the door an' keep
it shut. Give the baby a lump of brown sugar if he
starts to cry."

Dave thought about his infant son. Dave Junior, a
gift he wanted desperately after Myra had given him
two daughters. Darlene was much older. The others,
Melissa and Davey, hadn't been born until they
arrived in Kansas from Chicago to begin building the
store, in part because the trip westward had been so
hard on Myra, causing several miscarriages along the
way. A doctor in Kansas City had said it was the rough
ride on a Studebaker wagon seat that caused her to
lose the children. Myra's bleeding had scared Dave
half to death, because he hadn't known.

"They'll be here in a few minutes," he said, leaning
his straw broom against the doorjamb. "I'll put on
my clean apron so I'll look like a regular storekeeper.
If this is our lucky day we could sell plumb out of
whiskey an' coffee and licorice whips to boot. Most
hide hunters have got a real sweet tooth. Be sure you
tell 'em the Arbuckles has a peppermint stick in every
bag. Not just everybody knows that . . ."

Dave's freckled face twisted into a frown when he
got a closer look at the horsemen. "Somethin' about

'em don't look just right to me," he added softly, so
Myra couldn't hear. He didn't want to worry her. A
twelve gauge shotgun was hidden beneath the counter.
If these men gave any trouble, Dave was certain he
could handle it.

He went inside and put on a clean apron. While
Myra was busy dusting off whiskey bottles with a tur-
key-feather duster, he checked the loads in both barrels of his shotgun, oddly disturbed by the sighting
of so many men coming toward his trading post.

"Be sure you tell Darlene to pull the latch shut on
the door to the bedroom," he said, moving a glass
jar of peppermint sticks closer to the front of the
counter. Maybe the strange feelings he was having
were misguided. Days would pass without seeing a
soul during certain seasons, and he wondered if the
loneliness, the emptiness, was eating away at him at
that time of year.

"Why'd you say that?" Myra asked, halting in the
midst of her dusting chore.

He didn't want to worry her. "Just an ordinary
precaution when there's so many of 'em. Wouldn't
want some hide hunter to wander into the back by
mistake 'cause I know we'll be busy up front, sellin'
all sorts of things."

Myra walked to a window, shading her eyes from
the sun with a hand. "They *do* have an awful lot of
guns, Dave," she said with a trace of worry. "Nearly
all of 'em I can see are wearing pistols. They've all
got rifles too. Wonder who these men are and what
they're doin' here."

"Probably just hungry an' thirsty cowboys," he told
her. "I won't judge men by the number of guns they
carry. It could be a posse from Wichita lookin' for
bad men. You know this part of the Territory can

have some dishonest men crossin' on the way to other places. Don't worry, darlin'. Everything's gonna be okay, an' I've got the shotgun loaded. Get those whiskey bottles dusted off so they shine like new."

"I sure don't like the looks of 'em," she said, turning away from the window.

The sounds of horses came on gusts of wind as Dave gave his trading post a final glance, satisfied that everything was ready for new customers. It was with more than a little pride that he gave the interior of his store a look . . . it had taken a year to build the log structure, and all their savings to stock the store with staples, odd items travelers needed, and more. He and Myra were accumulating wealth by means of a swelling selection inside the store, and a small cash savings hidden in a baking soda tin underneath the rear porch.

Dave looked back at the window as dozens of riders came to a halt at the hitchrails. Smoothing the front of his apron, he came around the counter to welcome the new arrivals, walking out on the freshly swept porch.

A thin man dressed in gray Confederate pants and stovepipe cavalry boots swung down from his horse before the others dismounted. The man wore a battered Confederate cavalry hat, even though the war had been over for several years.

"Howdy, men," Dave said, smiling. "Welcome to the Cobbs Trading Post. What can I do for you, gentlemen?"

The fellow who left his horse ahead of the others had rather odd-colored eyes—gray, almost slate.

"Whiskey," the man replied in a rasping voice, like cold steel pulled across an anvil. He stared at Dave with no sign of friendliness.

"Got plenty of it. Six dollars a bottle an' it's fresh from Kentucky—the best money can buy."

"You got fatback an' beans?" the stranger asked, as his men came down to the ground amid the creak of saddle leather and the rattle of spurs and curb chains.

"We've got plenty of both," Dave replied, "and a fresh shipment of Arbuckles coffee beans."

"We'll take it," the gray-eyed man said. "All of it. You start puttin' it in towsacks."

"Sorry, mister, but I haven't seen the color of your money yet. You didn't even ask the price of the coffee or beans . . ."

It was then that Dave noticed a brace of pistols tied low around the man's waist.

"Don't care 'bout the price. We wasn't aimin' to pay for none of it anyways."

Dave took a step backward toward the door. "I've got a loaded shotgun inside, mister. You'll pay for the goods you want, or you'll get a taste of buckshot."

Several of the men who were gathered around the porch laughed.

"Buckshot?" a bearded man asked, grinning, like he didn't believe it. "What the hell is a little bit of buckshot gonna do to keep us from takin' what we want?"

Dave felt a tremor of fear run down his arms. "I'm warning you, gentlemen, I'm a good shot with a scattergun."

The man with the slate eyes spoke as he drew one of his guns from a worn holster. "You ain't gonna have time to fetch that scattergun, boy," he snarled, aiming his gun up at Dave.

"You won't get away with a robbery like this," Dave stammered with his palms spread helplessly.

"Who says?" another rider asked, pulling a pistol from the inside of his coat.

"We've got lawmen over in Dodge City, and a Territorial militia, and United States Marshals. You'll go to jail if you try to rob us."

"You keep sayin' *us,*" another newcomer said. "Is somebody else inside?"

"My wife. And my children. Now I'm warning all of you to get back on your horses and ride away from here unless you want serious trouble."

"Serious trouble?" the man in Confederate uniform asked. "I ain't exactly sure what you mean, mister."

"I'll shoot any of you who try to take supplies from our store without paying for them," Dave replied, with courage he did not feel, facing so many armed men.

"Like I said, son, you ain't gonna live long enough to get your hands on that gun. I'll put so many holes in you before you can turn around, you'll leak like a rusty bucket."

Dave tasted fear on the tip of his tongue. "This is the last time I'll warn you. Get back on your horses an' ride off before I'm forced to take drastic measures."

Laughter spread through the group of men standing around Dave's porch, and he sensed now just how deep the trouble was that he found himself in.

"I'm Bill Anderson," the gray-eyed stranger said, his gun still pointed at Dave's belly. "Maybe you've heard of me an' my boys. Some folks have taken to callin' me Bloody Bill."

Dave's stomach twisted into a knot, and his throat went dry, like sand. Everyone in the Territory knew about Bloody Bill Anderson and his desperados, but it was rumored he'd gone south to Texas. No one had spotted him or reported any of his recent exploits to the weekly newspapers—not for more than a year now—and it seemed to Dave it could have been longer. "Word was you went to Texas," he stammered, buying time, edging a little closer to the door. "We don't want no trouble, Mr. Anderson, but you can't just up an' take what's in my store without payin' for it."

Anderson seemed amused. A crooked grin revealed parts of his broken, discolored front teeth. "The hell you say. For a storekeeper you sure as hell can't count. There's twenty-seven of us an' ain't but one of you. I b'lieve they call it 'rithmatic.'"

Sweat beaded on Dave's forehead, forming on his palms. "I can count," he said weakly, staring briefly into the dark muzzle of Anderson's pistol.

"Let's see what kind of womenfolk you got inside," Anderson said, losing most of his grin now. "Some of my boys ain't been with a woman for quite a spell."

Dave took a brave step backward to block the doorway. "You won't lay a hand on Myra or Darlene!" he screamed, suddenly angry when his family's lives were clearly in danger.

"I'm done talkin'," Anderson snarled, his face becoming a mask of rage.

Dave was wheeling for the inside of his store to make a dive for the shotgun when a gunblast thundered behind him. Something passed through his ribs, and suddenly the front of his clean, white apron exploded, a burst of red showering the countertop and the floor as he began to fall helplessly, unable to control his legs.

He landed hard on his chest, his chin slamming against the floor where tiny droplets of his own blood covered the boards. He heard himself groan, a sound beyond his control as a searing, white pain spread through his body, dulling his brain so that it was hard to think clearly. A scream came from inside the building.

Booted feet stepped over him, all around him, the rattle of spur rowels dragging across floorboards echoing in his ears along with a curious ringing noise.

Dave tried desperately to raise his head as more men walked past him . . . he had to get up and reach his shotgun before these outlaws harmed Myra or Darlene and the other children. His vision was blurred and he couldn't see the men clearly, and neither could he push himself up off the floor. His arms and legs were like lead weights.

Then, as he was losing consciousness, he heard Myra scream at the top of her lungs.

A moment later Dave Cobbs slipped into a dark tunnel. He could feel himself falling, tumbling into a black void.

Chapter 4

The steers drifted easily across lower Colorado Territory valleys and grasslands, grazing as they traveled, losing little of the weight they'd gained on good pastures at Sugarloaf during the summer.

Smoke stopped on a wooded ridge overlooking Big Sandy Creek southeast of a tiny settlement called Last Chance. They'd been on the trail for three uneventful days, now entering some of lower Colorado's flatlands, where the countryside turned drier, making grass scarce, harder to find. It was also a region where occasional bands of renegade Osage warriors preyed on small wagon trains or widely scattered ranches, although most of the Osages were on reservations down in Indian Territory now. This had once been Ute and Arapaho country, sometimes frequented by roving bands of Cheyenne, until the treaties brought an end to most of the hostilities.

Things hadn't always been so peaceful, Smoke

remembered, in the days when he and Preacher had fought, and then made peace with the Shoshones and Utes. He was glad those days were behind him, yet there were times, when he was alone with his thoughts, when he missed that special closeness he felt toward Preacher.

Smoke scanned the valley below, passing an experienced eye along the creekbanks. All was quiet. Native birds fluttered among cottonwood and willow branches beside the water, a sure sign no danger was present.

He turned back in the saddle to motion Pearlie and Cal to bring the herd over the ridge, when he spotted Pearlie riding his way at a trot. Smoke pondered the reason why Pearlie would leave his spot riding drag and flank at the back of the herd.

Pearlie rode up and halted his favorite yellow dun gelding. He turned back to the west, squinting, aiming a finger in the same direction. "Seems like we got somethin', or somebody, who's followin' us. Every now an' then the blackbirds rise up all at once, maybe half a mile or so behind us. Then they settle back down till whatever it is moves 'em again. Could be a grizzly, I reckon, or it could be somethin' else. Whatever it is, it damn sure 'ppears to be followin' us the last couple of hours. I had it figured you'd want to know."

Smoke watched for sign of the blackbirds. For a few moments all was still behind them. "Can't see no disturbance now," he said. "Keep your eyes peeled. If it happens again, give me a sharp whistle and I'll ride back to see what's there. It won't be a grizzly in this low country so late in the year. They're headed to the High Lonesome to find places to hibernate for the winter by now. I 'spect it's something else."

"This country ain't known fer rustlers," Pearlie said, as he kept his eyes on treetops north and west. "Accordin' to what Louis told me this summer, hardly a thing happens down here, now that them redskins are cleared out."

"I hadn't heard of any trouble in this part of the Territory either," Smoke agreed. "Maybe it's a cougar. A hungry mountain lion'll sometimes follow a herd of cattle or buffalo for miles hoping to get a chance at a cripple or a calf. Just keep your eyes open and your rifle handy. Whistle if you see anything out of the usual."

"If it ain't nothin' but a big cat, I'll take a shot over its head to scare it off. No sense in killin' a graceful animal like that just 'cause it's hungry."

Smoke grinned. "We see things the same way, Pearlie. It was one of a thousand things Preacher taught me . . . never to kill an animal unless I needed the meat, sometimes a rogue grizzly if it gets man-hungry or develops a taste for beef. Same goes for a big cat. Most of 'em'll hide from the scent of a man." He took another look behind them. "That's why I don't think we've got a cougar following us. It would catch our smell an' leave us alone. Same goes for most wild creatures, even a bear. They don't look for man scent. Usually try to get clear of it quick as they can."

"It's the two-legged creatures I worry about," Pearlie said. "Some of them don't scare off so easy."

"You worry too much," Smoke told him, turning his Palouse to ride down toward the creek. "You're gettin' to where you sound more and more like Sally."

Pearlie wanted the last word on the subject. "There's times when things need a dose of worryin' over," he muttered, still watching the sky as he started back to the rear of the herd at a slow trot.

Following a gentle slope, Smoke rode to the stream and let his stud drink its fill. A few at a time, the gentle Herefords came to the water's edge.

Glancing backward, Smoke saw Pearlie and Cal bring the last of the steers over the rise, pushing them toward the creek at an easy gait. All seemed calm, quiet. Pearlie's concerns about being followed had come to nothing.

Suddenly, a swarm of blackbirds swirled into the sky behind them, circling, alarmed by something beneath them. Smoke's full attention remained on the birds for several seconds.

"Something is back there," he said under his breath, reining the stud around, pulling his Winchester .44 rifle from its boot below a stirrup leather.

He heeled the Palouse past water-seeking cattle to gallop to the top of the rise. Smoke found Pearlie on the ridge watching the blackbirds, holding his horse in check.

"That just ain't natural," Pearlie said, keeping an eye on the circling birds. "Somethin' got 'em scared. See how they won't settle back into them trees fer a spell? A blackbird ain't the spooky sort. Somethin's back yonder."

"I'll find out what it is," Smoke said, as Pearlie noticed his rifle resting on the pommel of his saddle. "Keep these steers bunched tight at the creek till I get back. Don't leave 'em for any reason."

Without waiting for a reply, Smoke urged his horse to a lope and rode back along the trail, searching the trees along hillsides and in deep arroyos for any sign of movement, any shape in the forests that did not belong. The blackbirds continued to fly in looping circles above the trees, unwilling to return to their perches.

It won't be a grizzly, Smoke assured himself. *Too late in the year.*

It was his Palouse that sensed trouble first, before he saw anything to cause him alarm. The big stud snorted and pricked its ears forward, slowing its gait, looking straight ahead at something Smoke couldn't see or hear above the rumble of galloping hooves.

Smoke's gaze swept the trees, and he trusted the Palouse's keen sight and hearing. He levered a shell into the firing chamber of his rifle and rested the stock on his thigh.

Four dim shapes, fanned out in an uneven line, appeared and then vanished in forest shadows, men on horses. He pulled the stud to a sliding stop, ready for trouble.

And then he saw clearly the outline of an Indian aboard a pinto pony, coming toward him at a trot, a long-barrel rifle in his hands.

Osage renegades, he thought, when he could see the shaved skull of the Indian, a trademark of the Osage tribe.

All four Indians were visible, coming at him from the trees, and all were carrying rifles. Smoke was out in the open in a grassy meadow, an easy target if he remained in one place.

He wheeled the stud to the left and drummed his heels into its sides, leaning over the Palouse's neck to make him harder to hit with a rifle shot.

The booming report of a heavy-bore gun sounded from a spot between tree trunks. The whistling passage of a lead slug went high above his head.

He rode hard for a stand of juniper, in order to be out of the line of fire. Another gunshot thundered, kicking up a plug of prairie grass in front of the stud's flying hooves.

He reached the pines just as two more shots bellowed from the line of trees. Molten balls of lead, meant for him, went singing among the branches.

Smoke swung to the ground, dropping the stud's reins to find an opening in the pines where he could take aim himself.

A lone Osage warrior, clad in buckskins, his skull shaved clean and painted black and yellow in some design, galloped his pony out of the woods. Smoke shouldered his Winchester, took quick but careful aim, and feathered the trigger.

The concussion of a .44 caliber shell filled the clearing where he'd ground-hitched his Palouse. In almost the same instant a yell echoed across the meadow. The Osage jerked in an odd way atop his racing pony, bending over, clutching a dark red spot in the middle of his chest. He flipped off the pinto's rump in a ball, tumbling, tossing his rifle aside to hold the mortal wound beneath his ribcage.

Another Osage came charging out of the woods, a rifle to his shoulder, screaming a war cry. Smoke calmly levered a cartridge into the chamber, took aim, and fired again.

The top of the Indian's skull seemed to come apart in a sort of slow motion, like syrup on a cold morning. Pieces of skin and bone went skyward, along with a spray of blood. The Osage's heels went up as he fell back across his black pony's croup, and for a time he appeared suspended there, until the rough gait of his horse sent him rolling off to one side.

The Indian landed in the grass limply, arms and legs askew, skidding across tufts of curly mesquite until he slid to a stop near the base of a slender oak tree that was shedding its colorful, fall leaves.

Another round went quickly into the chamber of Smoke's rifle when a third Indian swerved his sorrel pony toward the junipers where Smoke was making his stand.

"Damn fool," Smoke whispered to himself, drawing a bead on the Osage's chest.

When he pulled the trigger, the shock of it rocked him back on his heels a moment, and as a cloud of blue smoke cleared away from the muzzle of the Winchester, he saw the Indian topple over as his pony galloped away.

The fourth Osage brought his pony to a bounding halt more than a hundred yards from the junipers. He looked both ways at his fallen companions, as though he could not quite believe what he was seeing.

Then his head turned, facing Smoke, and the look on his face was one of pure hatred. He lifted his rifle, an old, single-shot musket, and shook it in the air defiantly, throwing back his head while he let out a shrill cry.

"Ayeee!"

Smoke grinned mirthlessly. He stepped around the juniper tree and held his Winchester over his head.

"Ayeee! Ayeee! Suvate!" he shouted, the Ute war song of victory.

As Smoke's cry filled the silent meadow, the Osage suddenly lowered his gun and stared at the white man.

For a time the two men stared at each other, neither moving or making a sound. The Osage was clearly puzzled, how a white man could know the war cry of his old enemy, the Utes.

"Suvate!" Smoke cried again, bringing his rifle down, then to his shoulder.

The Osage remained frozen where he was for a few seconds, then turned his pony around and made a hasty retreat toward the forest from which he had come, his pony's mane and tail flying in the wind until he was out of sight.

From the east, the rhythmic thump of a running horse's hooves came nearer. A moment later, rifle in hand, Pearlie came galloping across a row of low hills, ready to lend a hand in the fight.

Smoke stepped around the juniper so Pearlie could see him, waving his rifle over his head. Pearlie caught a quick glimpse of Smoke and reined his dun in that direction.

Pearlie galloped up and jerked his gelding to a halt.

"What the hell happened, boss? I heard all the shootin', an' I come a-runnin'."

"Four Indians. Osages, by their shaved heads. I dropped three of 'em. One rode off when he saw I wasn't gonna give him any special consideration."

Pearlie looked in the direction in which Smoke inclined his head. "I can see blood on the grass yonder. How come you didn't come after me an' Cal so's we could lend you a hand?"

"Didn't figure I needed any help, Pearlie. But you've got my thanks anyway."

"Damn near any man needs help up against four Injuns," was Pearlie's reply. He let his shoulders drop. "I reckon, knowin' you like I do, you'd be the exception."

"They had old, single-shot rifles. Wasn't much of a fight, really."

Pearlie looked down at Smoke, grinning. "Ain't

that just like you, Smoke Jensen, to make a fight where one man stands up against four Injuns an' he calls it not much of a fight. I'll swear . . ."

"They were young Osage bucks. Inexperienced. They came straight at me. It was like target practice."

Pearlie booted his rifle. "I reckon I'd best git back to the herd, afore you tell me that's where I'm s'pposed to be."

"You took the words right outa my mouth, Pearlie. Me and Sally aren't payin' you wages to sit here and jaw with me about Indians, or how they oughta be fought."

"Yes, sir," Pearlie replied, swinging his dun away from the junipers.

He rode off shaking his head.

Chapter 5

Cal squatted across the flames of their campfire, watching Pearlie ride slow circles around the steers until they bedded down for the night. Palming a tin cup of coffee to warm his hands in chilly night air, Cal listened to Pearlie sing a creaky version of "Little Joe the Wrangler." Singing, even as bad as Pearlie's voice could be, had a strange calming effect on cattle, a lesson every cowboy learned early on a trail drive.

"I swear, Pearlie sounds worse'n an axle needin' grease," he said. "It's a wonder it don't spook them steers into a stampede all the way to St. Louis."

Smoke grunted, blowing steam from his cup, glancing up at a clear, night sky sprinkled with stars. "It's a fact cows aren't much of a judge when it comes to music. Can't say as I ever heard a cowboy who could carry a tune. It's a blessing that cattle don't get all that particular about a melody, or most trail drives would be in trouble."

Cal looked at Smoke. "While we're on the subject of trouble, boss, tell me 'bout them redskins. Pearlie told me they was Osages, an' that you killed four of 'em."

"Pearlie's always been given over to exaggeration. I shot three that were coming straight at me. The fourth showed good sense an' rode off."

"I knowed we was gonna have trouble on this drive soon as that bay colt throwed me off. It was a message from the Almighty tellin' us to be ready for more'n a few difficulties. I never was all that superstitious 'bout such things, but when that bay pitched me over its head, I could feel it in my bones that we was headed into bad situations."

"What you felt in your bones, son, was the fall you took off that colt's back."

Cal looked down at his cup, a bit embarrassed. "It was more'n that, Mr. Jensen. I had the real clear sensation there was gonna be some shootin' on this drive, an' that whoever it was would be shootin' at us."

Smoke grinned. "If that happens, I'll take care of it. You handle your job with these steers, an' I'll handle any problems we run into."

"You figure that one Osage'll come back with some more of his friends?"

"Not likely. They were young renegades. Probably slipped off the reservation down in the Nations looking to get into a little mischief, maybe rob a rancher or two. They hadn't banked on runnin' into somebody who'd shoot back. I figure we'll have a peaceful drive all the way to Dodge . . . if you don't get bucked off that colt again."

"I sure do wish you wouldn't keep remindin' me. Pearlie still can't stop laughin' about it."

"He's only funnin' you 'cause he cares about you, son. If you can't take a little teasin' once in a while you'll never make it at Sugarloaf."

It was Cal's turn to grin. "I'm gettin' even with Pearlie tonight, boss. Just so you'll know, it's only a joke. He's been ridin' me so hard 'bout gittin' bucked off that I been thinkin' of ways to shut him up. Soon as he comes in from ridin' night herd he'll do what he always does—head straight fer this here coffee pot an' then sit down on his bedroll to pull off his boots. I found this great big cocklebur tangled up in that bay colt's tail whilst I was unsaddlin' him. I combed it out. Soon as Pearlie goes to sleep I'm gonna put that cocklebur in one of his boots. You ever notice the way Pearlie puts 'em on in the mornin'? First he stands up an' then he stomps one foot at a time into his boots. When he lands on that burr, we're gonna find out if Pearlie can dance as good as he can sing."

Smoke chuckled. "He'll try to get even with you. He'll know you put it there."

"I'm countin' on it. Maybe then he'll think twice 'bout remindin' me how high I was flyin' when I got throwed back at the ranch."

"You're liable to be in for a cussword or two. Pearlie knows more than a handful of bad words."

"But it'll be my turn to laugh, boss. My ears are plumb sore from listenin' to him heehaw me over gettin' pitched off that mornin'."

"The two of you are worse'n a couple of kids, like when he mixed castor oil in the syrup tin last year, knowing you'd be the first to cover your flapjacks with it and stuff your mouth full. I laughed so hard myself I nearly broke a rib."

Cal frowned. "Wasn't all that funny, you know. I swallowed a whole bunch of it before I got the taste.

I was in the outhouse nearly all that day, seemed like. Miz Jensen took to laughin' every time she seen me runnin' for the two-holer back of the barn. One time I almost didn't make it. She hadn't oughta laughed at me so much. Pearlie never did stop laughin' all day or the next mornin' either."

"It's because they like you, Cal. Sally loves you like you were one of her own. And remember, you got your revenge when you put a dead rattlesnake in his bunk under his blankets. I never heard such a yell as what came from the bunkhouse that night. I bet they heard it all the way to Big Rock."

Cal giggled. "Nearly busted the insides of my ears. Never heard so many cusswords strung together before. He cussed till he ran outa wind."

Smoke's thoughts went back to the ranch, wondering about Sally, wishing he could take her in his arms. It still amazed him that a woman could make him feel that way. He'd been sure he'd spend his life as a bachelor, until he met Sally. She had a power over him no one else ever had, if you didn't count Preacher, and that wasn't the same thing. They had a good life at Sugarloaf, surrounded by good friends and neighbors. It was more than Smoke had ever dreamed of having, after some mighty rough beginnings.

"Seems like you're distracted," Cal said after a bit.

"Thinkin' about Sally and the ranch, is all."

"If you'll pardon me fer sayin' it on account of it's personal, you've gotta be the luckiest man alive, Mr. Jensen, to have found yourself a woman like Miz Jensen. Times, I lay there at night wishin' I could find me a good woman like her. Don't reckon I ever will."

"You're young yet, son. Give it time. I never thought I'd find Sally. I suppose it's fair to say she found me. I was headed down some of the wrong trails when she came along. That little woman brought me up short like she'd put a spade bit in my mouth. Turned my whole life around.''

Cal cleared his throat. "Pearlie told me one time that you was a hard-nosed killer beforehand, that you were a shootist with a mean reputation."

"Maybe I was," Smoke allowed. "I never drew a gun on a man who wasn't goin' fer his gun first, if that matters. But I did some things fer the wrong reasons. Sally made me see the error of my ways. She can give a lecture that'd put any preacher in Colorado Territory to shame."

"I know that part real well, boss. When she gits on a mad an' starts shakin' that finger at me when I forgit sometimes to do chores just right, it's the same as bein' whipped with a willow switch. She can hurt a man worse with her tongue an' that finger than any woman I ever run across, even worse'n my Ma could."

"Sally can be tempermental," Smoke agreed. "Worst part is, she's always right about things. I keep wishing that, just once, she'd be wrong, so I could remind her of it."

"Then she's got that sweet side, like honey. She'll put her hand on my shoulder, or maybe just give me a certain look, an' I git plumb teary-eyed sometimes. When I had the whoopin' cough that time she mothered me like a hen. Like I said, you oughta count yourself as bein' mighty lucky to have her."

Smoke was truly distracted when, off in the night, Pearlie struck a particular sour note in the middle of a song. "I know how lucky I am, Cal. Never a day passes when I don't think about it. I'm gonna ask Sally to give Pearlie some singin' lessons as soon as we get back. Just now he sounded like a tomcat with his tail caught under a rocking chair."

Cal smiled. "Just wait'll you hear the noise he makes when he sticks his foot into the wrong boot tomorrow mornin'. It'll sound a lot worse than his singin', I promise you."

Smoke drifted toward sleep, entering an unwanted dream from his past. Smoke had been sitting on a rock, eating a cold biscuit when Kid Austin, as quick-handed a gunfighter as Smoke had ever faced, came striding toward him.

"Get up!" the Kid shouted. "Get on your feet and face me like a man!"

Smoke ate the last of his meager meal, then he rose to his feet. He was smiling.

The Kid kept coming, narrowing the distance, finally stopping about thirty feet away. He hunkered down like he was ready to make his play. "I'll be known as the man who killed Smoke Jensen," he snarled. "Me! Kid Austin!"

Smoke laughed at him.

The Kid flushed. "I done it to your wife, too, Jensen. She liked it so much she asked me to do it to 'er some more. So I obliged her. I took your woman, an' now I'm gonna take you!" He dipped his right hand downward.

Smoke drew his right-hand .44 with blinding speed, drawing, cocking, firing before Austin could realize what was taking place in front of his eyes. Two molten bullets entered the Kid's body—one in his belly, the other just above his ornate, silver belt buckle. The impact of two .44 shells dropped Austin to his knees while shock and then terror twisted his face. He tried in vain to pull his gun clear of its holster.

"I'm . . . Kid Austin," he croaked. "You can't . . . do this to me."

"Looks like I did anyways," Smoke said, turning away from the dying man to walk to his horse. Nicole, Smoke's first wife, and their son were dead by the hand of Kid Austin and his gang. He had tried to live in peace. The men who took what was near and dear to him wouldn't allow it.

He mounted Seven without looking back, until he heard the Kid cry, "It hurts, Momma! Help me!"

Austin was on his knees, rocked back on his haunches with his hands covering his belly, staring up at the sky. None of the other members of his gang were there to hear him begging. A loop of bloody intestine dangled from a hole in his shirtfront. Blood poured over the ground around him.

"Help me, Momma," the Kid said again, weakly this time as blood loss and pain began to claim him.

Smoke knew that Nicole must have begged for the gang members to stop before they killed her. Somehow, hearing the Kid beg for help wasn't enough justice for what he and his men had done to Smoke's family.

"I'm . . . Kid . . . Austin," he gasped, slowly toppling over on his side, curling into a fetal position. His Colt fell out of its holster, clattering on the rocks, glinting in the gauzy sunlight that was filtering into the canyon between the tall timbers.

"You can't . . . do this . . . to me," he groaned again, faint, hard to hear.

Smoke's jaw turned to granite. "Hell, I can't," he

spat, his teeth clamped together, holding Seven in check while he gave the gunman a final look.

One of the Kid's feet had begun to twitch in death. Smoke reined Seven away from the scene and started out of the canyon at a walk, his horse's hoofbeats echoing off canyon walls.

Behind him, the canyon was quiet. There was only the soft sighing of the wind passing through treetops where a corpse lay in a pool of crimson.

He rode back to the cabin in the valley and packed up his belongings, covering the pack frame with a ground sheet. He rubbed Seven down and fed him grain and hay.

Smoke cleaned his guns and made camp outside the cabin that night. He could not bear to sleep inside that house of death and torture and rape where Nicole and their son ended their lives.

His sleep had been restless, remaining that way for the week he stayed there, troubled by nightmares in which Nicole called out his name, and sounds of the baby crying.

The second week had been no better, his sleep interrupted by the same nightmare over and over again. Thus, when he kicked out of his blankets on that final morning in the valley, his body was covered with sweat. Smoke knew he could never rest until the men who rode with Kid Austin—the men who had violated Nicole and killed her along with the child—were dead . . . Potter, Stratton, and Richards.

He rode out of the valley, swinging north, bent on vengeance against the others. It had been the beginning of a long trail to track them down. And he was dreaming about it again, even after so many years. He wished the haunting dream would leave him alone.

Later, he awoke with a start when Pearlie came in from night duty with the herd.

"All's quiet, boss," Pearlie said, stripping his saddle off the dun.

"Sure glad to hear how quiet it is," he heard Cal say as the boy mounted to take Pearlie's place. "Sure do hope it stays that way tomorrow mornin'."

Smoke lay back down, grinning, knowing what Cal meant. And he felt good, being awakened from his awful dreams about a past he wanted to forget. Sally and Sugarloaf were his future, and he'd never been happier.

Chapter 6

False dawn brightened eastern skies when some inner sense awakened Smoke to danger. He reached for his rifle, turning over in his bedroll slowly, blinking sleep from his eyes. He lay for a moment, listening.

Off to his right, Cal rode slowly around the sleeping herd, until Smoke noticed that some of the steers were coming to their feet with ears cocked southward.

Smoke examined the southern skyline, passing a slow glance across each dark hill, every low spot. At first, he heard nothing at all besides the soft rustle of steer hooves on dry grass as more of the Hereford crosses stood up, hind legs first as was a cow's habit.

Cal stopped his horse, standing in his stirrups, also aware that something was wrong, something disturbing the cattle enough to bring them up before dawn.

Then Smoke saw what was frightening the steers. In a swale between two hills, a wolf pack trotted toward the cattle scent. In packs, timber wolves or gray wolves were often able to bring down a calf. Until the clever animals got closer they had no way of knowing the size of the cows they smelled on night winds.

Smoke came to his feet, balancing his Winchester in the crook of his arm. He stepped into his boots quietly, so as not to awaken Pearlie, and walked softly toward Cal.

"It's a wolf pack," he said when he reached the boy. "No need to worry. Soon as those smart creatures see how big our steers are they'll leave 'em alone. A wolf's too smart to take on any kind of animal this size, even when they're traveling in a pack like this bunch."

"There was that lobo a couple of years back, if you recall," Cal said in a quiet voice. "He came right up to the barns like he wasn't scared of nothin'."

Smoke remembered. "A big lobo timber wolf is a bit different. They aren't as afraid of a man's smell. These'll be gray wolves in this flat country. If they get any closer I'll fire a shot over their heads, and that'll be the end of it."

"How come you don't just shoot one of 'em?" Cal asked. "If you shoot one, the others'll sure enough hightail it out of here."

"No reason to kill it," Smoke replied. "They're doing what nature meant fer 'em to do . . . look for food. They scented these cattle on the wind, and to them, it's like a dinner bell. They wouldn't bother steers as big as these anyway."

"Not even in a pack?"

Smoke wagged his head. "They're too smart. A six-hundred-pound steer with a set of horns could kill a wolf easily, if it got the chance and if it was range-bred like ours. Wolves have instincts that tell 'em what to do, and what to avoid.''

"They sure do look spooky, trotting across that dark grass the way they are.''

Smoke watched the darker outline of the leader of the pack take the others upwind. "To me, they're beautiful animals. All they want is somethin' to eat. That big male will see what he's up against in a minute or two, and he'll signal that the hunt is over. Watch, and you'll learn something about wolves. Unless I'm dead wrong, that big male will stop shortly. He'll size up the situation and turn away. For two reasons. He'll smell men and the smoke from the coals in our firepit. And he'll know these steers are too big to bring down.''

Cal looked down from his horse, examining what he could see of Smoke's face in the semi-darkness. "You never are much when it comes to shootin' animals, I've noticed, even somethin' as dangerous as a wolf.''

"No need. I suppose it's because I've got respect for all of nature's creatures, even a polecat. A polecat don't have but one weapon, and that's his stink. He won't use it unless he feels threatened.''

"But a wolf eats meat, boss.''

"Only the meat it can catch and bring down. Keep your eyes on that big male. He's about to call off the hunt. Wait and see if I'm right about it.''

Almost at once the heavy male wolf halted in its tracks to sniff the wind, swinging its massive head back and forth to take on more scent. The wolf's tail went up as a silent warning to the others behind it, and just as suddenly, the other wolves came to a stop.

For half a minute or more, the wolves remained frozen to the spot, watching the herd of steers. Then, as Smoke predicted, the big male turned away and trotted off, leading his pack into a dry creekbed west of the herd.

"You sure were right about it," Cal said, a note of amazement in his voice. "They wasn't near as brave as that big lobo that came to the barns."

"A lobo is different," Smoke explained, turning to go back to the fire to start coffee. "He's alone for a reason. He don't think like other wolves, and that's why he doesn't run with a pack like those we just saw. A lobo is dangerous, but he's still real smart. Real hard to kill, in case you've never tried. Some way or another, a lobo can damn near feel a rifle's sights on him."

One of the steers let out a mournful bawl as cattle sometimes do when calling to each other. On the far side of the herd an answering bawl broke the silence.

"These cows don't seem agitated," Cal observed, as more of the steers came to their feet. "I reckon they didn't catch no wolf smell real strong, or they'd be millin' around, actin' like they was nervous about it."

"Sally was right about a Hereford being a gentler breed, an' it shows in the crosses. Takes a lot to spook 'em. Like I told you last night, Sally's right about damn near everything, and a mite too quick to remind me of it."

Cal chuckled, resting his elbow on his saddlehorn. "That's about the most halfhearted complaint I ever heard, boss."

"Wasn't a complaint, son, just a simple statement of plain fact."

A shadow moved near the firepit, and a split second later a shrill cry came from a figure hopping up and down on one foot.

"Damn, damn, damn, damn, damn!" Pearlie bellowed, slumping to the ground on his rump. "Feels like a damn porcupine decided to spend the night inside one of my damn boots!"

Cal got a sudden case of the giggles, trying to cover his mouth with one hand while they watched Pearlie struggle to get a boot off. Smoke grinned while witnessing Cal's sweet revenge.

"What the hell?" Pearlie exclaimed, holding something up to his face. Then his head snapped toward the herd where Cal was seated on his night horse. "Where the hell's that young 'un?" he snarled. "When I git my hands 'round his skinny little neck I'm gonna choke him plumb to death. . . ."

Cal could contain himself no longer and burst out laughing. Even Smoke had to chuckle out loud over Pearlie's outburst.

"What happened, Pearlie?" Cal asked as innocently as he was able, between fits of laughter. "Looked like you was dancin' a while ago, only I didn't hear no fiddler playin'. Where's the music?"

"I'm gonna kill you deader'n a gate hinge if'n I can git my hands on you, boy!" Pearlie shouted. "I could be a cripple the rest of my life for what you just done to me. Feels like there's blood in my boot . . . an' my sock's wringin' wet. I'm liable to bleed to death here, an' all on account of some snot-nosed kid who thinks he's done somethin' funny! Damn, damn, damn, that hurts!"

Cal let out a gale of heehaws, then he yelled, "Whoopee! I got you back, Mister Pearlie. Now who's doin' the laughin'?"

Smoke had heard enough, ambling back toward the firepit to get flames going for coffee and breakfast while Pearlie uttered a string of cusswords, rubbing his sore foot, swearing to have his revenge against Cal if it took him the rest of his life.

"Let's get this herd moving," Smoke said, tossing dry wood on the coals when Pearlie ran out of breath. "You boys can have at each other some other time, when we don't have cattle to get to market."

In the beginnings of flickering firelight licking up the sides of the woodpile, Pearlie gave Cal an angry glare. "I'm gonna git that boy next time," he muttered, to have the last word. "I swear I'm gonna fix him good . . . he's got no respect fer his elders, an' I'm gonna learn him some manners."

"Maybe he was remembering all those trips he made to the outhouse a while back," Smoke suggested, grinning.

Pearlie adopted an indignant look. "Have you plumb forgot 'bout that serpent he put in my bed? Any man who'd put a snake in another feller's bunk deserves to be shot. I didn't shoot him that night 'cause we was short-handed at the ranch. Otherwise, I'd have plugged him right then an' there."

Smoke was forced to laugh at Pearlie's mock rage. Pearlie and Cal were as close as brothers when there was work to be done or when the chips were down in a dangerous situation. Anyone who didn't really know them would think they were out to kill each other on a regular basis.

The herd stretched out for a quarter mile, moving slowly, grazing where the steers could find grass. The land yawning before them was empty, not a sign of civilization in this section of southwestern Colorado beyond a few widely scattered wagon ruts where seldom-used trails crisscrossed the countryside. Smoke rode point, guiding the way, using dead reckoning rather than a marked route to follow with the angle of the sun as a guidepost. Other than for the skirmish with the Osages, the trip was going peacefully enough. By Smoke's old standard, shooting three renegades bent on stealing a few beeves was a relatively mild irritation.

Off in the distance he could see a faint, green line, the Arkansas River where it wound its way across territorial boundaries into Kansas. This was land he seldom traveled, and the Kansas prairies were not to his liking—mile after mile of low flint hills without trees in most places, a featureless region where only the most determined settlers tried to establish farms and homesteads, raising a few cattle and sheep, living in sod dugouts, existing on small gardens and what meat they could raise during years when rains came. Thinking on it to pass time, Smoke supposed he'd been spoiled by the raw beauty of the High Lonesome in Colorado. He'd become a man with a kinship to the mountains and high valleys, never quite feeling at home anyplace else.

An hour later, when the river was in sight, he saw a lone horseman coming toward them at a long, ground-eating trot as if he were a man in something of a hurry.

"Maybe he's got troubles," Smoke muttered to himself, as the stud flicked his ears back when he heard his master's voice.

A quarter hour more and the rider approached Smoke, slowing his lathered horse a bit until he rode up and came to a halt.

"Howdy, mister," the stranger said, a man dressed in a badly worn business suit and bowler hat, a drummer by his appearance, although he had no packhorse or mule to carry whatever he might be peddling. "I saw your dust as I was crossing the river. I thought I'd warn you." The man carried a shotgun slung from his saddle by a leather shoulder strap, a hunting gun some men called a fowler's piece used for ducks and geese. The slight bulge of a small-caliber pistol showed beneath his coat.

Smoke scowled. "Warn me about what?"

"Robbers," he replied, taking off his hat to sleeve sweat and dust from his forehead. "By way of introduction, I'm Horace Grimes from Springfield. Be cautious as you cross over into Kansas. A gang of thieves and murderers is on the prowl to the east and south of Dodge City. It's an awful story, what happened to me, and to a shopkeeper and his family. I feel lucky to have escaped with my life."

"Tell me about it," Smoke said quietly.

"My personal experience with them was, upon reflection, very fortunate. My mule, along with all my buttons and fasteners, were stolen from my campsite while I was away hunting wild turkey for supper. I got back just in time to see a gang of twenty-five or thirty men stealing my mule. They were hard-looking characters, carrying an assortment of weaponry, so I remained in hiding up on a ridge while they scattered my inventory all over the ground in search of something more valuable, I presume. They took my mule and packsaddle, leaving me no way to carry what I sell. I'm a sales representative with the Springfield Fastener Company. I'm a peaceful man, heading for Dodge City to sell my wares. But the gang of thieves rode off in the direction of Dodge, leaving me no choice but to ride around the city. I've been looking for some sort of military outpost or a peace officer where I can report to the proper authorities what took place. There are no towns and no telegraph lines here. I must confess I'm utterly lost without a map or a road to guide me."

"What was this about a shopkeeper and his family?" Smoke asked, wondering who the thieves might be, traveling together in such large numbers.

Now Grimes's face turned pale. He reached inside his coat for a handkerchief to wipe his face. "Shortly thereafter I came upon a most dreadful sight, while trying to ride in another direction to avoid running headlong into the thieves. At a small stream I found the partially burned remains of a general store. It had been looted and burned. Among the ashes were the bodies of five people, a man and a woman, and the blackened corpses of three children. Some of the building was still smoldering. I must find a place to report this to the authorities as soon as possible."

Smoke gazed across the river into Kansas. "No place behind us, Mr. Grimes. You're welcome to ride with us back to Dodge City to file your report. There's a telegraph and a railroad line. Should be a few peace officers."

"But that was the direction this gang was riding, sir."

Smoke shrugged. "Like I said, you're welcome to stay with us to Dodge. You'll be plenty safe. You've got my word on it."

Chapter 7

Pearlie and Cal rode up to meet the stranger as the steers were crossing the shallow river . . . they both gave Grimes curious stares during the introductions.

"Name's Pearlie," Pearlie said. "This here's Cal," he added as the men shook hands. Then Pearlie frowned. "You was headed west, an' now you've done changed directions to ride with us. I was just curious about it."

Smoke was urging cattle into the shallows when Grimes gave his reply.

"I ran into a terrible situation," Grimes began. "I'm new to this part of the country, and I was seeking a military post or a town with a peace officer and a telegraph line to report more than one unlawful incident I had the misfortune to be a witness to. I was looking for someone with the legal authority to do something about it."

"That'd be Dodge City," Pearlie said, "only you're ridin' in the wrong direction. It's east."

"I know," Grimes answered, casting a look in the direction from which he had come. "I was heading for Dodge City when I was set upon by a gang of robbers. They stole my packmule and left the goods I was carrying scattered all over my campsite. Only that wasn't the worst of it. The gang rode toward Dodge, and I sought another route, hoping to find another town where I could report what had taken place. In the course of my travels, I came to a scene so brutal, so heartless, it rendered me ill. A small trading post beside a stream southeast of Dodge was burned almost to the ground. Among the ruins, I found five bodies, charred beyond recognition. A man and a woman, and three children, two of them hardly more than infants. The store's supplies had been looted. Empty shelves lay among the ashes. It was ghastly—the stuff of nightmares. I'm quite certain it was the same gang of highwaymen who robbed me, only I was more fortunate than members of that tragic family. They lost their lives."

Pearlie glanced over at Smoke. "Did you tell the bossman 'bout this here gang?"

"I did. He invited me to travel with you to Dodge City, so I could report what I saw to the proper authorities. He said there was a railroad and a telegraph there, and certainly a few peace officers. Your boss assured me I'd be safe with you."

Cal chuckled. "That'd be the truth if you ever heard it in your life. Do you know who our bossman is?"

"He did not bother to give me his name, however he is well armed and he seems quite sure of himself."

"He's none other than Smoke Jensen," Pearlie said.

Grimes frowned. "The name doesn't ring a bell."

"Well sir, it should," Cal said. "He's just about the most dangerous man with a gun in all of Colorado Territory, if he gits pushed. He was a gunfighter some time ago. Lives real peaceful now, runnin' a cow outfit, but I wouldn't wanna be the man who crosses him."

Pearlie nodded. "The name may not ring no bell with you, mister, but it damn sure does in these parts. Just ask around if you got any doubts."

"I'm from Springfield," Grimes said. "This was to be my first tour of this area, selling fasteners. While I've never heard of Mr. Smoke Jensen, it does not mean I have any doubts about his ability to protect me. I'm a fairly good judge of character. Mr. Jensen seems quite capable of handling himself. I do, however, have certain reservations. One man, or even the three of you, won't stand a chance against the men who took my mule and packsaddle. These were ruffians, lawless men by the looks of them, and what they most certainly did to that storekeeper and his family makes them cold-blooded murderers as well as thieves."

More cows crossed the river. Pearlie lifted his reins to lend a hand collecting those already on the far side. "Tell us 'bout this gang you mentioned. Did you git a look at 'em?"

"I saw them from a distance. There was so many, I remained hidden until they rode away from my camp with my mule and my packsaddle."

"When you say *so many*, just how many might that have been?"

"Perhaps thirty. Hard-looking men with pistols and

rifles. One appeared to be wearing an old Confederate uniform.''

"Thirty?" Pearlie asked. "Are you right sure you can count, Mr. Grimes?"

"At least that many. Possibly more. I was too frightened to get a closer look to be certain of their number. I knew I stood no chance against them."

Pearlie rolled his eyes in Cal's direction before he rode off to help Smoke with the strays. "That's a sizeable bunch of bad men," he muttered. "Hard to figure why there'd be so many travelin' together. It's also hard to guess why one of 'em would be wearin' a Confederate uniform so long after the war. That part don't make a lick of sense."

Cal rode up beside Pearlie to push the last of the steers across. "I've got this bad feelin' in the pit of my stomach, Pearlie," Cal said. "Somethin' tells me Smoke is gonna put us right where this outlaw gang is gonna be. You heard that feller say they was headed fer Dodge City, didn't you?"

"I ain't got no extra wax in my ears, Cal," he said with a touch of irritation. "You can damn well bet we're gonna be right square in the middle of a ruckus if them robbers happen to be in Dodge when Smoke Jensen an' the rest of us git there. May as well check the loads in yer pistol an' rifle right now. I can feel a fight comin'.''

"I warned you that mornin' I got bucked off, this was gonna be an unlucky trip. I felt it all the way to my bones."

"Them sore bones was on account of your fall, son. But when you ride with Smoke, you can lay long odds that we'll find a peck of trouble someplace or 'nother."

"Smoke said this was gonna be a peaceful trip,

that all we was gonna do was take these yearlin's to market.''

Pearlie made a face. "How many times, when we's gone someplace with the boss, have we set out on somethin' peaceful, only to wind up pickin' lead outa our hides?''

"Seems like a bunch.''

"Now you've got my drift," Pearlie said, urging a piebald steer into the river. "Ever watch buzzards circlin' in the sky, son? There'll always be somethin' dead underneath 'em. It's a harsh thing to say 'bout a good feller like Smoke, but the same can be said about trouble findin' him. You ain't been with this outfit long as I have. I've seen it a dozen times. We could set out to gather eggs in Miz Jensen's hen house, an' if Smoke happened to be along, there'd be some owlhoot with a gun hidin' behind them layin' cages, takin' shots at us.''

"You got this tendency to exaggerate, Pearlie," Cal said, reining his bay into the water. "It ain't always that bad, but there's been times when it seemed that way. The boss is tryin' to keep his word to Miz Jensen to stay away from other men's difficulties. He wouldn't intentionally break his word to her for anything. It just seems to happen, like a rainstorm that comes up all of a sudden.''

Pearlie urged his dun toward the shallows.

"You ever hear of a magnet, young 'un?''

"Yessir. It draws metal. I seen this feller in Denver on a street corner, peddlin' magnets. He claimed they was magic, that they had magical powers. Made sense to me, 'cause there ain't no other way to explain why one piece of iron would pull another up against it. It's gotta be some kinda magic. That peddler laid out a handful of horseshoe nails on this little table, and when he held that magnet over 'em, they jumped off the table like they was alive and grabbed hold of that magnet like they was stuck with glue. I was gonna buy one, just to show folks I could do magic myself, only they cost two bits an' I didn't have that much money.''

"It ain't magic," Pearlie said, when his horse reached belly-deep water. "It's a special kind of metal in 'em. And there's men who've got a special kind of drawin' power when it comes to guns an' gunplay. Smoke draws them hard-nosed types same as a magnet draws other kinds of metal. You wait an' see if I ain't right. I'm bettin' a month's pay that, by the time we git to Dodge, that outlaw bunch will be there, an' Smoke'll find 'em, unless they find him first. There's gonna be more bloodlettin' afore this ride is over."

"But I heard Smoke promise Miz Jensen he wouldn't get in no kinda trouble this time."

Pearlie chuckled, but with a touch of worry in the sound of it. "I'm dead sure he meant it when he gave her that promise, but that don't account for circumstances."

"Circumstances?" Cal asked in a way that made it clear he wasn't sure what Pearlie was talking about.

Pearlie took a deep breath, as though he'd grown frustrated trying to show Cal the logic behind his reasoning. "You think it might be just bad luck that a gang of murderin' thieves is headed fer Dodge same time as we are?"

"But how would they know we was comin', Pearlie? An' how would Smoke know?"

"It's called fate, young 'un. Some men have got the fates dead set against 'em. Smoke is one of 'em. Most other men can ride all the way from California to Dodge City without havin' so much as a loose horseshoe. Smoke don't hardly ever git that kind of peace. It's the hand of fate that keeps guidin' him toward a fight."

"All he aimed to do was sell these steers," Cal protested as they rode out on the far bank.

Pearlie let it drop, knowing Smoke could hear them now. He rode up and down the riverbank pushing steers into a bunch for the trail running beside the Arkansas River. A road of sorts following the course of the river would take them all the way to Dodge City.

Smoke got the lead steers turned east. Pearlie rode up to him just as the rest of the herd fell in behind the leaders.

"You hear what that feller said 'bout that gang?"

"He told me," Smoke replied quietly, paying more attention to the condition of their cattle, satisfied when he noted their bellies were full and hardly a one was traveling sorefooted in spite of sharp flint rock underneath their hooves.

"Did Grimes also tell you there was thirty of 'em?" Pearlie continued.

"He did," Smoke answered, counting steers as they went past him to see if they'd lost any on the trail—it seemed there were always a few strays that wandered off in the brush on any trail drive, no matter how carefully a group of cowhands tried to keep them together.

"Did he also tell you 'bout that one wearin' a Confederate uniform?"

Smoke stopped counting to look at Pearlie. "He didn't make mention of that part."

A slow recollection of something Louis Longmont told him a few years ago crept into Smoke's thoughts. Louis said there were rumors and occasional newspaper articles in Kansas City and a few Missouri papers that an infamous raider known as Bloody Bill Anderson had not been killed shortly after the war, as it was first reported after an incident at a farm house where possemen claimed to have killed Anderson, one of Quantrill's lieutenants, a madman who continued robbing and murdering Union sympathizers after the war ended. Despite what appeared to have been a positive identification of the body by men who knew Anderson, there were reports of sightings all over the Territories long after his supposed death, and numerous bloody scenes near the spots where folks claimed to have seen Anderson and his gang of looters. Louis had said it was hogwash, that Anderson was dead and that someone was merely impersonating him to shift blame for the raids and killings. Louis felt sure that Anderson was in his grave and that an imposter was using his name and reputation to hide his true identity. Louis Longmont was seldom wrong when it came to history, being a well-read, highly educated man.

"Louis told me there used to be rumors that Bloody Bill Anderson was still alive," Smoke told Pearlie, "some killer who dressed in a Confederate uniform, claiming to be Anderson. Bill Anderson was killed by a posse not too long after the war, an' men who knew him positively identified the body. That's what Louis said. I wouldn't pay too much attention to Grimes. It's more likely there were only a dozen men or so who stole his mule . . . probably a bunch of drifters and saddle tramps who found easy pickings. Same goes for the folks who were robbed and killed at that tradin' post. It's more likely the work of a gang of misfits and cowards. One of 'em just happened to be wearing pieces of an old Confederate uniform."

"I remember hearin' all about Bloody Bill Anderson and Quantrill's raiders," Pearlie said. "You said Louis told you there were rumors he was still alive."

"Louis said they were *rumors*, Pearlie. Stories written up in a newspaper."

"I sure as hell hope that's *all* they are," Pearlie said as a frown creased his dust-caked forehead. "Him an' Quantrill was supposed to be real mean hombres."

"You pay too much attention to a man's reputation," Smoke said, swinging his Palouse to head for the point position at the front of the herd. "Most times, that's all it is—a batch of made-up stories designed to scare folks. Now let's get these steers to the railhead before they die of old age while you're worrying about other things. Louis told me Bloody Bill Anderson was dead, and that's good enough for me . . . and even if he ain't, he's just another man who bleeds and dies if a bullet hits him in the right spot."

Chapter 8

"We'll need more mules an' packhorses to haul off the gold an' banknotes," Bill said, holding a half empty bottle of whiskey by the neck while he stared into the fire, a bottle taken from Dave Cobbs's store. "With two banks, there's gonna be plenty of money needin' to be hauled off in a hurry. We'll head south to Indian Territory an' lay low for a spell, like we was doin' up 'til now. There'll be plenty of law dogs out to hang us, an' the army'll be lookin' for us too. Ain't hardly no law in the west part of Indian Territory. We'll be safe enough if we stay outa sight, send one or two men to the closest settlement to buy the things we need."

"We're gonna be rich," Sammy said, after taking a sip of whiskey from a bottle he shared with his brother. "Won't be no more poor days fer none of us."

Claude nodded in agreement. "It's flat country all

the way to Dodge from here, Bill. A few hills. Maybe five miles to the outskirts of town. When I scouted it today, Dodge looked real quiet. Hardly any herds there yet. This train came in from the east, an' I watched it with my field glass. Six soldiers got off the baggage car, carrying cash boxes of loot down to one of the banks, four of 'em did, whilst the others guarded the shipment with rifles. You was right 'bout them banks bein' full. There's money comin' on every train, most likely."

"Maybe we oughta wait a day or two," another man suggested from the far side of the firepit. "If there's money comin' damn near every day, that's more fer us."

"I ain't in the mood for waitin'," Bill said. "We ain't got hardly any cash money an' I'm ready to stuff my pockets full of Yankee gold."

"We never did find that storekeeper's money," Jack Starr said in a sour voice. "The woman wouldn't talk even when I told her I was gonna bust her baby's skull with the butt of my gun 'less she told where it was."

Sammy chuckled. "She was screamin' too loud to talk," he said. "When Claude tore her dress off, 'bout all she would do was scream her head off. Even when ol' Billy Ray was havin' his way with her, all the bitch did was scream an' try to fight them ropes while we was holdin' her legs. She was a lot stronger'n we figured."

Bill took another swallow of whiskey. "We got most of what we needed . . . this here redeye—twenty bottles of it—an' enough in the way of food to keep us fed for weeks while we're hidin' from the law. Storekeeper like that, he wouldn't have much cash money anyhow."

"He sure did try an' git back up after you shot him, Bill. I never seen a feller try so hard in all my borned days. He come up three or four times, shakin' like a cold pig, only he fell back down from his hands an' knees every time," Claude remembered.

Sammy chimed in. "That sure was a pretty fire, boys. Them flames jumped higher'n hell. Real pretty, too . . . yellow colored with plenty of smoke, making them poppin' noises when the jars of pickled peaches busted. We shouldn't have left so many of them peaches behind."

"Wasn't enough packhorses to carry everything," someone offered. "We got most of the good stuff, like this here bottle of whiskey an' all them others."

Anderson looked up from his idle contemplation of the coals in the pit. "Who's out ridin' guard tonight?" he asked, as if it had suddenly occurred to him that their camp might need watching.

"Lee an' Sonny are up north," Jack Starr replied. "That's where somebody's most likely to stumble onto our camp headed to Dodge. Dewey an' Roy are ridin' circles south, just in case anybody comes from another direction."

"Good idea," Bill said, "only it appeared Roy was too damn drunk to sit in a saddle just before dark. Maybe this cold night air'll sober him up."

Someone belched loudly outside the circle of fire-light, a supper of boiled beans and fried fatback not resting well with a bellyful of whiskey.

Claude said, "We hadn't oughta take no chances. If Dewey an' Roy's both drunk, maybe somebody oughta go relieve 'em on night watch."

Bill nodded. "We sure as hell don't need to be takin' no chances, not with all that's at stake in them banks. Two of you boys who can mount a damn horse go fetch Roy an' Dewey back to camp. Don't want no slipups on this job, boys. This'll be the biggest payday of our lives. Any sumbitch don't do his job right an' I'm gonna shoot him myself. I want that understood real clear."

"Let's you an' me go, Sammy," Claude said, coming to his feet slowly, rubbing one knee while he held a bottle of whiskey in the other.

"It's cold out yonder, away from this fire," Sammy protested as his brow formed a frown. "Let somebody else go."

Bill drew his right-hand pistol and aimed it across the fire directly into Sammy's face. "Get on your damn horse," he said, thumbing back the Colt's hammer, "or you ain't gonna notice the cold much longer."

Sammy came abruptly to his feet. "All I was sayin' was, it's cold," he said, backing away from the muzzle of Bill's gun with fear widening his badly crossed eyes. "I sure never said I wouldn't go. No sir, I never said that . . ." He wheeled as he was speaking and hurried off toward the picket lines where their horses were tethered. Claude followed him into the darkness as a silence gripped the camp. Everyone knew that Bill Anderson would shoot one of his own men over the slightest provocation, and as often as not, for no clear reason at all.

Bill put his pistol away. "Some of you boys need to be reminded it takes discipline to hold an outfit together. Well I'm damn sure here to remind any sumbitch who forgets."

As Sammy and Claude were saddling their horses, a sound came from the northwest—horses moving toward the fire at a trot.

"That'll be Lee an' Sonny," a voice said. "Wonder what the hell they's doin' comin' back?"

Bill saw three men outlined against a star-sprinkled sky as they rode over the crest of a rise above the hollow he'd selected for a campsite, where travelers couldn't see the glow of their fire from a distance.

"There's three," another member of the gang said. "Who the hell've they got with 'em?"

"Looks like they've a prisoner," Jack Starr's deep voice answered. "The stranger's got his hands tied behind him. . . .I can see that from here."

Bill stood up, resting one palm on the butt of a pistol, the other hand wrapped around the neck of his whiskey bottle. "Bring the sumbitch to the fire," he said lowly, his right gunhand tensing while his fingers curled around his walnut pistol grips. "I want a damn explanation for why they brung him here. Don't them two fools know we'll have to kill him, now that he knows where we's camped?"

"Must be a reason," Starr muttered under his breath, making his way toward the silhouettes of Lee and Sonny and a newcomer with his hands behind him. Starr drew his Dance revolver and held it at his side.

"Who've you got there?" Starr demanded when the three riders were at the picket ropes.

Sonny's tinny voice resounded from the tether lines as he dismounted. "Just an old man, Jack, but he was headed this way an' we had to stop him or he'd have rode right up on this here fire."

"Pull him down an' bring him over to the light where Bill can see him," Starr replied.

The figure between Bill's night guards was jerked out of the saddle, landing with a grunt on his face and chest near the front hooves of his horse.

"Git up, you ol' geezer," Sonny demanded, "or I'll shoot a hole through the backside of your skullbone."

The man struggled to his feet despite his bindings, and then he was shoved toward the firepit at gunpoint. Sonny held his .44 against the man's spine, prodding him with it.

A slope-shouldered man in his sixties with flowing gray hair came to the fire, his eyes roaming the assortment of hard faces staring at him.

"Who the hell are you?" Bill snapped. "An' what the hell are you doin' out here in the middle of nowhere so late at night on a damn horse?"

The old man refused to answer at first. A bloody gash left a trickle of crimson running down his left cheek into his gray beard.

"Says his name is Smith," the gunman named Lee Wollard said when he walked up to join the others. "Hell, if we was to make ourselves believe every sumbitch who said his name was Smith is a relative of the Smith family, wouldn't be nothin' but Smiths in this whole Territory. I slapped him across the face with the barrel of my gun, only he won't say no more. He just stared up at me, sullen like a damned mule so his jaw won't work when it's supposed to."

"I can loosen that jaw some," Bill snarled, walking slowly around the fire until he stood in front of the old man. "I can put a little grease on it, so to speak."

Having said that, Bill swung his Colt in a wide arc, landing it squarely across the stranger's lips. The old man staggered back and fell down on the seat of his pants, yet he still glared at Bill defiantly, slitting his eyelids.

"He ain't the real talkative sort," Sonny said. "Maybe if I was to stomp on his belly some with these here stovepipe boots he'd find some words inside his mouth.''

"Suit yourself," Bill remarked. "Kick the hell out of him a few times. Let's see if it works.''

Sonny lifted a booted foot with a silver spur tied to the heel and smashed it into the old man's stomach. A groan came from the downed man's tightly closed lips despite all his efforts to prevent it.

"Kick him again, Sonny," Lee said, grinning in the poor light. "Ask him what the hell he's doin' out here so late. We got a right to know, seein' as this is our camp he was fixin' to ride up on. The bastard ain't got no manners or he'd have rode off in 'nother direction. Kick him real hard this time, so he'll know we mean business.''

Sonny, a razor-thin cowboy with deeply bowed legs, swung his foot into the old man's ribs with all his might. A rush of air came from the nostrils of the man who called himself Smith, and still he did not utter a word.

"Tough ol' sumbitch," someone witnessing the affair said when it was clear the man wouldn't talk yet. "You're gonna have to hurt him real bad, I'll bet, afore he says anything.''

Bill gazed down at the old man's face. "I'll hand it to you, Mr. Smith. You damn sure know how to take a little pain without complainin' about it. But we ain't done. Before we get through, you'll talk. I'll promise you that much. You see, we gotta know if you was out here spyin' on us. You got no choice but to tell us what we need to know, or you're gonna die. Is that part gettin' through your thick skull?''

Blood oozed from the old man's mouth, dribbling into his beard, falling in tiny damp circles on the ground underneath him, but his lips did not move. He took a deep breath.

"Kick him again, Sonny," Bill demanded. "Make it right near one of his kidneys. In case you ain't never been kicked there, it hurts like hell an' you'll be passin' blood fer days afterward."

Sonny swung his boot toe into the man's lower back, and all who were standing there heard the thud of the blow. Smith winced, twisting his face with pain, until he coughed up a huge mouthful of blood. He said nothing.

Bill looked at the men closest to him. "Some of you boys get mounted. We need to make damn sure this old man was alone, that there ain't others out there lookin' for us. Word of what we done at that tradin' post may have reached the law over in Dodge."

"He was by hisself," Lee insisted, looking to Sonny for agreement. "We checked for half a mile in every direction 'fore we brung him back here."

"I want ten men in saddles," Bill said. "Scour every damn inch of these hills. If word gets to the law dogs in Dodge that we're close to town, they'll form up a posse an' come lookin' for us."

In twos and threes, gunmen left the fire to saddle their horses, spurs clanking across rocky ground.

Bill looked down at the bloody, bearded face resting on the ground near his feet. The old man's eyes were fixed on his in a steady, unwavering stare. "You know we have to kill you, old timer," he said, with what could have been a suggestion of respect in his voice. "You might tell other folks where we are if we let you go. I'll agree you're a tough old son of a bitch, to take that kickin' without spillin' your guts. Just so you'll know, it ain't personal. I'm Bill Anderson. Some have taken to callin' me Bloody Bill. We're gonna rob them banks in Dodge City, an' we can't have the whole damn town expectin' us. This is just business, old man. I gotta make sure your mouth stays shut.''

Smith's eyes closed. He nodded once, as though he understood.

Bill aimed down at Smith's forehead and pulled the trigger. The report from his .44 was like a clap of thunder rolling across the Kansas prairie southeast of Dodge.

Chapter 9

Smoke felt some satisfaction over their crossbred steers and the way they handled the trail. Despite his initial worries that the Hereford blood in them would make them difficult to drive over long distances, their longhorn characteristics prevailed in ways he hadn't expected.

He spoke to Pearlie. "Those short legs don't seem to make all that much difference in the way these steers travel. I had it figured otherwise."

Pearlie nodded as the cattle wandered over a grassy flat, grazing hungrily. "It's that Meskin longhorn in 'em," he said with certainty. "The Hereford makes this bunch gentler, but I'd hate like hell to have to round 'em up if we have a stampede on our hands."

"That don't seem likely," Smoke offered, gazing across the eastern horizon. "These cattle are pretty well trail-broke by now."

"Hearin', or seein' the wrong thing'll spook 'em,"

Pearlie insisted. "I ain't gonna start countin' no chickens till we got eggs in a basket at Dodge."

"We should be there tomorrow," Smoke said, "if I remember this country right."

Pearlie gave him a sideways look. "You think there's anything to that story Grimes told us 'bout them raiders, an' maybe it bein' Bloody Bill Anderson?"

Smoke gave him an indifferent shrug. "Don't see how it matters to us, so long as whoever it was don't try to steal any of our beeves."

Pearlie looked eastward. "It's after you pocket the money fer these steers I'm worryin' about."

"You worry too much, Pearlie."

"It's my nature. My pappy was a worrier. Momma said it was what put him in an early grave."

Smoke turned back in the saddle. Grimes and Cal were driving the last of the steers over a swell in the prairie. A few steers were limping some after so many miles traveling on flinty soil. "I hope you don't worry yourself to death the way your pappy did," Smoke said absently, his mind on the lame cows bringing up the rear of the herd. "This ground's too damn hard to dig a grave. We'll have to cover you up with your bedroll and leave you on top of one of these hills. We didn't bring a shovel, and I won't dig in this flint with my bare hands. I'll get Cal to say a few words over you, but that's about the best we can do if you cross over here due to worryin'."

"I ain't dead yet," Pearlie growled, "an' I damn sure ain't gonna be happy to have that sneaky young 'un sayin' a damn word over my dead body if it *does* happen. My foot's still sore from that cocklebur. I've been thinkin' real hard about ways to git even with the little runt. If I had any poison, I'd put it in his coffee tonight. A man don't realize how bad he needs two good feet 'til some sneaky little owlhoot puts a burr in his boot. I swear by the moon an' stars, I'm gonna git even."

"The two of you are like a couple of kids," Smoke said as he urged his stud forward with his heels.

Pearlie wasn't ready to give in. "That boy's got a mean streak. I aim to cure him of bad habits, some way or 'nother. I ain't done with him yet, not by a long shot."

Smoke decided it was time to intervene. "Save your trickery 'til we get these cattle to market, Pearlie. I don't want anything to keep us from getting our beeves sold. On the way back you can have your fun. Meantime, let's get the steers in a bunch and push 'em a little harder. Their flanks have filled out over the last hour or two. We need to make up for lost time as much as we can."

Pearlie spurred his dun to a short lope to circle the lead steers for a push. Smoke headed for the point position while forcing wandering cattle back into a tighter group. If memory served him they were a day and a half west of Dodge City—he had begun to recognize familiar landmarks, a rocky knob to the north and cottonwood groves along the Arkansas River where he'd made camp before.

When the steers were strung out in good trail fashion he allowed himself to relax against the cantle of his saddle. It had begun to seem like the drive would end peacefully, until he heard a distant shout behind him.

Cal was shaking out a loop in his lariat rope, yelling to Pearlie, "Watch out fer that maverick!"

A mottled longhorn cow trotted over a hilltop near the rear of the herd, shaking its massive, six-foot spread of horns. Smoke knew what lay in store unless someone could turn the renegade cow away from the crossbreds. The wild longhorn, a maverick that had escaped from some earlier trail drive, would frighten the gentler cattle into a stampede. A purebred Mexican longhorn could be among the most unmanageable animals on earth. The big cow coming toward the herd could have been running wild across empty Kansas prairies for years.

Cal spurred his bay into a gallop, swinging his loop over his head. Smoke halted the Palouse, reining around to lend a hand, for he knew the colt that Cal was riding hadn't been taught the finer points of holding a heavy cow at the end of a rope.

He sent the stud into a hard run, taking down his own lariat as he saw Pearlie wheel his horse toward the maverick. Pearlie and Cal would arrive at the hilltop at roughly the same time and Smoke hoped that Pearlie, riding an older ranch horse, would be first to get a noose around the longhorn's neck.

The stud's thundering hooves beat out a rhythm on hard soil as Smoke closed the distance. The spotted longhorn came to a sudden stop, snorting, waving its dangerously sharp horns back and forth as a warning to the approaching cowboys. An old mossy horn of this type could seriously injure a horse or a cowboy if things went wrong. Pearlie would know how to avoid a calamity, but young Cal had little experience with wild range cattle.

It was a blessing when Pearlie reached the longhorn cow first and swung his loop, just when the spotted creature made a turn to escape. Pearlie's noose settled over the cow's horns in expert fashion.

Cal galloped up, slowing the bay at almost the same instant when the wild cow suddenly turned around to charge Pearlie's dun horse.

"Look out!" Cal cried.

Pearlie got his dun stopped a moment too late. The cow made a charge for Pearlie with horns lowered while Pearlie was dallying his lariat around his saddlehorn.

The maverick was quick, and wise to the ways of cowboys and ropes. Lunging to one side, it kept coming toward Pearlie at a full charge before Pearlie could collect himself or free the rope from his saddle.

The spotted cow struck Pearlie's dun gelding full tilt, all its power in its hindquarters, driving one horn into the dun's ribs.

Pearlie toppled from his saddle as his horse staggered from the force of impact, a thousand pounds of angry longhorn rushing into the side of the dun.

Smoke asked his Palouse for all the speed it had, drumming his heels into the stud's ribs while shaking out a loop to catch the heels of the maverick—if only he could get there in time to rope the longhorn's back legs before it turned on Pearlie.

But it was Cal who came to the rescue. He threw a loop on the ground just in front of the longhorn's rear hooves as it was goring Pearlie's horse with a razorlike horn, blood squirting from a deep wound in the gelding's side.

Cal jerked the bay around and took off in the opposite direction with his loop securely fastened around the maverick's hocks.

When the bay colt hit the end of the rope it stumbled momentarily, but at the same time the longhorn was pulled backward, freeing its horn from the dun. Pearlie lay helpless on the ground beneath his horse, in real danger of being trampled to death.

Cal yelled, "Pull, you bay son of a bitch!" as he drove his spurs into the colt's hide.

The longhorn bellowed as it was jerked off its feet by the power of the bay's efforts to drag it away from Pearlie and the injured dun. The cow fell over on its side, bawling, swinging a blood-drenched horn back and forth, unable to rise to its feet again as Cal dragged the enraged beast away by its hind legs.

Smoke galloped up on the stud and threw his noose over the cow's horns. The Palouse, with thickly mus-cled hindquarters and gaskins, had an easy time of it pulling the head of the downed maverick to one side until the animal lay, stretched out between Smoke's rope and Cal's, bellowing for all it was worth, fighting the pull of both ropes in a futile effort to get free.

Smoke quickly examined the dun as Pearlie came staggering to his feet. The horse's wound was serious, but with luck and a bit of careful attention, the geld-ing would mend.

He turned his attention back to the cow, then to Cal. "Nice work with those heels, son," he cried above the angry roar of the thrashing maverick. "You may have saved Pearlie's life. One of these wild, mossy horns can be damn near as dangerous as a wounded grizzly."

Cal's face was the color of milk. "Didn't know what else I could do, boss," he stammered. "Wasn't no other place I could put a rope 'cept fer them back feet."

Pearlie bent down to pick up his hat, dusting it off quickly before he walked around his dun to inspect its wound. "I owe you, young 'un," he said, frowning, tracing a fingertip over the bloody hole in the geld-ing's side. Then he turned to Smoke and drew his pistol. "If it's all the same to you, Smoke, I'd like to put a bullet in that damn maverick's brain fer what it done to my best cowpony.''

Smoke wagged his head. "We don't need the meat, Pearlie, and what this cow did was what nature intended—tryin' to join our herd when it caught the scent. I've got my rope around its horns, and this stud is heavy enough to drag the cow off for a ways. We ain't gonna shoot it for doin' what came natural to an animal.''

"But it damn near killed me an' my dun!" Pearlie exclaimed, with an accusing finger aimed at the cow.

"That isn't what matters, Pearlie,'' Smoke told him as he swung the stud around to pull the downed longhorn away from the herd. "There's a difference between killin' a dumb animal and a man. Animals act out of instinct—they don't bear grudges or kill for no reason. Same can't be said for some breeds of men. Put the gun away. I'll haul this cow over the hill yonder and take off these ropes. Get back to the herd, or they'll drift all the way to creation.''

Pearlie, even as mad as he was, was wise enough to know when to be quiet. He mounted his horse and gathered up his reins to ride away, holstering his Colt. "I'll tend to this horse's wound as soon as me an' Cal git them cows collected,'' he said, a change in his voice. Then he looked at Cal. "You done yourself proud, boy, an' I won't forgit it. I was aimin' to git even with you fer that cocklebur, but I reckon we'll call things square, least for now.''

Cal gave Pearlie a sheepish grin. "Wasn't you I was tryin' to help, Pearlie,'' he said. "I got to feelin' real sorry for that yellow dun horse, havin' a horn stuck in him. If that horn had been stuck in the same feller who put castor oil in the syrup tin back at Sugarloaf,

I might not have been so inclined to tie my rope to
a mad cow."

Pearlie shook his head. "I shoulda knowed it was
a waste of perfectly good air to pay you a compli-
ment." He swung his horse back toward the herd,
mumbling to himself.

Smoke spoke to Cal. "Shake your loop off this
critter's legs, an' I'll yank her out of sight. You're
making a right decent cowhand, Cal. That heel loop
is mighty hard to throw."

Cal shook slack into his lariat, and the noose
opened just enough to allow the longhorn's hind legs
freedom.

The Palouse plunged forward when it felt Smoke's
heels, and the rope went taut between Smoke's saddlehorn and a maverick that could have caused the
Sugarloaf brand a stampede.

A few seconds later the longhorn scrambled to its
feet and snorted, shaking its head but harkening to
the pull of Smoke's rope to keep from choking.

The stud struck a slow trot ahead of the cow, turning its head just enough to keep a wary eye on the
horned beast behind it. The Palouse was a seasoned
roping horse, bearing the scars of close calls with
other wild cattle.

"That was some demonstration," Grimes said at
their evening camp fire, waiting for coffee to boil.
He was speaking to Smoke when he said it. "The
young man named Cal showed courage when he came
to Pearlie's rescue."

Smoke was occupied slicing strips of fatback into
a small cast-iron skillet on a rock beside the flames
as darkness came to the Kansas prairie. "Cal's got

the makings of a top cowhand. He lacks a bit of experience, maybe, but that'll come with time. He has what it takes.''

Grimes gazed at the pair of pistols belted around Smoke's waist. Smoke saw him from the corner of his eye.

''Your men tell me you are experienced with those sidearms you carry,'' Grimes said.

It was a subject Smoke didn't care to discuss at the moment. His thoughts were on Dodge City, and cattle buyers he would find there. He ignored the drummer's remark. ''Coffee's near 'bout ready, Mr. Grimes. Hand me a couple of those tin cups.''

Chapter 10

Dodge City had grown considerably since Smoke had last seen it a few years earlier, before the railroad line came. A stockyard stretching for half a mile lay beside the end of a railroad spur ending in Dodge. Row upon row of false-fronted, clapboard buildings lined dirt streets in the business district. A few stores and drinking parlors occupied large, canvas tents. Sod houses and woodshacks had been built in virtually every direction around the business sector, but it was easy to see that the heart of Dodge was the cattle market, plank corrals and loading ramps where beef on the hoof could be driven into cattle cars on a number of rail sidings.

Fall winds kicked up dust from nearby barren hills, clouds of alkali chalk sweeping over the town in irregular gusts that swirled across everything. Smoke tugged his hat down to keep it from blowing off as he led the steers toward the west end of the cow pens, where empty corrals would hold his beeves until a price could be struck with a cattle buyer.

It was late, approaching sundown, when he pointed the herd across a rusty set of rails into an alleyway between livestock pens. A couple of young cowboys who worked for the market had begun to open a number of gates so the Sugarloaf cows could be herded into corrals with water troughs and haystacks.

Weary Hereford crosses walked quietly into the alleys and then into the pens, scenting water and sweet prairie hay. The last half-dozen steers at the back, evidencing various stages of sorefootedness, limped into corrals and went straight for the hay and water. A pink-cheeked cowboy with a tally book and a pencil came up to Smoke as he was dismounting from the stud.

"Howdy, mister," the boy said. "I reckon you know the way it's done. You take a head count, an' I'll do the same. If we come up with the same number I'll enter it in the book an' you sign your name to it. Can't be no disagreement over how many you brung that way."

"I understand," Smoke replied, tying off his horse's reins. "I'll start on this end. Should be three hundred an' seven by my count earlier this morning."

"Those sure are fine steers, mister. Don't get many with Hereford breedin'. We've got buyers in town who'll jump at the chance to buy 'em. Ol' Crawford Long is a cranky cuss, but he said one time a drop of Hereford blood in a cow gives it twice as much meat as a longhorn. I figure he'll be your top bidder. I can send word to him when we're done with this count, if you want."

"Sounds good to me," Smoke said, distracted by

the sight of Grimes talking to another cowboy working the pens. He could hear part of the conversation.

"They murdered the whole family," Grimes said. "Burned the place to the ground. They stole my mule. Are you certain you haven't seen a gang of rough-looking men coming to Dodge in the last couple of days?"

"No sir, I sure ain't. It's been pretty quiet. The big herds comin' up from Texas ain't arrived yet, so it seems like Dodge is half empty. Everybody woulda noticed if some big gang rode into town. Couldn't hide somethin' like that. But we got us a good City Marshal. Wyatt Earp's his name. He don't act scared of the devil hisself."

"Can you direct me to his office?" Grimes asked. "I need to report my stolen mule and what happened at that trading post east of here."

"The Marshal's gone right now lookin' into some kinda trouble at Cobbs Store. A muleskinner said he saw it got burnt plumb down, just like you said. He didn't say nothin' 'bout findin' no bodies."

Grimes seemed frustrated. "Is there anyone else I can report the theft of my mule to?"

"A deputy by the name of Sims. He can send off a telegram to the army over at Fort Larned . . . tell 'em to be on the lookout for that big gang you told me about."

"Where's the Marshal's office?"

"Right up Main Street, across from Garner's Mercantile. You can't miss it."

Grimes rode off toward the center of town. Smoke began his count of the steers while Pearlie unsaddled to apply another coat of fatback drippings to his dun's wound.

Cal swung down and stretched his legs before he

unsaddled his horse to put it in one of the smaller pens.

"Three hundred and seven," the cowboy said, frowning at a page in his tally book. "Just sign your name right here at the bottom of the page."

Smoke scribbled his name and handed back the pencil. "We need a good meal and a decent room for the night," he said as he loosened the cinch on his stud.

"The Drover's Hotel has got the best of both. Best chicken an' dumplin's in the whole world, an' real soft beds. Miz Cox can make the best apple pies you ever ate too. Don't miss out on the pie, if she's got any today. You're kinda early to be comin' with a herd, mister. Be a few more weeks before the big bunches get here, so Miz Cox don't fix as much till more hungry cowboys show up."

"I'll remember to ask for the pie," Smoke told him, swinging his saddle over a fence rail, then taking down his warbag. "You can tell that cattle buyer I'm ready to sell and head back for home."

"Just curious, mister, but where's home?" the cowhand asked as his gaze fell to Smoke's pistols.

"Colorado Territory, at the foot of the Rockies. Can't say as this part of Kansas is nearly so pretty to look at."

The young man shook his head. "There ain't no reason on earth to live here, 'cept for a job. Cold as hell in wintertime an' hotter 'n blazes in summer. There's this sayin' among cowboys who come up from Texas: 'Kansas has got three suns.' "

When no more was offered, Smoke asked for some sort of explanation, "Three suns?"

"Yep. The sun over your head, sunflowers, an' ornery sons of bitches."

The Drover's Hotel was a two-story affair made of wood planks, with peeling white paint. A wooden porch ran the length of the place. Smoke, Pearlie and Cal carried their saddles, gear, and guns up a set of sagging steps to go inside. Smoke could already smell something good coming from a cafe off to one side of the hotel lobby.

"I got wind of chicken an' dumplin's just then," Pearlie said.

"That wrangler at the cow pens said to be sure to try the apple pie," Smoke replied as they walked through a pair of glass-paned doors.

"I'm so hungry I could eat boot leather," Cal said as they rested their saddles on the polished hardwood floor.

Smoke pulled off his hat when an elderly woman came to the desk.

"Do you gentlemen wish to hire a room?" she asked.

"Three of 'em," Smoke answered. "On the second floor, if you don't have no objections."

"None at all," she replied. "Each room is a dollar a night, and it's payable in advance."

He placed three silver dollars on the desk. The woman gave him three keys. Pearlie hesitated before heading for the stairs.

"Ma'am, could that be chicken an' dumplin's I smell?"

"It is indeed. Made this morning, and we have apple pie for dessert."

"Lordy," Pearlie exclaimed, rolling his eyes. "I've done died an' gone to heaven."

Their dinner was delicious, every bit as good as the wrangler said it would be. But when big slices of apple pie—made dark with cinnamon and sugar—were placed in front of them, it was Cal who whistled softly through his teeth.

"It can't be as good as Miz Jensen's, I'll bet, but it looks mighty close."

Smoke had to admit the pie was mighty close to being as good as Sally's, but the thought of a comparison reminded him of how much he missed his wife. He cleaned his dish quickly and took a sip of strong coffee, forcing his thoughts away from Sally and Sugarloaf to the business at hand. "We made it, boys," he said after a moment of silent contemplation.

Pearlie, forgetting his manners, licked his pie plate clean and set it down sorrowfully. He looked at Smoke. "I overheard one of them hands tell Grimes there wasn't no gang of strangers in town. Maybe Lady Luck is gonna smile on us this time. No more shootin' or duckin' lead."

Smoke glanced at a front window as dusk came to Dodge City. "Seems nice and quiet. Come sunrise I'll make the best deal I can for our beeves, draw our money from the bank, and we'll head out. To tell the truth, this flat country just don't suit me none at all."

"Me neither," Cal said, tossing his fork down when the last of his pie was eaten. "Ain't nothin' but dust an' hard rock in Kansas. Can't wait to git back home."

Pearlie's expression turned wary. "We ain't started in the direction yet, young 'un. There's still time for plenty of things to go wrong."

"Like what?" Cal asked, frowning.

Pearlie was watching the front windows.

"Any number of things," he told him.

"But you ain't said what they could be," Cal persisted, as if he needed to know what was on Pearlie's mind. "Them steers can't stampede 'cause they's locked up in corrals. Ain't no redskins gonna ride into Dodge to cause trouble."

Pearlie leaned back in his chair, folding his arms across his belly. "I've got this feelin'," he said quietly. "I sure do hope I'm wrong."

Smoke emptied his coffee cup and pushed back his chair. "Let's check on the steers and our horses before we turn in. After sleepin' on this hard Kansas ground, I'm ready for a bed that's a little softer."

"Sounds mighty good to me," Cal agreed, standing up to rub his stomach. "Only trouble is, I'm so full I may not be able to walk plumb down to them stockyards. Pearlie, I was wonderin' if you'd mind carryin' me part of the way?"

Pearlie grunted, made a face, and walked away from the table without uttering a word, his spurs making a clanking noise over the cafe floor.

Smoke paid for their meal, thinking about the next day. A two-year breeding program at Sugarloaf would be weighed by the price he got for their steers. He hoped Sally wouldn't be disappointed with the result.

Strolling down Dodge City's main street, Cal and Pearlie were unusually quiet. Off in the distance they could hear a steam locomotive chugging toward town from the east. Smoke had to guess the train was bringing empty cattle cars for the herds coming up from Texas. He felt content, missing Sally more than he expected.

"Train's comin'," Cal said.

"I got ears, boy," Pearlie remarked. The edgy feeling he complained about earlier was showing.

Cal gave Pearlie a look. "Kinda grumpy, ain't you, fer a man with a bellyful of apple pie an' dumplin's?"

Full dark was spreading over the hills and flats by the time they came to the cattle pens. Smoke gave their horses a quick inspection, satisfied. The steers were busy nibbling mounds of hay.

Pearlie had his hands on a top fence plank, taking his own look at the animals. He spoke to the others. "Full bellies all 'round. Us too. But come to think of it, I could sure use a spot of whiskey to settle my nerves before we turn in."

Cal chuckled. "You've sure been havin' plenty of nerve troubles lately. I was the one who was worried 'bout that feelin' in my bones that this trip was gonna be a bad one. It turned out I was plumb wrong."

Smoke swung away from the fence as Pearlie said, "I said it before an' I'm sayin' it again. We ain't got back to Sugarloaf yet with any cow money."

"We'll get back okay," Smoke said as they walked back toward the lights of town. "The only part that ain't clear yet is just how much money I'll be handing over to Sally."

"It'll be plenty," Cal assured him. "Those steers are near fat as ticks on a hound dog. They'll fetch a handsome price from a cow buyer with good sense."

Smoke wasn't ready to agree, not until an offer was made, yet he kept quiet about it.

"Speakin' on the subject of men with or without good sense, I ain't seen that Grimes feller since we got here," Pearlie said. "He rode off to the Marshal's office soon as he found out where it was."

"Can't say as I miss him all that much," Cal said. "All he talked about the whole time he was helpin'

me ride drag was the button an' fastener business.
Can't think of anything I care any less about than
buttons or fasteners.''

The train was in sight, puffing, pulling a long line
of cattle cars with a lone oil lamp on the front of the
locomotive, showing the engineer the tracks. Smoke
stopped suddenly at the beginning of Main Street,
but not because of the train's arrival or anything he
could identify. For reasons he couldn't explain, the
small hairs on the back of his neck were rising, and
it sure as hell wasn't on account of the weather.

Chapter 11

Smoke drifted off to sleep in a comfortable room at the Drover's Hotel, uneasy for reasons he did not fully understand. And as he slumbered, his dreams were strange, scenes from his boyhood, events that ultimately brought him to where he was now—and the nickname he'd carried with him since he and his father ran across a grizzled old mountain man who simply called himself "Preacher."

Kirby Jensen, at sixteen, found his young mind full of questions his father, Emmett, could not answer. But the old mountain man, Preacher, seemed to understand his curiosity.

It was an odd time to be asking questions, locked as they were in mortal combat in a remote section of northwestern Kansas with a bloodthirsty band of Pawnees, but that did nothing to prevent Kirby from

asking Preacher about the Sharps .52 caliber rifle or
how to shoot it.

Preacher gave him a terse reply. "Boy, you
heeled—so you gonna get in this fight or not?"

"Sir?"

"Heeled! Means you carryin' a gun, so that makes
you a man. Ain't you got no rifle 'cept that chunk of
scrap iron?"

"No, sir."

"Take your daddy's Sharps, then. You seen him
load it, you know how. Take that tin box of tubes,
too. You watch out for our backs. Them Pawnees—
and they is Pawnees, not Kiowas—is likely to come
'cross that crick. You in wild country, boy. You may
as well get bloodied."

"Do it, Kirby," his father said. "And watch yourself.
Don't hesitate a second to shoot. Those savages won't
show you any mercy, so you do the same."

Kirby, a little pale around the mouth, took up the
heavy Sharps and the box of tubes, reloaded the rifle,
and made himself as comfortable as possible on the
rear slope of the slight incline, overlooking the creek.

"Not there, boy!" Preacher corrected Kirby's position. "Your back is open to the front line of fire. Get
behind that tree 'twixt us and you. That way, you
won't catch no lead or arrow in the back."

Kirby did as he was told, feeling a bit foolish that
he had not thought about his back. Hadn't he read
enough dime novels to know that? He chastised himself. Nervous sweat dripped from his forehead as he
waited.

And he had to go the the bathroom something
awful.

A half hour passed, the only action the always blowing Kansas winds chasing tumbleweeds, the south-

ward-moving waters of the creek, and an occasional slap of a fish on the surface.

"What are they waiting for?" Emmett asked the question without taking his eyes from the ridge.

"For us to get careless," Preacher said. "Don't you fret none . . . they still out there. I been livin' in and 'round Injuns the better part of fifty year. I know 'em better—or at least as good—as any livin' white man. They'll try to wait us out. They got nothin' but time, boys."

"No way we can talk to them?" Emmett asked, and immediately regretted saying it as Preacher laughed.

"Why shore, Emmett," the old mountain man said. "You just stand up, put your hands in the air, and tell 'em you want to palaver some. They'll probably let you speak your piece; they polite about that. A white man can ride right into nearabouts any Injun village. They'll feed you and give you a place to sleep. Course, gettin' out is a problem.

"They ain't like us, Emmett. They don't come close to thinkin' like us. What is fun to them is torture to us. They call it testin' a man's bravery. If'n a man dies good—that is if he don't holler a lot—they make it last as long as possible. Then they'll sing songs about you, praise you for dyin' good. Lots of white folks condemn 'em for that, but it's just they way of life.

"They got all sorts of ways to test a man's bravery an' strength. They might—dependin' on the tribe— strip you, stake you out over a big anthill, then pour honey over you. Then they'll squat back and watch, see how well you die."

Kirby felt sick to his stomach.

"Or they might bury you up to your neck in the ground, slit your eyelids so you can't close 'em, and let the sun blind you. Then, after your eyes is burnt blind, they'll dig you up and turn you loose naked out in the wild . . . trail you for days, seein' how well you die.''

Kirby positioned himself better behind the tree and quietly went to the bathroom. If a bean is a bean, the boy thought, what's a pea? A relief.

Preacher just wouldn't shut up about it. "Out in the deserts, now, them Injuns get downright mean with they fun. They'll cut out your eyes, cut off your privates, then slit the tendons in your ankles so's you can't do nothin' but flop around on the sand. They get a big laugh out of that. Or they might hang you upside down over a little fire. The 'Paches like to see hair burn. They a little strange 'bout that.

"Or, if they like you, they might put you through what they call the run of the arrow. I lived through that . . . once. But I was younger. Damned if'n I want to do it again at my age. Want me to tell you 'bout that little game?''

"No!'' Emmett said quickly. "I get your point.''

"Figured you would. Point is, don't let 'em ever take you alive. Kirby, now, they'd probably keep for work or trade. But that's chancy, he being nearabout a man growed.'' The mountain man tensed a bit, then said, "Look alive, boy, and stay that way long as you can. Here they come.'' He winked at Kirby.

"How do you know that, Preacher?'' Kirby asked. "I don't see anything.''

"Wind just shifted. Smelled 'em. They close, been easin' up through the grass. Get ready.''

Kirby wondered how the old man could smell anything over the fumes from his own body.

Emmett, a veteran of four years of continuous war, could not believe an enemy could slip up on him in open daylight. At the sound of Preacher jacking back the hammer of his Henry .44, Emmett shifted his eyes from his perimeter for just a second. When he again looked back at his field of fire, a big, painted-up buck was almost on top of him. Then the open meadow was filled with screaming, charging Indians.

Emmett brought the buck down with a .44 slug through the chest, flinging the Indian backward, the yelling abruptly cut off in his throat.

The air had changed from the peacefulness of summer quiet to a screaming, gunsmoke-filled hell. Preacher looked at Kirby, who was looking at him, his mouth hanging open in shock, fear, and confusion.

"Don't look at me, boy!" Preacher yelled. "Keep them eyes in front of you!"

Kibry swung his gaze to the small creek and the stand of timber that lay behind it. His eyes were beginning to smart from the acrid powder smoke, and his head was aching from the pounding of the Henry .44 and the screaming and yelling. The Sharps he held at the ready was a heavy weapon, and his arms were beginning to ache from the strain.

His head suddenly came up, eyes alert. He had seen movement on the far side of the creek.

"Right There! Yes! he thought. *Someone, or something was over there!*

I don't want to shoot anyone, the boy thought. *Why can't we be friends with these people?*

And that thought was still throbbing in his brain when a young Indian suddenly sprang from the willows by the creek and lunged into the water, a rifle in his hand, a war cry echoing from his throat.

For what seemed like an eternity, Kirby watched the young brave, a boy about his own age, leap and thrash through the murky water. Kirby jacked back the hammer of the Sharps, sighted in on the brave, and pulled the trigger.

The .52 caliber pounded his shoulder, bruising it, for there wasn't much spare meat on Kirby. When the gunsmoke blew away, the young Indian was face down in the water, his blood staining the stream.

Kirby stared at what he'd done, then fought back waves of sickness.

The boy heard a wild scream and spun around. His father was locked in hand-to-hand combat with two knife-wielding braves.

Too close for the rifle, Kirby clawed his Navy Colt from the leather, vowing he would cut that stupid flap from his holster after this was over.

He shot one brave through the head just as his father buried his Arkansas Toothpick to the hilt in the chest of the other Indian.

And as abruptly as they came, the Indians slipped away, dragging as many of their dead and wounded with them as they could. Two braves lay dead in front of Preacher; two braves lay dead in the shallow ravine with three others killed in the first attack.

The boy Kirby had shot lay in the creek, arms outstretched, the waters a deep crimson. The body floated slowly downstream as the current carried it away.

Preacher looked at the dead buck in the creek, then at the brave in the wallow with them—the one Kirby had shot. He lifted his eyes to the boy.

"Got your baptism this day, boy," he said. "Did right well, you did."

"Saved my life, son," Emmett said, dumping the bodies of the Indians out of the buffalo wallow. "Can't call you 'boy' no more, I don't reckon. You be a man now, after what you done here today."

A thin finger of smoke lifted from the barrel of the Navy .36 that Kirby held in his hand.

Preacher smiled and spat tobacco juice.

A moment of silence passed, until Preacher spoke as he was looking at Kirby's ash-blond hair. "Yep," he said, taking his own sweet time saying what was on his mind. "Smoke'll suit you just fine."

"Sir?" Kirby finally asked, when he was able to find his voice.

"Smoke," Preacher said again.

Emmett was watching Preacher. "Smoke?" he also asked, as if the word bewildered him.

"Smoke," Preacher drawled for a third time. "That's what I'll call you from now on. Smoke."

Kirby whispered the nickname. "Smoke. Smoke Jensen." He liked the sound of it, and of course he was flattered that the old mountain man thought enough of him to give him a monicker, one that he'd earned by shooting two Pawnees. Preacher wasn't the sort to show respect for a man unless he'd earned it, and Kirby was only sixteen when Preacher dubbed him with a handle showing bravery in the heat of battle.

"I reckon it suits him," Emmett said, after a moment or two of thought.

"It do for a fact," Preacher remarked. "Judgin' by what the boy showed today, he'll live up to it as time goes by. Some men has got a natural talent with a gun. Seems this boy come to be a man real sudden-like. Be the last time anybody'll call him boy. Like I said, he got his baptism here today. From now on we'll be ridin' with Smoke Jensen, Emmett. He done hisself proud when the chips was down."

* * *

Smoke awakened suddenly from a light sleep, turning his gaze to an open hotel window beside the bed, shaking off the memory of that Indian fight with his father and Preacher. That was so long ago, or so it seemed.

He swung his feet off the bed, oddly disturbed by something he couldn't identify. Was it merely the recollection of the dream because it was so vivid? Or was it something else his keen senses detected in the darkness beyond the window?

Smoke went to the windowsill and leaned out, giving the dark outlines of Dodge City a sweeping glance, scenting the wind while he listened to the night sounds.

"Somebody's out there," he told himself quietly. "I can damn near feel it. Or maybe it's like Preacher did that time when he smelled those Pawnees slippin' up on us in the grass."

Yet no matter how carefully he examined the shadows beside every building, the silent streets after the town had gone to bed, he couldn't find anything amiss—nothing he could put a finger on.

Later, he lay back down on the mattress and closed his eyes for a time, still listening to the distant cry of an owl somewhere to the south, the occasional lowing of a cow coming from the cattle pens.

Could be just my imagination, he thought, knowing better. A sixth sense always warned him of danger, and he had that feeling then. No matter how hard he tried he couldn't shake it off or put it to rest.

A slow hour passed, and when he opened his eyes the window was graying with the light of false dawn.

It was senseless to lie there, wondering about the odd feeling stirring the hairs at the back of his neck.

Smoke got up and strapped on his pistols, then pulled on his boots. Cradling the Winchester .44 in the crook of an arm, he let himself out into a dark hallway and went quietly down the stairs.

Chapter 12

Twenty-three-year-old City Marshal Wyatt Earp yawned and stretched when he got out of bed. He'd gotten to bed late after visiting the ruins of Cobbs Trading Post. What he found there was gruesome. Five charred bodies among the remains of the log store, including three children. And when Wyatt got back to send out a burial party early this morning, his deputy told him about the drummer who'd lost his mule to a gang of outlaws too numerous to take lightly, if the report was true. The incident had taken place only a few miles from the trading post.

Probably an exaggeration, he thought, crossing his bachelor quarters behind the jail in his stocking feet to light a lantern, then the potbelly stove so he could boil coffee. Outlaw gangs usually numbered no more than five or ten. Thirty was a ridiculous figure, the result of fear on the part of the drummer. So many men in one bunch would attract too much attention.

He lit the lamp, adjusting its wick to a soft glow, then he put kindling in the potbelly and struck a lucifer to it. As soon as he'd blown the flames to life he opened the flue and put water in his coffee pot, then a handful of pan-scorched coffee beans.

Beyond the windowpane of his single room, Dodge City was still dark. And quiet. The tracks of a great many horses had gone south away from Cobbs Trading Post, away from Dodge, he remembered. He'd taken it as a good sign that no trouble was headed this way.

Late the night before, Wyatt had gotten off a telegram to the army about the killings, although he expected little from Fort Larned in the way of action. The army seemed indifferent to all but the most glaring atrocities in Kansas Territory. It was unlikely that the slaying of a storekeeper and his family would be given much attention from the commander at Fort Larned—at best a cursory examination and a meaningless report forwarded to Washington.

Wyatt wondered what he would do if any real trouble came to Dodge. He had two part-time deputies, recently unemployed cowboys who were no great shakes with a gun. Wyatt had his own doubts about facing down a bunch of hardened killers. Most of the troubles in Dodge City came from rowdy cowhands with too much whiskey behind their belts. Senses dimmed by alcohol, they were seldom difficult to control, and most were easily bluffed by Wyatt when he showed his calm exterior, a steely-eyed look and grim determination to settle a dispute or haul a man to jail for the night if he gave too much argument.

He paused at the window again, peering out, when a tall, angular cowboy wearing two pistols and carrying a repeating rifle strode past his office toward the shipping pens.

"He's out early, carryin' enough weapons to fight a war," Wyatt said under his breath. It seemed a strange hour to be on the streets with so many guns.

Simple curiosity got the best of him. He stomped into his boots and strapped on his Colt Peacemaker before shouldering into his coat to walk outside. The stranger was half a block away.

"Hey mister!" Wyatt cried. "Hold up there just a minute!"

Before the first word had left his mouth, the stranger had begun a rapid turn, one hand close to a pistol. He relaxed when he saw Wyatt standing in front of the marshal's office.

Wyatt started toward him. The man's reactions had been as quick as lightning, and he'd been ready to go for a gun, a sure sign the stranger understood dangerous situations. In the half dark it was hard to see his face until Wyatt walked up to him and halted a few feet away.

"Name's Wyatt Earp. I'm the City Marshal. Just curious as to why you're carryin' so many guns at this hour."

"Smoke Jensen," the big man replied evenly. "I was headed down to check on a herd I brought in yesterday. As to the guns, I rarely go anywhere without 'em. Old habit, I reckon."

Wyatt nodded when he heard the explanation. Jensen was even bigger than he first appeared, looking lean and hard, a tough customer by all outward signs. "It's my job to ask questions now an' then, Mr. Jensen. Like when a stranger comes to town with a good-sized collection of arms. But if you're a cattleman like you say, you'll get my full cooperation. We aim to make sure our peaceful visitors enjoy their stay.''

"I'm peaceful," Jensen replied. "Just careful, is all.''

Wyatt grinned. "I understand bein' careful. When the big herds come in, a man with a badge don't want to turn his back on anybody.''

Jensen understood. "It's a mighty good idea not to turn your back on any stranger . . . 'less you got eyes in the back of yer head.''

Wyatt wondered if the stranger might have seen anything at Cobbs Trading Post. "Which way did you come into Dodge?" he asked.

"From the west. Colorado Territory," Jensen replied.

"Did you happen to see a big bunch of riders along any of the trails you took?''

"Hardly a soul, Marshal, 'cept for the drummer who claimed his mule got stolen. He said somethin' about a sizable bunch of bad men takin' his mule while he was off hunting. His name was Grimes, best I recall.''

Wyatt nodded again. "Grimes filled out a report with one of my deputies. He said a gang of nearly thirty men rode up to his camp an' stole his mule . . . he saw them from a distance an' stayed hid. Then he came upon that burnt-out tradin' post at Cobbs Creek. I rode out there late yesterday to verify the report we got from a muleskinner. Five bodies lyin' in the ashes. A man an' his wife an' three children. I'm sendin' a burial party out this morning. Could be it was the work of that same bunch Grimes reported.''

"We didn't see anybody," Jensen said again.

"A gang that big would stick out," Wyatt said. "Be hard as hell to miss 'em, unless that drummer had trouble gettin' the right count. Coulda been 'cause he was scared."

"I didn't question him much on it," Jensen added. "I'm here on business—cattle business. I figured that stolen mule and what he saw at the tradin' post was a job for the law or the cavalry."

"You've got it guessed right," Wyatt agreed, "only I won't get much help from the army. Whoever was responsible is probably headed deep into the Indian Nations by now. It don't seem likely we'll see 'em here in Dodge."

Jensen aimed a glance at the darkened front of the Cattleman's Bank across the street. "If it's outlaws, that many of 'em, a bank full of cattle buyers' money could draw 'em here."

"It's possible," Wyatt said. "We've got two banks in Dodge City, and cattle buyers, along with their money, are beginnin' to arrive on the train."

"I know I'm early," Jensen said, "but I'm from cold country up near the Rockies. Wanted to get my business done and get back to the ranch before the snow flies."

Wyatt turned to head back into the office, remembering his coffee. "Enjoy your stay in Dodge, Mr. Jensen. Sorry to have delayed you, but it's a part of my job to be suspicious of any newcomers."

"I understand," Jensen told him, swinging toward the railroad tracks and shipping pens, balancing his rifle in his left hand as he walked off down the street.

Wyatt went back inside, closing the door behind him, left with the distinct impression that Smoke Jensen was a man who could handle himself. Some gents had a way about them, a quiet confidence that was a subtle warning to others who might be inclined to test them.

As he was pouring coffee the front door opened. Jim Bob Watley, one of his deputies, came striding in, wrapped in a green plaid mackinaw.

"Mornin', Wyatt," he said, taking a clean cup from the drainboard. "I just walked past the undertaker's place. Seen Mr. Starnes had five coffins loaded in the back of his wagon, two of 'em real small like you told him. He's takin' Clifford to dig them graves. Had pickaxes an' shovels loaded."

"That's mighty hard ground to dig," Wyatt said, blowing steam from his cup.

Jim Bob poured his own coffee. "Who you reckon coulda done somethin' so awful as that . . . killin' them kids an' all, then get 'em burnt up in a fire?"

"Hard to say, Jim Bob. This territory can be full of men who take what they want by any means available. The tracks went south toward the Nations."

"Then we ain't formin' up no posse to go after 'em?"

"I'm a City Marshal, Jim Bob. That's a job for the army or Federal Marshals. I intend to send a wire to Fort Smith over in Arkansas, to the U.S. Marshal's office there. Trouble is, we got no description of who done it."

"That drummer saw 'em," Jim Bob replied. "He damn sure wants his mule back. But when I asked him if he could identify any of the bunch, he told me he was too far away to see any of their faces."

Wyatt took a sip of scalding coffee. "Probably wouldn't do any good. Like I said, the tracks were headed due south."

"Was there really thirty of 'em?" Jim Bob asked. "I had a hard time makin' myself believe there could be so many."

Wyatt recalled what he'd found on the south side

of the creek. "There were plenty of 'em, all right. Maybe not thirty, but a helluva big bunch."

"I'm sure glad they ain't comin' here, Wyatt. Don't know what we'd do if thirty mean-natured men showed up in this town with their minds made up to raise hell."

Wyatt wondered about it. "We'd be badly outgunned, that's for sure."

The front windows of the office brightened as dawn came to eastern skies. Cody Wade, Wyatt's other part-time deputy, walked in as Wyatt was talking to Jim Bob.

"Mornin'," Cody said, his face somewhat ashen in spite of the cold wind. He went over to the stove to warm his hands and get coffee. "Marshal," he said, looking at Wyatt, " I just seen this feller I recognized. He was down at the railheads lookin' over a bunch of white-faced cattle."

"Who is he?" Wyatt asked, for it seemed like a number of people were out and about early that morning.

"A gunfighter by the name of Smoke Jensen. A damn killer is what he is. Hails from up in Colorado. It's been ten years since I seen him tangle with a shootist by the name of Sundance. Can't recall no more of Sundance's name."

Wyatt turned to Cody, frowning. "I talked to this Smoke Jensen a half hour ago. He introduced himself and said he was a cattleman."

Cody wagged his head. "Maybe a cattleman is what he's callin' himself now, but back in them days he wasn't nothin' but a hired gun. This Sundance feller, he was supposed to be fast as greased lightnin' with a pistol. Jensen drew on him an' shot off part of his ear . . . before Sundance ever got his gun clear of leather.''

"Then Jensen *lied* to me,'' Wyatt said, his eyelids narrowing as he remembered the stranger, who was wearing two pistols and carrying a rifle.

Cody poured himself a cup of coffee. "All I'm sayin' is, it ain't no good sign that a feller like Smoke Jensen is in Dodge City. We can look for a good-size share of problems if he's of a mind to use them guns of his.''

Wyatt put down his cup, glancing over to a gun rack filled with shotguns and rifles near the office door. "Maybe I can talk him out of causin' any trouble,'' Wyatt said, ambling over to the gun rack, taking down a twelve-gauge shotgun, breaking it open to load both tubes.

"Like I said,'' Cody continued, "that Jensen is meaner'n two mad rattlesnakes. I'd be careful, Marshal, if I was you.''

"He didn't seem like he was on the prod,'' Wyatt answered in a quiet voice, thinking out loud.

"Maybe he ain't. But I figured you'd want to know he was in town.''

"I knew he was here . . . I just didn't know who he was or what he was.''

"He's a killer, by reputation,'' Cody assured him. "He ain't no cattleman . . . leastways, he wasn't ten years ago.''

"A man can change,'' Jim Bob offered, sounding like he hoped Wyatt wouldn't ask them to back his move against Jensen.

"An apple don't fall very far from the tree,'' Wyatt gave as his reply.

Cody seemed perplexed. "Ain't much we can do unless he starts somethin', is there?''

"I can warn him," Wyatt replied, sauntering over to the door with the shotgun aimed at the floor.

Cody looked at Jim Bob, and it was clear that the same thought was in each deputy's mind.

"You want us to go with you?" Cody asked.

Wyatt shook his head. "I can handle it. If he's a cattleman like he claims to be, there won't be any trouble. But if he's a paid shootist who has his sights on the money in both of our banks, then that's another matter. I recall he *did* make some mention of the bank across the street."

"One man ain't gonna try an' rob the Cattleman's Bank," Jim Bob said. "It'd take at least three or four."

Wyatt opened the door and stepped out into a coming sunrise. "I'll find out if he's got anybody with him," he said, starting off down the boardwalk in front of the office, aiming for the cow pens beside the railyard.

Chapter 13

Smoke leaned against a corral plank, examining the condition of his steers as the first rays of sunlight beamed above the horizon. The cows' flanks were full. They were in almost perfect, market-ready flesh. Sally had been right about how a Hereford crossed with a longhorn. These were beefy cattle, the type any meat company would want to buy, and despite Smoke's earlier misgivings, they trailed well, covering distance while staying in good shape.

Just thinking about Sally made him lonely, and when he felt it, that emptiness, he chuckled softly to himself. He would not have dreamed of missing a woman in his early years. It was proof of how much he had changed—how much she had changed him.

He heard footsteps behind him. Marshal Earp was coming to the shipping pens, and now he carried a double-barrel shotgun.

Smoke turned away from the fence, wondering why Earp would be headed in his direction.

Earp walked up, the shotgun's barrels aimed at the ground in a way that helped Smoke relax the hand he held near one of his pistols.

"Mr. Jensen," Earp said when he came to a halt a few yards away, "one of my deputies said he recognized you . . . that you're a gunslick—a hired gun."

Smoke didn't like the sound of Earp's voice. "That might've been true of me some years back," he said.

Earp seemed uneasy, his gaze flickering from the pair of Colts around Smoke's waist to the Winchester he held loosely in the palm of one hand. "We don't tolerate any gunplay in Dodge City," the Marshal said.

"I'm not here to use a gun," Smoke answered. "These are my crossbred steers. I'm here to sell 'em, get my money, and ride back to Colorado Territory. Ain't no law against that in Dodge, is there?"

"No, sir, there ain't," Earp replied, "but my deputy said you were a dangerous man. He did make mention of some incident he saw a few years ago . . . maybe he said it was five years, give or take."

"What incident was that, Marshal?"

"I reckon it was a shootout of some kind. Some guy called Sundance. I believe he told me the gent's last name was Morgan, just before I left the office to come down here an' ask you about it."

"I did have a little difficulty with Sundance Morgan. He came after me with a gun. I put a little notch in his ear, just to remind him it was a mistake."

"Then you're sayin' it was self-defense?"

"That's exactly what it was. He brought up this gang of gunnies from the Mexican border, offerin' 'em money to bring me down. Him and his boys weren't particulary good at what they set out to do."

"When we talked earlier," Earp continued, "you made some mention of the bank. It would be a natural conclusion on my part if I wondered about you takin' a notion to rob it, seein' as you have this mean reputation as a shooter an' all."

Smoke felt he understood the Marshal's concerns, however he wasn't going to be pushed. "The only thing I'm interested in at that bank is the money a cattle buyer is gonna pay me for these pens full of steers. I've never taken a dime of money that wasn't mine." Smoke took a shallow breath, one eye on Earp's gun hand, and the other on the shotgun. "Your deputy was right to tell you I'd tangled with Sundance, but that was quite a spell in the past. I came to Dodge with steers to sell. I mind my own business these days. Don't stick my nose in another man's troubles, and my guns ain't for hire. I don't rob banks for a livin' and I've never drawn a gun on a man who didn't draw on me first, if it'll put your mind to rest."

Earp appeared to relax some. "I've never been one to hold a man's past against him, Mr. Jensen. I've been in a scrape or two that could have been called a killin', or self-defense. There's times when a man has to do what his gut tells him, or he's liable to wind up dead."

"It was the same with Sundance Morgan," Smoke told him. "It was him an' his boys, or me. I did what I had to do, and the Sheriff at Big Rock in Colorado can verify my side of things. I caused a lot of blood to be shed, but Morgan and his shootists didn't leave me with no selection."

Earp nodded. "I reckon that's good enough for

me. It's just that report we had about outlaws and the drummer's stolen mule, on top of the killings at Cobbs Trading Post, that've got me on edge a little. There was a bunch of tracks leadin' south where that family got massacred.''

"Grimes told me about it. Grimes told one of my cowboys he saw a man with 'em who wore an old Confederate uniform, and there was some talk that it could have been Bloody Bill Anderson. I've been told Anderson was killed over in Missouri long years back. You know how folks can worry when a rumor starts.''

The muscles in Earp's jaw tightened some. "We've had one or two reports come down the wires that Anderson was sighted, only nobody could verify it, and that was a year or two ago. Could be somebody wantin' folks to think it's him. But there was truth to the stories about raids in southeastern Kansas last year. A town got sacked, and more'n a dozen citizens were killed by a gang of misfits. The army looked into it and couldn't find a trace. A handful of survivors swore the leader looked like Bill Anderson, but folks get scared when lead's flyin', and sometimes they can't be all that sure of what they saw.''

Smoke knew that eyewitness reports were often unreliable. "I can vouch for that. A man who's scared don't always see what he thinks he sees.''

Earp made a half turn to leave. "I'm still curious as to why you're out an' about so early, totin' that rifle. It's like you're expectin' some kind of trouble.''

Smoke decided he would confide in the Marshal, even though he had no basis for his worries. "I woke up early with a feelin' in my gut that something wasn't quite right. I've learned to trust that feelin' over the years. Appears it wasn't anything, just my nature to be suspicious when somethin' gnaws on me like it did last night and this morning."

Earp gave Dodge City and its surrounds a passing glance as buildings and the hills beyond brightened with dawn. "Seems real peaceful to me, Mr. Jensen. Hard to ask for a town to be any quieter."

He didn't want to concern Earp, since he really didn't have anything solid to base his vague uneasiness on. "Maybe that was it," he said, giving the hills his own careful examination. "It may be too quiet. I suppose I'm accustomed to noisy towns, and when a town ain't noisy, it don't seem natural."

"Just wait a few weeks," Earp told him, giving a weak grin. "Soon as the big herds start comin' in, you'll get all the noise your ears can stand. After a bunch of cowboys have been on the trail for weeks without seein' a woman or havin' a bottle of whiskey, they get a little carried away when they ride into Dodge an' find plenty of both. A man can't hardly sleep at night for all the music and hell-raisin', but for the most part it's just honest cowhands lettin' off steam."

"To tell the truth, I'm glad I won't be here to see it," he said. "I've gotten used to the peace and quiet up in the High Lonesome."

Earp gave Smoke a curious stare. "You don't sound like a man who used to throw lead for a livin'. If my deputy hadn't recognized you, I'd've never guessed it."

Smoke leaned back against the fence. "Plenty of men've taken the wrong fork in the road, Marshal. 'Specially when they were younger."

The Marshal was still looking at him, sizing him up, or so it seemed. "What was it changed you, if you don't mind me askin' you?"

Smoke grinned. "A woman."

"A woman?" he asked, clearly surprised. "I was expectin' you to say you'd done a little jail time, or maybe had a run-in with the law someplace."

"A woman came along, a real special woman. She's my wife now."

Earp shrugged. "Can't say as I've ever met a woman who'd make much of a change in me," he said.

"I was lucky. I've thought about it plenty. I was headed for an early grave, most likely, until Sally came along. It don't matter how careful a man is when he's in the gunfighter's trade—he's always got a backside."

Earp was grinning again. "Same goes for a man who wears a badge. Some son of a bitch decides to come gunnin' for you, it ain't possible to hide from it for long. Best thing to do is face up to it. You gotta hope you're just a fraction faster with a gun."

Smoke offered his opinion on the subject. "Bein' fast ain't all there is to it, in my estimation."

The Marshal frowned. "It can make the difference between livin' and dyin', if you ask me."

Smoke wagged his head. "Gettin' off the first shot don't amount to much if you can't hit what you're aiming at. If I had to chose between bein' fast and having the best aim, I'll take the latter every time. 'Course, it helps if you got both speed and accuracy."

"Sounds like you figure you've got both," Earp replied as he shouldered his shotgun for the walk back to his office.

"I get by," was all Smoke said as Earp took off toward the center of town.

He watched the young Marshal walk away with a mixture of impressions. Earp had nerve—it was easy to see that. Most men wouldn't have walked up to

Smoke looking for a confrontation as to his gunfighter's reputation—not anyone who knew about his past. But there was also something about the way Earp carried himself that showed he lacked some confidence, as if in his own mind he hadn't been fully tested yet.

Smoke turned back to the cow pens when he heard a man wearing spurs clanking down an alleyway between corrals. He appeared to be checking float valves on water troughs, filled by several windmills on both sides of the shipping pens, that filled a storage tank beside the railroad tracks.

Satisfied that all was as it should have been with the herd, Smoke pushed away from the fence to find a place where he could buy coffee and breakfast.

A gust of wind swept across Dodge as daylight came, and when it did, Smoke paused to look at the southern horizon. A lone horseman sat on a hilltop more than a mile away as though he were watching the town.

"Wonder why he ain't moving," Smoke whispered, unable to make out any detail from such a distance. A rider headed for Dodge wouldn't be sitting still like that, he reasoned.

Smoke stood frozen, watching the horseman for almost half a minute before the rider turned away and rode out of sight.

The feeling returned, stronger than ever, that something was looming beyond the horizon, and he'd just seen possible proof of it. Could the raiders who struck Cobbs Trading Post be setting their sights on a town the size of Dodge?

It could only mean one thing, if this were true; the gang was as big as Grimes said it was, perhaps as many as thirty men. It would take a small army to strike a town of this size with any hopes of shooting their way in and out, exchanging gunfire with armed citizens and lawmen. A handful of men, no matter how well armed or brazen they might be, could never pull it off.

Smoke continued up Main Street when no one else appeared on the hills south of town, wondering if he might be jumping to conclusions. Lengthening his strides to make the hotel so he could wake up Cal and Pearlie, he halted again when he saw Marshal Earp standing on the boardwalk in front of his office, looking south.

Earp spoke to him. "Did you notice that gent way out yonder on the top of a hill, Mr. Jensen?" Earp asked.

"I did," Smoke replied. "Seemed kinda outa the ordinary to me, that he wasn't headed into town. He sat there for about a minute an' then turned back."

"I was thinkin' the same thing," Earp offered, with his gaze fixed on the hills.

"Could be a lookout," Smoke suggested.

"We're in agreement on the possibility. Just to be on the safe side I'll tell my deputies to load their rifles and sidearms. Don't hurt to be careful."

"I'll have my two wranglers climb outa bed and strap on their pistols," Smoke said. "They've got Winchesters and plenty of shells."

He noticed that Earp swallowed hard . . . his Adam's apple rose and fell.

"I sure hope we're both wrong about it," Earp said, as he turned for his office door.

"Same goes for me," Smoke agreed, walking on with a bit more haste to reach the hotel.

* * *

"Wake up, Pearlie," Smoke said. "Get dressed and check the loads in your pistol and rifle. Then get Cal out of bed and tell him to do the same."

Pearlie sat up in bed quickly, rubbing his eyes. "We got trouble?" he asked.

"Can't say for sure," Smoke answered. "All the same, I intend to be ready if there is any."

Chapter 14

Bill Anderson addressed his men in the pale gray of dawn as they sat their horses in a swale southeast of Dodge City. Bill could feel his heart pumping. "Pass out the ammunition, Claude, an' make damn sure everybody has extra shells. I want every gun fully loaded. Don't spare no lead when we get to town. Shoot any sumbitch who ain't runnin' for cover. Kill anybody who's got a gun out if he's actin' the least little bit like he's ready to use it."

Claude stepped down from his sorrel and went to a packhorse to begin passing out cartridges. Solemn-faced men began loading weapons—pistols, shotguns, rifles of every description, depending upon the preferences of the men who used them.

"We'll split into two parties," Bill continued. "Jack's gonna lead the bunch comin' from the north. We'll give him half an hour before ten to get around. Then we ride in slow, like we ain't up to nothin'.

Folks won't be none the wiser 'til we get to them banks an' start shootin', most likely. But if some sumbitch yells or makes a fuss, kill him right where he stands. Jack's gonna take four men in one bank with him while me an' Sonny an' a couple more hit the other bank, the one on the west side of that main street. That'll leave nine or ten men outside to cover us. Jack'll have a packhorse an' that mule to load the money on. We'll have two packhorses. I want Claude leadin' the string of packhorses that comes with us. Dewey's gonna lead the other horse an' the mule. Six men stay with each string of packhorses to guard the rear whilst we're clearin' out of Dodge City. There's gonna be a helluva lot of lead flyin', so stay low in the saddle an' keep your eyes open. We start ridin' into town at ten o'clock so the bank vaults'll be open."

"What about that Marshal?" Sammy asked. "I thought we was gonna stay an' string him up, then set the whole damn town on fire."

Bill gave Sammy a look. "That fire's your job, Sammy, you an' Roy. Find some kerosene an' toss it on some of them walls. Strike a match to it an' then get mounted. The wind blowin' like it is, Dodge is gonna burn plumb to the ground."

Jack thumbed cartridges into his spare pistol and stuck it in his belt before he loaded his sawed-off shotgun. "If we kill enough of 'em real early, the rest are gonna run like rabbits," he said.

"Jack's right," Bill agreed. "Don't show no bashfulness when it comes to the killin' part. I want them streets to turn red with blood."

Lee Wollard, a lantern-jawed man from Mississippi, holstered his Colt .44 and took a lariat rope from his saddlehorn. "Me an' Sammy an' Buster can ride up to the lawdog's office an' blast him out. I'll put this here rope 'round his neck, an' we'll drag him to the closest tree to string him up, if we don't have to kill the bastard first. Come to think of it, we'll hang him anyway 'cause he's gonna wind up dead, one way or another.''

Some of the men chuckled while they were putting rounds into their weapons.

"I'm puttin' you in charge of the Marshal, Lee," Bill said, before he took a swallow of whiskey. "Kill the sumbitch any way you have to, but just make damn sure he's dead.''

The click of loading gates on all manner of weaponry filled a moment of silence. Brass-jacketed shells clattered while going into place.

Bill looked at his father's pocket watch. "It's near seven right now. Pick out the men you want, Jack, an' get headed up to the north. Stay out of sight behind these hills. Don't want 'em to know we're comin' if we can help it. Harley said the town looked real quiet. No train's due 'til noon, if it's on schedule like it has been all week.''

Harley Woods urged his horse closer to Bill's. "Hardly no sign of life on them streets. Most of them cow pens is empty, only I did see some real strange-lookin' cattle. White heads, damn near every one, an' the rest of their bodies was solid color or they had stripes on their hides.''

Bill opened his Greener shotgun and made sure both ten-gauge tubes were loaded. "We ain't interested in cows, Harley. It's them banks we're after. Who the hell cares what color a damn cow is, anyways?''

"They was just unusual," Harley said quietly, like he wished he hadn't mentioned it.

Bill snapped his shotgun closed, booting it at the

front of his saddle in a sleeve that was tied to the cantle. "All right, boys," he said. His Winchester came out of a boot beneath a stirrup leather as he spoke, jacking a cartridge into the firing chamber. "Let's move out."

Jack Starr led fourteen men in a circle, heading back down the swale. The metallic sound of armament, bits, and spurs was the only noise accompanying the whisper of hooves through dry grass as they moved away.

"Pass out the whiskey," Bill said, taking another swallow from the bottle he held in his fist. "Don't want none of you runnin' out of nerve when the shootin' starts."

Claude walked among the mounted men, passing out fresh jugs of whiskey. He paused when he passed Bill's horse.

"You want a new one, Bill?" he asked.

Bill examined the contents of his bottle. "I'm okay for now I reckon. We've got plenty of time. Them banks won't open 'til ten. We gotta make sure we don't kill nobody inside 'til them vaults are open."

Claude moved on, handing bottles up to several more men. He felt confident of his plan to take Dodge by storm, Bill did, and his instincts were seldom wrong. Surprise would be a part of their success that morning, but overwhelming firepower would be the most important thing. City folk weren't usually inclined to shoot back when they were being shot at.

Homer Suggins swung his dappled gray over to talk to Bill. "One thing would be a help, Bill," he said, his face twisted in thought. "If some of us rode up to the back of them buildings an' got up on the roof where we could shoot down at the street, we'd be able to keep any local heroes from makin' a run fer one of them banks while the men are inside.''

"Good idea," Bill said. "You an' Sikes are good shots with a rifle. Take him an' get up on a couple of rooftops. You'll have cover, an' any sumbitch who comes out in the street'll be a sittin' duck.''

"Just thought it made good sense, Bill.''

"It does for a fact. Soon as you boys see the money is on our packhorses, climb down an' head out to the south. Jack's gonna help cover our escape with heavy doses of lead. You ride down them alleys an' join us quick as you can.''

Homer smiled. "It's gonna be like old times again, ain't it? Like when me an' Sikes was with Quantrill when we hit Lawrence. We shot every man an' boy in sight. Them newspapers claimed we killed a hundred an' fifty in Lawrence. If you recall, Frank James was with us then.''

I remember,'' Bill said. "That was before Jesse, when he was just turned seventeen, joined up with us. Jesse an' Frank James rode with me when we hit Centralia, Missouri, in '64, an' that was when we stopped that Wabash an' Pacific train by puttin' crossties on the rails.''

"I heard you got three thousand dollars off'n that train, afore you gunned down twenty-five Yankee soldiers.''

"That's when Jesse James shot the Union commander right off his goddamn horse," Bill said.

"Wasn't no better fights than them two—Lawrence and down at Centralia," Homer agreed.

Bill's face turned hard. "It was that damn Order number eleven that done it," he said.

"We burned more houses an' barns in this Territory an' Missouri when we come across Yankee sympathizers than any other outfit. Damn proud of it, too. If it hadn't been for Bobby Lee givin' up so quick, we'd've won that war a piece at a time."

"You ever hear from Jesse or Frank?" Homer asked.

Bill wagged his head. "They both think I'm dead. They shot the wrong man over in Missouri, them Yankees did, an' somebody did me a favor."

"A favor?"

"They claimed it was me. Somebody said he was positive it was me they killed. I owe that feller."

"Jesse an' Frank an' them Younger boys have sure made a name for themselves."

"We're liable to do the same thing," Bill promised, "after we pull off this robbery in Dodge. It's gonna be in all the newspapers."

" 'Specially if we hang that Marshal," Homer said, with an eye to the north where Dodge lay just beyond a string of low hills. "They'll sure as hell talk 'bout that, the way they's talkin' 'bout Jesse an' Frank an' Cole."

"We're fixin' to make news," Bill said, taking a swallow of whiskey. "It's time we quit hidin' from them bluebelly sons of bitches."

Homer scowled a little. "They'll come after us hard, Bill. We ain't got enough men or guns to hold 'em off like we done in the old days."

Bill thought about it. "We'll hire us some gunmen from down in Mexico with part of this bank loot, Homer. With money, we can buy the best gunmen there is, south of the border, if we make the right offer."

"I never did trust Meskins much."

Bill shrugged. "Don't have to trust 'em. Pay 'em good wages an' kill the sons of bitches who don't take orders from me like they should."

Homer's scowl softened. "Down in Lawrence we couldn't miss with a bullet, Bill. There was folks all over the place, runnin' like hell in every direction. All a man had to do was shoot in the general direction an' somebody'd go down. I still remember it like it was yesterday. Seemed like we killed more'n a hundred an' fifty. Maybe them newshounds can't count all that good."

"We're gonna have us some more of them good times," Bill said. "Startin' in about two hours . . ."

Homer lowered his voice. "We've got a few with us who ain't so good with a gun, Bill, an' some of 'em don't have much in the way of backbone." He said it quietly, after making sure no one was listening.

Bill glanced over his shoulder. "Some men get more backbone when they've got a bellyful of whiskey. That's why I had Claude pass them bottles around."

"Maybe, then, they can't shoot straight?" Homer wondered aloud as he took a drink of whiskey himself.

Bill gave Homer the eye. "What the hell difference does it make if we lose a few? Some of these farm boys ain't worth the gunpowder it'd take to kill 'em. Like Tom the other night—a goddamn crybaby. I was glad to be rid of him."

"I can hardly wait for the shootin' to start," Homer said with a wistful expression glazing his eyes. "I can hear them city folks screamin' right now, when they see us ride off with their money."

"It's gonna be easy," Bill said. "We ride in shootin' every sumbitch in sight. Jump down an' clean out them safes. Then we ride like hell for the Nations."

"The army's gonna follow us."

Bill's mouth drew tight across his teeth. "Let 'em come. I got a plan for that, too."

"What sorta plan, Bill?"

"You'll see, when the time comes. There's this place down in Choctaw country, a real narrow canyon."

Homer grinned. "We'll get up on the rim an' shoot 'em down like caged turkeys. Right?"

"They'll follow our tracks, an' we'll make 'em real plain so they can't miss us. We can settle a few scores for the stars an' bars, even if the damn war is over."

"Sounds like a good plan to me."

Homer had been with Bill since the war, and he trusted him in tight spots. "You keep one eye on Jack Starr," he said, keeping his voice low.

"Why's that, Bill?" Homer asked.

"It's simple enough. We're gonna have us four horses loaded with Union money. There's lots of men who'd shoot a man in the back for that much loot. Jack was born natural mean. He can't be trusted plumb to the core when there's too much hard money at stake."

"He ain't never showed no sign of bein' a snake. . . ."

"That's on account of us not havin' enough to be worth takin' the chance. All that's about to change."

"You figure he'd shoot you in the back? Honest?"

"He might. You keep an eye on him after we pull this job. Be ready to kill him if'n he so much as touches his gun when he's around me or that money."

Homer let a bubbling swallow of whiskey slide down his throat. Then he sighed, sleeving his lips dry. "I'll kill him if'n he does, Bill. You can count on it."

"I knowed I could trust you, Homer. You been sidin' with me since the war. Ain't many in this outfit I'd say the same thing about."

Homer looked around them before he said any

more. "There might be more'n one who'd get greedy," he said. "I never did trust Dewey or Roy all that much."

"When there's a pile of money involved, not many men can be trusted. You remember that, Homer."

Chapter 15

Crawford Long, a dapper man in a business suit and silk vest introduced himself to Smoke at nine o'clock sharp down at the shipping yards while Pearlie and Cal kept an uneasy watch in all directions from a top rail of a corral fence, rifles resting on their laps.

"Pleased to meet you, Jensen," Long said, passing his eye over Smoke's offering of steers after they shook hands. "These are top-notch cattle. I come to Dodge City early every year to get my pick of what comes in. I'm with Chicago Beef Company, and I can assure you I'll pay top prices for your steers."

"How much might that be?" Smoke asked, his rifle leaning against a corral post within easy reach, just in case the trouble he sensed early that morning, after seeing the lone rider turn away from the horizon, actually arrived.

Long, in his fifties with a paunch straining the buttons on his vest, screwed his face into a frown.

"An ordinary longhorn in good flesh fetches eight or nine dollars a head. I'll double that for this bunch. How many have you got?"

"Three hundred and seven," Smoke answered. "That's what's in the railyard tally book."

"I'll stick my neck out an' pay eighteen dollars apiece," Long offered.

"I'm holding out for twenty, but I appreciate your offer," Smoke told him. "I'll show them to a couple more buyers, and if your offer is tops, then I'll sell to you. On the way down here I was guessing they'd bring twenty-five a head. It's choice beef, and any experienced cattleman can see that. Not much waste on a carcass."

Long chewed his fleshy bottom lip a moment. "I'll pay the twenty, then. That comes to six thousand one hundred and eighty dollars, by my calculations."

Smoke quickly did the numbers in his head. "Sounds right to me, Mr. Long."

Long turned away from the fence. "Then we'll shake hands on it an' our bargain is sealed. As soon as the Cattleman's Bank opens we'll go draw your money. I'll write out a bill of sale while we're at the bank. Sheldon Herring, the bank president, is a friend of mine. We can use his office to finish our business. I come here every year since the rail spur was built. I'll start arranging for cattle cars right away. I'd like to get these cows to Chicago as quickly as I can."

Smoke shook with Long, thinking how pleased Sally would be when she heard the news. Their Hereford crosses had more than doubled their income from beef production over previous years. "It's done, then," Smoke said. "We've got a deal at twenty per head."

"It's a pleasure doing business with you, Jensen,"

Long said with a smile. "I'll meet you in front of the bank at ten. In the meantime I'll check with the yard foreman to get cars ready for the three o'clock train back east. The locomotive gets here at noon, usually. Then it takes time to make that turnaround and fill the boiler. After you pocket your money, the yard foreman can start pulling empty cattle cars to the loading chutes with teams of mules. See you at the bank, Jensen."

Crawford Long hurried off, his head bent into the wind to keep from losing his bowler hat.

When Long was out of earshot, Pearlie said, "That's one fine price fer a batch of steers, boss." He squinted in the sun's early glare, watching the hills a moment. "It sure don't appear them owlhoots are gonna show up in Dodge today. Maybe that feller you saw was just some drifter. . . ."

"The day ain't over yet, Pearlie," Smoke said. "I've still got this funny feelin' down the back of my neck."

Smoke ran across Marshal Earp and his two deputies on Main Street—the three lawmen were walking around Dodge carrying shotguns, and one deputy had a Winchester rifle. Smoke left Cal and Pearlie to watch the herd.

Earp spoke to Smoke first. "No sign of any strangers or anything unusual goin' on. Seems real quiet."

"It does for a fact," Smoke agreed.

"Did you get your cattle sold?" Earp asked.

Smoke nodded. "Made a deal with Crawford Long from the Chicago Beef Company just now. Soon as the bank opens I'll draw my money and we'll be headed back home."

Earp gave his deputies a sideways glance. "Just to

be on the safe side, I'm puttin' a deputy at the front door of both banks armed with shotguns and pistols, while I keep movin' around with an eye out for strangers.''

"Good idea," Smoke said, although he felt sure that experienced bank robbers would make short work of two deputies standing out in plain sight, making easy targets. "My men are down at the cow pens keeping an eye on things until my business with Long is finished."

"Can your cowboys shoot?" Earp asked.

"I was about to ask you the same thing about these two deputies," Smoke replied.

Earp seemed a little embarrassed. "I'd say they're fair hands with a gun."

Smoke wasn't all that impressed with the looks of either one, and yet he kept his opinion to himself. As he was about to leave the Marshal, he happened to spot a pair of cowboys riding along the railroad tracks, coming from the east, still almost a mile away. "Here comes a pair of newcomers," he said. "Maybe they're just passin' through, but it wouldn't hurt to keep one eye on 'em until we know what they're up to.''

"We get saddle tramps passin' through all the time," Earp said, "and there ain't but two. No sign of that big bunch the drummer told us about."

Smoke slitted his eyes to keep out the sun, still watching the pair. "They might come in quiet, in twos an' threes. It'll pay to watch 'em."

"You've got a suspicious nature, Mr. Jensen."

Smoke nodded. "It's what has kept me alive all these years, Marshal."

He strode off down a side street, a knot forming

in his gut, telling him something was about to go wrong.

At a corner where he had a view of open land to the east, he stopped long enough to watch the two riders approaching Dodge by following the rails.

"Unusual," he said to himself, his voice lost on a gust of wind.

Playing a hunch, he walked back a dozen paces and slipped into an alley running between rows of buildings in the business district. As it was early, shadows offered him a place to stay out of sight.

Pausing near the back wall of a harness shop, he rested against the boards, waiting, holding his rifle down beside his leg.

A quarter hour later one of the cowboys he'd seen reined his horse into the alleyway. He stopped his mount, gave a look toward the rooftop above his head, and drew a rifle, stepping to the ground, tying off his brown gelding to a rain gutter. The stranger looked both ways up and down the alley, then he pushed an empty flour barrel against the building and began climbing up on the roof.

He's going to cover the street, Smoke thought, *while the bank is being robbed.*

There wasn't time to alert Pearlie or Cal or Marshal Earp to what was going on. . . .

Hatless so as not to show himself, a rawboned cowboy lay on his belly peering over the false front of a dry-goods store with a view of Main Street. Smoke crept up behind him on the balls of his feet, pulling his gleaming Arkansas Toothpick from a sheath inside his right boot. The cowboy's rifle lay beside him, next to his battered Stetson.

"Nice view, ain't it?" Smoke whispered, when he was a yard or two away.

A square-jawed man whirled around, clawing for a pistol he had buckled to his waist, his eyes rounded with surprise.

A ten-inch blade sliced into Clifton Sikes' chest, snapping cartilage and bone. His mouth flew open to cry out in pain when a huge hand covered his face, smothering his shout.

Sikes arched his back, trembling, his gun hand clamped around the butt of a Walker Colt .44. Blood squirted from the knife blade when Smoke pushed it all the way to the hilt into the gunman's ribs.

"Stings a little, don't it?" Smoke asked, a mirthless grin twisting the corners of his mouth, his palm still covering the man's quivering lips, silencing the sound bubbling in his throat.

The gunman's eyelids batted, then closed. His body relaxed on the rooftop. Blood pooled around him as Smoke took out his knife, leaving a gaping wound over Sikes's heart.

"One more," Smoke said, ducked down behind the false front of the store, wiping blood off the blade before inching backward to climb down to the alley.

He broke into a run when his feet touched ground, heading for the side street where he had left his rifle hidden behind a barrel of trash. Smoke rounded the corner at a dead run, aiming for Main Street.

He saw Marshal Earp standing next to a hitchrail with his face turned northward. "Marshal!" he cried, running as hard as he could, rifle in one hand, bloody knife in the other.

Earp wheeled at the sound of his name. He saw Smoke coming toward him.

"What the hell? . . . Where'd you get all that blood on your sleeve?" Earp asked, eyeing the knife.

Smoke raced over to him, slightly out of breath. "One of those strangers we saw followin' the tracks into Dodge climbed up on that roof yonder with a rifle. He was gonna cover this street while the bank's bein' robbed."

Earp tensed, pointing to the hills north of town. "I see a dust cloud comin'. Takes plenty of horses to kick up so much dust."

"They're comin' for the bank, whoever it is," Smoke warned as he sheathed his bowie. "There's one more of 'em somewhere on a rooftop. I killed the first one I found. Tell your deputies to get to cover—and you'd better do the same!"

Earp appeared frozen momentarily. He looked across the road at the bank. "The Cattleman's just opened. I'd better warn them to close the safe an' get to a safe place."

Smoke gave the dust sign a closer look. "If it's as many as old man Grimes said there was, no place is gonna be safe, Marshal. Tell 'em to lay down on the floor behind somethin' while I find that other owlhoot who's gonna cover the street from a roof somewheres."

"Son of a bitch," Earp sighed, his face gone white. "Here it is, a goddamn bank robbery in Dodge, an' I've got just two green deputies."

Smoke turned away, sighting along the rooflines of stores and shops on Main. "I'll help all I can, Marshal," he said over his shoulder as he broke into a run, turning down another side street to reach an alley across from the smaller Dodge City Savings Bank farther down the road.

* * *

Homer Suggins took a drink of whiskey and set the bottle down beside him, removing his sweat-stained Confederate cavalry hat to peek over the wood front of Martha's Eatery. He'd been very careful crossing the roof, so as not to make noise that would alert anyone inside. He put his Henry repeating rifle by his side, rising up on his elbows to see what was happening on the street below.

He saw a sign reading, "The Dodge City Savings Bank" and quickly lowered his head. He had a perfect view of the front, which would allow him to kill anyone who challenged Jack Starr or any of his men when they went inside for the robbery—and of far more importance, to cover them when they came out.

Homer felt a strange tingling of excitement in his chest, like he did back when William Clark Quantrill signaled that a raid was about to begin. That was so many years ago, and he'd missed the feeling, the rattle of guns, the screams of wounded and dying men all around him. Bill Anderson was too cautious, staying far from any chance of a real showdown. This raid on Dodge was more like it.

He thought he heard the whisper of feet behind him, although he knew it wasn't possible—hell, he was hidden up on a roof, and no one had seen him climb up that pile of wooden crates at a back corner.

Homer glanced over his shoulder, merely to satisfy himself that it was his imagination.

What he saw made his blood run cold. A towering giant of a man loomed above him, a bloody Arkansas Toothpick in one hand and a pistol in the other.

"Let me guess," the tall stranger said, his voice like a horseshoer's rasp across an anvil, grating. "You came up here with that rifle to go bird huntin'. I've heard it's a good time of year for whitewing doves.''

Homer's heart stopped beating altogether for a moment or two, as he heard the deadly tone behind the wisecrack this big man had just made.

"I . . . I was gonna fix a leak in this roof,'' Homer explained with his voice breaking. "Honest, I was. . . .''

In a blinding movement the stranger's blade penetrated Homer's belly. White-hot pain raced through his chest and abdomen when the blade twisted. Something popped inside him, and it hurt like hell.

"I never met a man who fixed leaky roofs with a rifle an' a bottle of whiskey,'' the same voice said, as Homer felt himself slipping into a black void. The stranger's shape was fuzzy, indistinct.

His eyes closed. Then Homer Suggins began the long sleep.

Chapter 16

Smoke saw dust rise above hills south of Dodge as he wiped blood off his Toothpick on the dead man's pants leg. "Comin' from two directions," he muttered, wheeling in a crouch to hurry back across the rooftop and to climb down to the alley. He needed to warn Marshal Earp and to have him clear the streets. Otherwise any number of innocent citizens could have been killed.

He dropped to the ground and took off in a run, rounding a corner where he spied Earp on Main Street, positioning Deputy Cody Wade in front of the Dodge City Savings Bank.

"Get everybody inside!" Smoke yelled, causing Earp to swing around suddenly. "Another bunch is comin' from the south!"

Earp looked southward as Smoke ran up to him.

"Son of a bitch!" Earp exclaimed. "Two bunches!" He turned to Deputy Wade. "You an' Jim Bob start

yellin' for everybody to take cover inside someplace.
I'll tell both bankers to close their safes an' get to
cover. This is gonna be a war, Cody, an' I want you
an' Jim Bob inside one of these buildings so you don't
get shot all to pieces!''

"I'll go fetch my men," Smoke said, breaking into
a run for the cow pens. He cried over his shoulder,
"We'll get up on the rooftops like they aimed to do
and shoot down at 'em!"

He didn't wait for Earp's reply, running hard until
he sighted Pearlie and Cal at a corral fence. Both
men were looking at the dust rising from hills south
of town.

"Bring your rifles!" Smoke bellowed, waving them
away from the railyard. "Hurry it up! Trouble's
comin'!"

Cal and Pearlie took off in awkward runs with Winchesters clamped in their fists. Cal was the first to
reach Smoke.

"Is it that big gang Grimes told us about?" Cal
asked, out of breath from his sprint.

"Looks like it. You boys get extra boxes of hells
from our gear and climb up on one of them roofs
with a false front, so you'll have some protection from
a bullet. I'll get on that roof across from the savings
bank. The minute any shooting starts, be damn sure
you aim for a bank robber. Don't take no chances if
you can't be sure your target is one of 'em.''

"Lordy," Pearlie said, glancing over his shoulder.
"I knew this wasn't gonna be no peaceful trip. . . ."

"So did I," Cal added, swallowing hard, "right after
that bay throwed me off.''

"Get going!" Smoke commanded. "Bring me
some spare shells an' we'll pick out the best places
where you can shoot.''

As Pearlie and Cal took off for the hotel, Smoke saw Crawford Long heading into the Cattleman's Bank. He shouted across the road at the cattle buyer. "Find some cover, Mr. Long! Me an' the Marshal think there's a gang of bank robbers headed this way. Stay out of sight 'til it's over. We'll conduct our cow business soon as we can settle this."

Long's face went slack. "Right!" he cried, making a fast turn away from the bank, hurrying as quickly as his chubby legs could move down the boardwalk, entering a smaller hotel named the Palace, with his coattails fluttering in the breeze.

Now Deputies Wade and Watley were shouting to everyone to get off the streets. Women and children and men of every description made dashes for doorways on either side of Main Street.

Cal burst out of the hotel cradling extra boxes of cartridges against his chest. All of their Winchesters were .44s, and the same shells fit the cylinders of the pistols they carried.

Smoke took a box of shells as Marshal Earp trotted up with his shotgun. Pearlie came clumping out of the Drovers Hotel as Smoke was speaking to the others.

"I'll get back up on the roof of Martha's Eatery," he said, "on account of it gives me the best view of the Dodge City Bank. I want you an' Pearlie across the road an' get up where you can cover the front of the Cattlemans. An' watch your backsides when the shootin' starts, so nobody can slip up behind you. We'll have 'em caught in a crossfire when they ride into town. If they don't know we're ready for 'em, maybe we can drop a good-sized handful before they get the wiser."

"What about our steers, boss?" Pearlie asked, pushing brass cartridges into the loading gate of his rifle until the tube was full, jacking one into the firing chamber.

"They ain't after cows, Pearlie. They've come for the money we aimed to get for our herd, an' every cent that's in them bank vaults besides. We ain't gonna let 'em just ride in an' take the profit out of a year's worth of ranching at Sugarloaf. Soon as the first shot gets fired, start killin' outlaws . . . only remember to stay down so you don't wind up dead or wounded."

Pearlie and Cal hurried across the street as the dust to the north and south grew thicker, moving closer rapidly. In minutes the gangs would be in sight.

Marshal Earp spoke. "I'll take up a position inside my office, along with Cody, so we'll have a good view of the street in both directions. I told Jim Bob to hide behind that brick wall next to the blacksmith's shop. He's got plenty of ammunition, an' he don't have to be all that good a shot, usin' a double scattergun."

Smoke nodded, preparing to run back to the alleyway to get on the roof of the cafe. "Just keep your heads down. I'll get as many as I can, maybe move around a bit if they find cover in town instead of pullin' out."

Earp gave him a weak grin. "I sure hope you're as good with a gun as Jim Bob said you was, Mr. Jensen. We're gonna need all the help we can get."

Smoke took off without a word, his mind focused on what was to come. A battle was about to be waged in the streets of Dodge City, if he was any judge of such matters. He could feel it coming as he ran into the alley to make the climb to the roof of Martha's Eatery.

He found the dead outlaw just where he had left him, a few feet behind the false front of the building. Blood encircled the corpse and already the blowflies were feeding on it, buzzing over the body in swirling black clouds.

Ignoring the green-backed flies, Smoke took off his hat and rested against the wooden front of the building, only his eyes visible above the boards where a sign was painted, with the words: "The Best Grub in Dodge."

Now there was nothing to do but wait, and see what kind of move the bank robbers made when they hit town. It would depend on how experienced they were, how much savvy they had.

In the back of his mind he wondered if this bunch could be led by Bloody Bill Anderson. Louis had been so sure of the report that Anderson had been killed in Missouri many years ago, not long after the war was over. But Smoke found himself with a nagging feeling of doubt, until he decided it really did not matter either way. He'd been up against men with tall reputations before, and most of them had turned out to be ordinary men who died just as quickly as nameless gents with guns. The trick was to be first with a bullet in a critical spot, something Smoke had learned before he was old enough to shave—he'd had one hell of a good teacher, a withered old mountain man who understood the business of living and dying better than anyone he'd ever known.

He thought of his promise to Sally the day they left the ranch with the herd—to swing wide of trouble whenever he was able. She'd understand this sudden turn of events, he told himself. How could he have known a gang of bank robbers had planned to strike Dodge City at the same time they arrived to sell their steers? It was the luck of the draw, a coincidence.

Peering above the boards, he could see riders now, more than a dozen heading for Dodge at an easy trot from the north. To the south, where more hills stretched to the horizon, all he could see was dust, thickening, like storm clouds moving over Kansas prairies.

Brushing blowflies away from his face, he studied the men riding toward town. By being watchful, paying attention to things out of the ordinary, he'd been able to kill two of them before the robbery attempt had begun. Like so many parts of his nature that were regular habits, he'd learned this watchfulness from Preacher.

As Smoke gazed south, a line of horsemen appeared below the dust, maybe fourteen or fifteen men, spread out in a ragged line. It was plain that these riders were after something, splitting into two groups, arriving at the same time.

Keeping his rifle barrel hidden behind the planks so that sun light wouldn't reflect off it, giving him away, he settled in to see what would happen next.

Sounds from the street below quieted as everyone in the business district of Dodge hid behind closed doors. And in the silence, Smoke could hear the distant drum of hoofbeats coming closer to town.

"There's gonna be a lot of blood spilled here," Smoke said under his breath, sure of it. A gang of this size would not be easily discouraged.

The most important factor in evening the odds against them would be to wait until all the robbers were in range. If anyone fired a shot too early, the raiders would be warned and their plans might change. If they spread out across the town, killing and looting, Smoke and his cowboys and Earp and his deputies would stand little chance of thinning the outlaws' ranks.

"Here they come!" someone cried from down

Main Street. It sounded like Deputy Watley. The deputy was too green to know how to win a fight like this.

Smoke took a chance, raising his head slightly above the top of the roof. "Stay quiet!" he yelled as loudly as he could. "We don't want 'em to know we're ready!"

As the sound of his voice faded away, an eerie silence came to Dodge. Only the constant buzzing of the flies hovering over the corpse behind Smoke reached his ears, save for the distant rumble of approaching horses.

Hidden in the shadow that was cast by the false front of Martha's Eatery, he could lean away from the boards to get a view of the riders coming from the south. When he slitted his eyes to dim the sun's glare, he saw a man riding at the front, wearing an old Confederate cavalry officer's hat and a gray tunic.

"Maybe it's some gent tryin' to make folks think he's Bill Anderson," Smoke said to himself. "Damn near every Southern soldier's got parts of an old Rebel uniform."

And Smoke could also make out the rifles and shotguns these men were carrying, evidence they were headed into Dodge without a peaceful purpose.

"It won't be long now," he whispered, as a change came over him. It was always like this before he engaged in a fight—the tingling down his arms, his tongue going dry, the slight increase in the beat of his heart when his muscles tensed, ready to do battle with an enemy.

The horseman in the gray hat and tunic was clearer now, at a distance of less than a quarter mile. He rode with a stiff spine, in soldier fashion.

"Maybe it is Bloody Bill," he whispered. "It don't make a damn bit of difference to me who he is. . . ."

The gang picked up speed, urging their horses to a lope as they neared the outskirts of town. Smoke raised his Winchester to his shoulder, keeping the muzzle low, out of sight.

"Welcome to Dodge, Mister Bloody Bill Anderson, or whoever the hell you are," he hissed, clamping his teeth, cords of hard muscle standing out in his neck. "We've got a little surprise waitin' for you."

The men rode past small houses and shacks at the edge of the business district. The raiders coming from the north were entering the other side of town—Smoke could hear their horses pounding hard ground with shod hooves.

Only a minute or two more, Smoke thought, drawing back out of sight behind the planks.

Suddenly, the roar of a shotgun blasted from the far side of Main Street, probably an edgy deputy of Earp's who couldn't wait for the right moment.

"Damn!" Smoke snapped, his hands gripping the stock of his Winchester. Someone had given their ambush away to the gang of highwaymen, too soon to give them the benefit of the element of surprise.

As Smoke rose up to join the fight, a deafening series of gunshots filled Main Street, thundering off buildings lining the roadway. Guns began cracking and popping from so many directions, it was impossible to tell who was doing the shooting, although it was clear the shots came from the street and buildings on both sides.

A horse screamed when shotgun pellets riddled its hide. A sorrel fell over in front of the Dodge City Savings Bank, pinning its rider's left leg.

Smoke found a target, a man on a rearing horse

with a rifle in his hands. Aiming quickly, Smoke fired a .44 caliber slug into the man's ribs, sending him toppling from the saddle.

A brass cartridge case tinkled hollowly near his feet when he worked the Winchester's lever . . . he scarcely noticed it in the melee.

A scattergun exploded from a window of the Marshal's office, sending another raider plunging off his horse with his face a red mass of pulpy tissue and blood.

Smoke heard a rifle crack from a rooftop across the street, where Pearlie was making his stand. A gunman with a flop-brim hat let out a yell and rolled backward off the rump of his steed.

The fight was on. Smoke fired at a slender rider aboard a pinto gelding. The man disappeared into a cloud of dust churned up by so many horses' hooves.

Chapter 17

A storekeeper ran out on the porch in front of Burns Hat & Boot Shop, shouldering a long-barrel goose gun, taking aim at the first riders to come up Main from the south. Just when he had his feet planted and was ready to fire, a woman's voice shrieked, "No, Henry! Come back inside!"

The concussion of a shotgun blast bellowed from a gun in the hands of a raider on the back of a galloping, black stud. Smoke was too far away to return fire accurately and he didn't want to give his position away yet, not until he had plenty of targets he knew he could fell.

Henry Burns was torn from his feet, his shopkeeper's apron shredded by shotgun pellets, bloodied when a full charge struck him in the chest and face. His goose gun flew from his hands as he toppled off the porch, clutching his belly, landing in the dirt on his side, screaming in pain, his feet kicking helplessly while he thrashed about at the edge of the road.

"Damn," Smoke whispered, wondering why anyone would run out to face a gang as large as this, armed only with a hunting gun. Some would call it courage—Smoke classed it as stupidity when the odds were so long.

Suddenly the leader of the raiders spurred his horse into a full-tilt charge, headed for the front of the Cattlemans Bank at top speed, his men spurring their mounts behind him. One of the raiders fired a sawed-off shotgun into a storefront window, and the sounds of shattering glass accompanied the thunder of hooves echoing off buildings lining the road. Inside the Ladies Fine Dress Shop, a woman wailed at the top of her lungs when glass fragments and a pair of dress dummies were blown into the interior of the building. In another part of town a child began to cry incessantly, frightened by the explosions.

Smoke raised his head and shoulders above the false front of the cafe, aiming for the leader of the bunch aboard a racing sorrel gelding. His sights came to rest on the center of the man's gray Confederate tunic when fate took a hand. The sorrel stumbled, then quickly regained its footing just as a raider on a chestnut moved between the leader and Smoke. Too late, Smoke triggered off a reflexive shot, feeling the Winchester's stock slam into his shoulder.

A bearded bandit atop the chestnut jolted when Smoke's slug passed through him. He teetered dangerously in the saddle and then fell off to one side, where he was trampled by running horses behind him, his limp body twisting and turning every time a flying hoof struck him.

Smoke levered another round into the chamber as

rapidly as he could, but the raiders had him pin-pointed. Pistols and rifles fired up at the roof of Martha's place, forcing Smoke to duck for cover.

Splintering boards and the crack of dry wood announced the impact of a dozen bullets meant for him. The element of surprise was gone for Smoke and the others trying to defend the town and its banks. Things would quickly settle into a game of hide-and-seek, with death as a reward for the loser.

Moving on his haunches, he crept to another spot on the roof as guns opened up across the road, the unmistakable bang of a .44 caliber rifle amid the roar of several shotguns. Answering fire came from the street until the air was filled with the noise made by dozens of pounding guns—the whine of lead passing overhead was hard to hear above the sounds of exploding gunpowder.

From the north, pistols chattered and rifles popped when the second group of robbers hit town. Now and then a stray bullet would strike the storefront where Smoke was hidden, some glancing off, others becoming embedded in sun-warped planking. Smoke was too wary to rise up again until the time was right—he'd have been a fool to have made a target of himself again. The time would soon come when the fully loaded guns in the raiders' hands were empty. Then Smoke could make each shot count from his perch above the cafe.

A shotgun thundered close by. A window just beneath Smoke was blasted to pieces, bits of glass tinkling to the boardwalk below like tiny musical chimes.

"Son of a bitch!" a muffled voice cried from some-where in the cafe, then the sounds of scurrying feet moved toward the back of the place.

A lessening in the booming gunfire brought
Smoke's head up just in time to see Marshal Earp's
deputy, Jim Bob Watley, rise above his hiding place
behind the brick wall at the blacksmith's shop to aim
his shotgun. He fired point-blank into the side of a
running horse, knocking the animal off its feet, sending it crashing down on its side, legs flailing, kicking
up dust while its rider raced for cover with a rifle in
his hands. But before the robber could make the
corner of the telegraph office, a pop came from Pearlie's rifle on a rooftop. The outlaw staggered, trying
to keep his balance and run at the same time, until
he sank to his knees with blood pumping from the
front of his shirt. He dropped his rifle to clutch his
wound in a feeble effort to stem the flow of blood.

Smoke came up quickly, turning his Winchester
on a man in a stained leather vest, leading a pair of
packhorses. Smoke fired at precisely the right
moment, when his gun sights were steady. The cowboy
flew forward over the pommel of his saddle, diving
head-first toward the ground with a pistol still
clamped in his fist. His gun went off when his skull
landed in a dry wagon rut, the bullet plowing a furrow
in the dirt near him. He collapsed in a heap with his
head twisted at an odd angle after he fell, lying still.

Smoke ducked just in time to escape a hail of bullets
coming from the street when some of the raiders
heard his gun. The pop and crack of lead riddled
the boards above Smoke's head for a time, until more
gunfire from another rooftop took their attention
away.

Smashing glass at the front of the Dodge City Savings Bank forced Smoke to peek over the planks
again. Three robbers were down off their horses,
shooting out the bank's front windows with shotguns.

Women were screaming inside the building, then a man cried out in agony a split second after another shotgun blast.

Smoke watched the outlaws rush in, climbing over a brick ledge that had once supported big panes of glass. He couldn't see what was going on inside, or hear any more voices when a lull in the shooting abruptly ended.

"They're inside," he growled angrily. "They'll kill everyone in the bank, or take some as hostages. . . ."

Marshal Earp fired sporadically from a broken window of his office, wounding another horse when he downed a raider with the shotgun. Two wounded, dying horses lay in the street. Smoke counted the bodies of five bank robbers sprawled in the dust and dirt. One wounded outlaw was crawling toward safety behind a water trough, leaving a trail of red in his wake.

The leader of the gang was nowhere in sight. Guns thundered in front of the Cattlemans Bank as more robbers tried to shoot their way in.

He heard Cal open up with his rifle, firing five shots in quick succession down into the street. Tiny wisps of gunsmoke lifted from the boy's firing position.

He finally found his nerve, Smoke thought with no rancor. A boy like Cal had never been in the midst of a war like the one going on in Dodge City then.

Smoke backed away from the edge of the roof to move again, to the far side of the cafe in order to keep the gunmen who were in the road guessing where he was. Inching across the roof, he could not help thinking about what must be going on inside the Dodge City Savings Bank, where hapless citizens of the town had made the mistake of doing their

banking business that morning. Smoke was sure that
members of the gang would be smart enough to take
hostages, probably women, believing that no one
would take a shot at them if the women were used
as human shields.

He came to the corner and glanced over his breast-
work of planks to see what was going on. Gunfire
rattled and boomed up and down Main Street with
no signs of lessening.

We're badly out-gunned, he thought, spotting loose
horses trailing their reins and galloping in every direction. Some of the raiders were on foot, making them
easier to stalk—easier to kill when he came down off
the roof to go after them one or two at a time.

One thing was in their favor: he and his cowboys,
and Earp and his deputies, had been as ready as they
could be for the robbery—behind cover with plenty
of ammunition. Things would likely have been over
already had it been otherwise. But the truth was, the
fight to save Dodge City's money was far from being
won or lost. It was a pitched battle, one-sided as hell,
yet Smoke had not begun to thin the robbers' ranks,
as he had planned to do, when opportunity came.

A heavy-bodied raider jumped off his nervous,
brown mare to make a run for the broken front windows of the bank. He stood at a hitchrail to tie his
horse in front of the building just long enough for
Smoke to draw a bead on his head.

The Winchester spat out its deadly load, banging
so near Smoke's right ear that he was deafened for
a moment. The gunman was midway through looping
his reins around the hitch post when he stiffened his
spine. His left foot came off the ground in a most
curious way, suspended as though he intended to
remain balanced on his right leg. His stetson flew off

amid a cloud of crimson mist, and it appeared that a plug of his long, black hair went with his hat.

"Gotcha, asshole," Smoke whispered, dropping back down out of sight at the same time the gunman's right knee buckled. He sank to the roadway, arms windmilling, his right shirt sleeve bloodied. He dropped the shotgun he carried and went over on his face, his chin landing hard on the boardwalk in front of the bank's shattered windows.

Smoke was barely ahead of answering fire from the street below. Bullets thudded into the boards between him and the war going on beneath him, some slugs sizzling over his head.

His senses warned him before his ringing ears actually heard the sound behind him. Whirling around, clawing for a pistol, he was just in time to fire at a head that was peering over the back of the rooftop.

His bullet struck a bearded outlaw in the throat. Pale blue eyes bulged in their sockets, eyes locked on Smoke's. For a time the man seemed frozen, gulping mouthfuls of his own blood, until he let out a groan and fell to the alleyway below, making a deep, thudding noise when he landed, followed by another groan that was louder than the first.

I've got to move, Smoke thought. The robbers were closing in on his position.

Bent over in a crouch, he ran to the back of the cafe, only to find another gunslick staring up at him.

Smoke's Colt belched flame and lead. His aim was true, in spite of the fraction of a second he had to shoot his adversary while staring into the dark muzzles of a shotgun.

A sandy-haired cowboy flinched when a ball of lead entered his forehead, knocking his hat to the ground. The outlaw took a half step back, still gazing up at the roof with a blank look in his eyes while the rear portion of his head came apart. Pieces of skullbone and twists of hair spiraled away from a spot just above his shirt collar. Bloody droplets splattered over the dirt alley where he stood, then suddenly his shotgun discharged. A swarm of speeding buckshot went skyward harmlessly, making a soft, whistling noise after the roar from both barrels filled the space between the rears of several buildings.

As if an anvil had been dropped on his chest, the raider was driven flat on his back in the alleyway, a delayed reaction to the fatal wound that had split his head open. His lips moved, trying to speak, although no words came out—only more blood coursing down his cheeks.

Smoke swung over the eave, letting himself down slowly, with his rifle tucked between his knees. The steady bang of guns had lessened somewhat up and down Main by the time he reached the ground.

Instinct kept him still for a moment, until he was certain no one was watching him from either end of the alley. On nothing but a hunch, he ran north, toward the rear of the harness shop, leaving two dead men in his wake.

At the corner leading into a side street, he paused to look and listen, getting his bearings, when he caught a glimpse of a rider spurring relentlessly away from the battle that was raging from one end of Dodge City to the other. A bandit wearing a Confederate infantryman's cap urged his horse to greater speed, looking back over his shoulder with a revolver gripped in his fist.

"Drop the gun!" Smoke shouted. "You can leave yer friends, but you ain't taking any guns with you."

The outlaw whirled around in the saddle to face

the voice he heard, and just as quickly he swung his pistol in Smoke's direction.

Smoke fired his rifle as the words "I warned you!" came loud and clear from his mouth. The Winchester thudded with all the power of a .44, its recoil jarring Smoke's right thigh as the bullet rocketed from the barrel in a spit of orange flame and a cloud of gunsmoke.

The robber's horse shied as the loud report clapped in front of it, and in the same instant a Confederate soldier's cap went into the air as the head on which it had been perched was driven backward. The man fell twisting, tumbling to the street.

A woman in a blue, ankle-length dress tried to escape out a side door of Brown's Bakery at a corner on the far side of Main. One of the raiders fired his pistol from atop a prancing horse, shooting her in the back before he spurred out of sight.

Sudden rage filled Smoke when he saw the woman go down. It was time to send these yellow bastards a message.

Chapter 18

Bill Anderson ducked into the Dodge City Savings Bank with a pistol in his right hand, a twin-barrel sawed-off shotgun in his left. Lee, Sonny and Dewey were positioned behind a polished, oak counter next to the door of a massive safe. Lee held a gun to the head of a trembling, balding man in front of the vault, obviously the banker in charge of things. The vault was closed. Sonny had a woman in front of him, his fingers wound into her long, dark hair so that her head was pulled back. Her palms were raised, and they shook uncontrollably. Outside, at a hitchrail, a gunman called Lucky held both nervous pack-horses, trying to calm them in the midst of all the shooting while staying hunkered down, to be out of the line of fire while Dewey and the others were inside the bank.

"He won't open it, Bill!" Lee growled, glancing out broken front windows when another wave of gunfire filled the street. "I swore I'd kill the sumbitch if he don't."

Bill noticed two bodies on the floor—a farmer dressed in overalls surrounded by blood, and an elderly woman in a faded, calico dress, her deeply wrinkled face pockmarked by shotgun pellet wounds oozing more blood onto waxed hardwood flooring. It appeared that the woman was still alive—he heard her soft whimpering above the thunder of gunshots outside.

"What's your name?" Bill asked, looking at the banker. He didn't like what he saw—a pampered man with fear written all over his face.

"F ... Feagin," the banker stammered. "David Feagin. I'm the only one who knows the combination to the safe ... and I ... won't open it. The money belongs to the townspeople of Dodge City."

Bill crossed a floor that was covered with broken glass and bloodstains, walking around the counter. He went up to Feagin with a snarl widening his lips. "Then I'm gonna have to kill you an' dynamite your vault. . . ." His gaze wandered to the woman with her hands raised in the air. Sonny held a gun against her ribs. "Or I can shoot this pretty lady, Mr. Feagin. You can watch her die, an' then I'll give you one last chance to open your vault. You ever see a woman die from a bullet hole right before your very eyes? There'll be this big hole, plumb through her, and her blood's gonna run all over this here floor. She'll scream real loud right at first, an' then she'll make softer noises after she falls on the floor. Her blood's gonna be on your hands, Feagin, unless you open that goddamn safe right now."

"Dear God," Feagin whispered, sweat running down his pale cheeks, dribbling on the front of his brown suitcoat and vest. "You wouldn't simply execute her . . . would you?"

Bill nodded as the rattle of guns quieted briefly out in the road. "We sure will, Mr. Banker, 'less you open that damn iron box real quick."

A sudden blast of shotgun fire bellowed from a spot not far from the bank.

"What the hell was that?" Bill demanded, inclining his head toward the windows. "See what it was, Dewey."

Dewey stepped cautiously to a shattered window. He stood still for a moment, peering out. "It's Jack an' Sammy an' a few more boys. They just shot their way into that other bank up the street. Yonder's some kid, maybe fourteen or so, runnin' with his hands coverin' his bloody face. Appears he caught a faceful of buckshot. Acts like he's blind. He just fell over a water trough outside, an' he can't stand up no more." Dewey gave the south end of Main a closer examination. "Somebody musta shot ol' Claude, 'cause the packhorse an' that mule is wanderin' loose, draggin' lead ropes. There's sure a bunch of dead folks layin' all over the place. . . ."

"May the Lord have mercy on us!" Feagin said, as if he knew his time had come. "Please don't kill any more people! Order your men to stop shooting, and I'll open the safe. Please don't kill any more women or children."

At that precise moment a shotgun erupted, then a shrill woman's voice screamed farther down Main.

"Roy shot this woman in the back of her head," Dewey said tonelessly. "She was tryin' to run from that store across from the bank. I swear, if it don't look like Roy shot her head plumb off . . . I didn't know we was gonna kill womenfolk this time."

"Please ask them to stop!" Feagin cried. "You can have all the money! Please don't kill anyone else."

"Start twistin' that dial," Bill snapped. "Soon as it's open, maybe I'll think about havin' my men stop shootin'. The longer you wait, the more folks is gonna die."

Two pounding shotgun blasts came from the Marshal's office, almost in unison. Then a wall of answering fire boomed from all directions, bullets cracking against the front of the building in a staccato of ear-splitting noises.

As Feagin began working the combination dial on the front of the safe, an eerie quiet settled over Dodge for a moment. Not a gun sounded for several seconds. The silence caught Bill's attention until another noise came from a rooftop almost directly across the street.

It sounded like a charging buffalo bull's roar at first, as a man stood up behind the false front of a bullet-riddled cafe called Martha's Eatery, hoisting what appeared to be a lifeless body over his head. He made the roaring sound with his head thrown back, then, demonstrating tremendous strength, threw the body over the wooden front of the building and disappeared.

The body landed on Main Street will a dull thud. Bloody Bill Anderson's eyelids narrowed, staring at the prone form. "Goddamn!" he exclaimed bitterly. "That's Homer! Some son of a bitch went an' killed Homer Suggins!"

Dewey blinked. "That is Homer," he said softly, with a note of disbelief. "Homer was 'bout the most careful feller I ever knowed in my whole life . . . how the hell did anybody git up on that roof behind him without him knowin' it? Homer could hear a damn sewin' needle drop."

"He's damn sure dead," Lee said, his gun jammed into the woman's ribs while he glanced out the glassless windows. "He ain't so much as moved a muscle."

Anderson's jaw clamped. He looked up at the rooftop of the cafe. "One of you go find that half-breed scout, Scar Face. Tell Scar Face to hunt down that son of a bitch who killed Homer an' bring me his goddamn scalp. Tell that breed the bastard's up on that roof yonder. Run an' fetch that breed, Dewey, an' tell him what I said. While you're out there, have somebody grab up the packmule an' that horse so we can haul our loot outa the Cattlemans Bank."

"What about Claude?" Dewey asked.

"Who cares about Claude?" Bill said. "Get goin'."

Dewey stepped carefully over a low windowsill and turned up the street, hunkered down with his gun aimed in front of him, not taking any chances that a stray bullet might hit him.

Bill turned back to Feagin, fighting the fury he felt inside for losing a good man like Homer Suggins, one of the few in his band he truly trusted. Homer had been with him since the war, and he'd always carried his share of the load. "Get that safe open!" he shouted. "Or you'll be the next sumbitch lyin' out there in that road dead as a fencepost."

Feagin's fingers quivered, turning the dial as Bill wondered who the brazen bastard was who tossed Homer's body down to the street—an act of outright defiance. And there was that strange yell Bill gave to attract attention to himself while he did it, a man who needed to be taught manners.

A rifle cracked from a rooftop near the Cattlemans Bank, and the sound made Bill grin. Sikes was still up there, gunning down resistance. Losing Homer wasn't good news, but they had another expert marksman firing from a good position, keeping any lawmen in town pinned down.

"Hurry up!" Bill said to the banker, when the safe had not yet been opened.

The crackle of pistol fire came from inside the Cattlemans Bank. Jack Starr was probably after revenge for what had happened to Homer, Bill thought, killing townspeople unlucky enough to be in the bank when it was being robbed. And Scar Face, the half-breed Pawnee, would take care of the loudmouth on top of the cafe in a short while. The breed was good at stalking ... not much at long distance shooting, Bill remembered. Scar Face could read horse sign the way some men read a book. He'd find that big, murdering bastard who had somehow slipped up behind Homer. Throwing his body down in the street was a form of insult that Bill wouldn't take without exacting revenge.

Feagin said, "I must have gotten part of the combination wrong. It won't open. I'll have to try again."

Bill whirled around, showing his teeth. He spoke to Lee. "Give Mr. Feagin a reminder of what'll happen if he gets it wrong again."

Lee drew back his pistol and whacked the banker on the top of his head. Feagin's eyes rolled upward, and he sank to the floor, out cold.

"Goddamn, Lee!" Bill cried. "Why the hell'd you hit him so hard? We ain't never gonna get that money 'til he wakes up."

"Sorry," Lee muttered, reaching down to pick Feagin up by his coat lapels. "I'll slap his face 'til he comes around."

Lee backhanded the banker's left and right cheeks several times, yet nothing seemed to revive Feagin at the moment. Lee gave Bill a quizzical stare. "What do you want me to do with him now?" he asked.

Bill cocked his .44 angrily. "I've got no use for a man who's too damn stupid to know what to do," he said, and at the same time, he pulled the trigger.

A bullet tore through Lee Wollard's left ear, coming out the other side amid a splash of crimson that spattered all over the door of the vault. Lee was slammed against the wall beside the safe as though he'd been kicked in the head by a mule. He slid down to the floor with his eyes wide open and his lips moving, trying to form the word *no*.

Sonny flinched when he saw Bill shoot Lee through the head, but he held his tongue when Bill glared at him. Lee let out a final groan and went still.

"Ask the bitch real nice if she wants to live," Bill said, struggling to control his temper. "If she opens that safe I'll spare her life. Otherwise, we're gonna kill her right here an' now."

"You heard what Bill said," Sonny snapped, punching the barrel of his gun a little deeper into her side. "Open it, or we'll kill you."

"I . . . don't . . . know . . . the combination," the woman stuttered, her eyes about to pop from her face. "I swear before God, I do not know how . . . to open it."

"You want I should shoot her?" Sonny asked.

Bill looked down at Feagin. "Let's try one more time to wake this bastard up. This is takin' way too long. We should already be headed out of town by now. Put the bitch on the floor an' find a pitcher of water. There's gotta be some water 'round here some place."

Sonny shoved the terrified woman to the floor and stalked off to locate a pitcher of water, entering an office to one side of the bank lobby. He came back a few moments later, as Bill was listening to the slackening gunshots up and down Main Street, a sure sign that Dodge City's lawmen were already dead, or pulling back when they saw that the odds were against them.

"Here's some water," Sonny said, carrying a small ceramic pitcher over to Feagin. He bent down and splashed the water on the banker's face. "Wake up, you son of a bitch!" Sonny snarled before he tossed the pitcher to the floor, smashing it, drawing his pistol again.

Feagin's eyelids fluttered. "What . . . happened?" he asked in a groggy voice.

"You went to sleep," Sonny replied, showing the banker the muzzle of his Colt. "Now git up an' open that safe or I'll kill the woman yonder. Better make it quick, too."

Feagin shook his head. He came slowly, unsteadily, to his feet, swaying dizzily, reaching for the combination lock once again. "Please don't kill Miss Peabody," he croaked, twirling the dial. "She doesn't deserve to die. She's only an employee of the bank."

Sonny waved his gun barrel near the banker's face. "But she is gonna die 'less you git this open."

"I'm doing the best I can."

While Feagin twisted the lock, Bill sauntered over near one of the front windows, glancing up at the roof of Martha's Eatery. It was all he could do to control himself, his blinding rage, when he saw Homer's body lying in the street. Gunshots were fewer now in Dodge, and he consoled himself with that fact. They had taken the town by storm, and soon they would empty every pocket in the entire place by cleaning out the two vaults.

"It's open," Sonny said, passing a quick look over Lee's motionless form. "We're gonna need some help gettin' all this money outside into them packs."

Bill saw Scar Face trotting down the boardwalk in front of a small harness shop. He ignored Sonny for a moment, going to the window to catch the half-breed's eye with a wave. When Scar Face saw him, he came to a halt.

Bill pointed to the roof of Martha's Eatery. Scar Face gave a nod in return and headed down a side street toward an alleyway.

He spoke to Lucky, who was holding the horses outside. "Tie 'em off an' get in here to help us load this money. Most of the shootin's stopped anyhow."

Scar Face turned into the alley with a bowie knife gleaming in one hand, a Colt pistol in the other. Bill gave a grin without any humor behind it. "That'll teach the sumbitch, whoever he is, not to tangle with Bloody Bill Anderson," he added softly.

Chapter 19

Wyatt knelt beside the remnants of an office window, being very careful when he peered over the sill to see what was going on at the Cattlemans Bank. Cody lay on the floor, groaning, his left shoulder seeping blood around the bandanna Wyatt had tied over his wound. For several minutes Cody had been unable to shoot, in a state of mild shock after the bullet had grazed his flesh, peeling his skin open so it looked like a gash made by a knife.

"I'm seein' stars, Marshal," Cody whispered, blinking. "It feels like I'm gonna faint."

"You'll be okay," Wyatt said. The shooting had all but stopped on Main Street. Half-a-dozen bandits were inside the bank. Three more were outside, hidden behind stone water troughs with rifles and shotguns. All seemed lost. There weren't enough guns in Dodge to halt a bank-robbing gang of this size, and with the corpses of innocent women and the Wilkins boy lying in the road in spreading pools of blood, it was unlikely that any civic-minded citizens would rush to their aid with hunting rifles or shotguns. Henry Burns lay dead in front of his store. The bodies of four outlaws lay farther to the south, although one appeared to be alive, barely able to crawl, trying to reach safety.

He wondered about Jim Bob. Watley's shotgun had been silent for several minutes. Every now and then, one of Jensen's cowhands would fire a shot at a robber from a rooftop. Neither man seemed to be much of a marksman.

"Jesus, this hurts," Cody sighed, resting his head on the floor, watching the flyspecked ceiling through pain-hooded eyes. "Wish I could get over to Doc Sanders' house."

"Ain't no back door," Wyatt reminded him, seeing shadows move inside the bank. Suddenly, coming from the north, a bandit came down the street leading a horse and a mule bearing packsaddles.

Wyatt raised his shotgun over the windowsill and thumbed back both hammers, determined to stop the pack animals from hauling off the money if he could. But the bandit walked between the pair of animals, using them as shields, preventing Wyatt from taking a shot that wouldn't harm the four-legged creatures.

"Hellfire," he said quietly, waiting for the right opportunity. "I can't shoot him without hurtin' the horse or the mule. I reckon I oughta shoot 'em anyways, so they can't carry off the money. Seems a damn shame. . . ."

A rifle cracked from a rooftop up the street, kicking up a cloud of dust in front of the bandit who was leading the animals. And at the same time, a terrific shotgun blast came from Jim Bob's position behind the wall at Joe's Blacksmith Shop.

The mule brayed, lunging forward as shotgun pellets struck its rump. It jerked the leadrope free of the bandit's hand and took off down Main at a gallop.

The bandit quickly put himself behind the plunging, rearing, bay packhorse, trying to settle it so he would be safe standing behind it. Two men rushed out of the bank with rifles before the horse calmed down.

One raider took aim at Jim Bob's hiding place and fired a Winchester .44 in Watley's direction. The boom of the outlaw's gun echoed off buildings while the second robber aimed for the same spot.

Another rifle cracked from a rooftop. One bandit staggered and went down on one knee, dropping his rifle to grip his right thigh muscles. Wyatt wasted no time. He pulled the trigger on one barrel of his Stevens twelve-gauge.

The kneeling robber was swept off the roadway by a swarm of heavy buckshot, spinning him around like a child's top while his dust-covered, gray hat was torn to shreds, flying off his head in bits and pieces. The outlaw's face appeared to melt, changing shape as skin and blood were ripped off his skull while he was twisting in the air. Before he fell he became a ghostly apparition, a man with a grinning skull for a head, toppling over on his back between a pair of dry wagon ruts.

Wyatt ducked down just in time. Four or five rifles banged away at his ruined office windows, sending singsong balls of lead speeding through the office until they struck the rear wall, where dozens of wanted posters were nailed up around a doorway that led to jail cells at the back. A slug pinged into the potbelly stove, bouncing harmlessly to the wood floor. Another shattered the globe on Wyatt's desk lantern, sending tiny glass shards all over his desktop and the floor. Then the shooting died down and finally ended, bringing on another moment of quiet, which Wyatt guessed would be short-lived.

"We're gonna git killed, Wyatt," Cody said in a high-pitched voice. "They's gonna storm this jail, an' then we's done for."

Wyatt was annoyed, despite his young deputy's lack of experience. "It'd be a help if you got up an' fired out one of these windows once in a while. Two guns are sure as hell better than one. You ain't hurt so bad you can't shoot, an' it might discourage 'em from rushin' us."

There were tears in Cody's eyes when he came trembling to his hands and knees. "I'm scared, Marshal," he whimpered, taking up his shotgun again. "No sense denyin' it . . . I'm scared I'm gonna die."

"Shoot at 'em every once in a while an' then get back down out of sight," he said. "It ain't over yet. That big feller, Jensen, has killed the hell outa four or five. He just tossed one off the roof at Martha's, an' you never heard such a yell as when he done it. Jensen may be every bit as mean as you said he was. He damn sure don't act like he's scared of nothin. . . ."

Wyatt fell silent when he saw an Indian dressed in buckskin leggings and a sleeveless vest hurry around a corner farther up Main. The redskin wore a derby hat with a feather stuck in the hatband, and he was carrying a long knife and a pistol. "Looks like they've sent somebody after Jensen," he said, keeping his head low near a corner of the sill. "He'll be headed to that alley behind the cafe so he can climb up to where he's got a shot at Jensen. No tellin' how many

of 'em Jensen's killed. Sure don't seem there's near
so many robbers as there was when they rode in.
Jensen sure must be a quiet feller on his feet, to be
so big. He slipped right up on them two who came
in ahead of the others to get on rooftops. Killed 'em
both with that huge knife he's got. The blade had
blood all over it, an' so did Jensen's shirt sleeve."

Cody winced when he put the shotgun to his right
shoulder, even though his wound was to the other
arm. "Jensen used to be one bad hombre, Marshal.
Sundance Morgan an' his gang wasn't no bunch of
greenhorns. I heard later on that Jensen killed damn
near every one of 'em, before it was over. Maybe
Jensen's a little older now, but I still wouldn't care
to tangle with him. Sure as hell am glad he's on our
side, him an' his two cowboys, only it ain't likely to
be enough. I counted damn near thirty men ridin'
into town a while ago. To my way of thinkin', we
don't stand a chance against so many, not even with
Smoke Jensen sidin' with us."

Wyatt took a quick look at the Cattlemans Bank
before pulling back. "The real tough part is gonna
be when they try to ride outa here with the money,"
he said, thinking out loud, reloading the spent tube
in his Stevens. "We'll have to kill as many as we can
without bein' killed ourselves ... maybe scare 'em
into leavin' some of the money behind. With Jensen
an' his men shootin' down from the roofs, an' Jim
Bob doin' the best he can along with the two of us,
maybe we can make a difference." His face twisted
in a frown. "That is, if that damn redskin don't get
Jensen first with that knife or the gun."

"You seen a redskin with 'em?" Cody asked.

Wyatt nodded. "At least a part-blood. He was
wearin' this ol' derby hat with a feather in it, an'

deerskin leggin's. I saw this big scar down one side
of his face."

Cody turned, facing the back wall. "Holy cow, Marshal!" he exclaimed, pointing to a wanted poster that
was fluttering in a soft wind that was coming through
broken windowpanes. "That'll be a gent they call
Scar Face Parker. We got his reward poster last month,
if you'll remember. Came from the U.S. Marshal's
office over in Fort Smith on the train, along with a
handful of others. He's wanted for murder in Indian
Territory. Seems like that poster said he was a half
Pawnee. Said he'd be armed an' dangerous to catch
. . . that he killed two Deputy Marshals from ambush
while they was on his trail some place down in the
Nations."

Wyatt pursed his lips. "It don't make a damn who
he is, Cody. Right now he's got a knife an' a gun, an'
he's headed for the roof where Jensen tossed down
that body. Could be we're about to find out if Mr.
Smoke Jensen is as dangerous as you say he is, if the
redskin I saw is this Scar Face Parker."

Cody turned back to the window, peeking above
the sill. "He won't be no match for Jensen, Marshal,
if Jensen's the same man he used to be."

"Time's gonna tell," Wyatt replied, taking his own
quick look at the front of the bank. "They've got one
packhorse tied to the rail over yonder. Best we can
do is shoot any son of a bitch who comes out carryin'
bags of money. Smoke Jensen'll have to take care of
himself."

A shotgun roared from Jim Bob's spot behind the
wall, and the clatter of pellets rattled off the front of
the bank harmlessly.

"Jim Bob couldn't hit the side of a barn," Wyatt

muttered. "I wish we had one or two more men who could shoot straight."

Now Cody's cheeks began to turn red. "It ain't so much that my aim is bad, Marshal. I'm just afraid of dyin', is all. I got two kids to feed, hardly more'n babies yet. Beth wouldn't know what do to fer money if I wasn't here to help her raise 'em up like I'm supposed to, bein' their daddy."

"I understand, Cody," Wyatt told him quietly. "Just do the best you can. The more lead we throw at 'em, even if it ain't all that true, will be a help."

"My arm's hurtin' somethin' awful," Cody added, as though he needed to explain.

Wyatt let it drop, bending his head around an edge of the windowframe to see what was going on.

A muffled pistol shot came from inside the bank, and right after that a woman's voice let out a mournful wail.

"That was Miz Meeks," Cody said. "Wonder if they shot her? Can't see no reason why they'd shoot a nice ol' lady like Miz Meeks."

"They didn't shoot *her*," Wyatt explained. "She's frightened. I imagine they shot Sheldon Herring for some reason or another. Maybe he tried to argue with 'em over takin' away all the bank's money."

"Lordy," Cody sighed. "Now they've gone an' killed the president of the bank. Whoever this bunch of outlaws is, they's sure as hell bad men."

Wyatt thought about it. "I figure we've just had a visit by Bloody Bill Anderson, even though some folks believe he's been dead since the war. It's just a guess, but it looks like we've got proof on our hands that Bloody Bill is still alive, robbin' an' killin', just like he used to. It would explain what happened to Dave Cobbs an' his family down at the tradin' post the other day. It was easy to see that the store was looted before they burned it plumb to the ground, an' they killed Cobbs an' his whole family so there wouldn't be no witnesses alive to talk, to tell who done it."

Cody bowed his head, fingering traces of tears from his eyelids. "Beth's been tellin' me all along I hadn't oughta took this job. She said I could find work at the shippin' pens durin' the trail drive season, an' that we'd live off what we could grow in our garden between times. Right about now I sure do wish I'd listened a little bit closer to what she was sayin'."

"It's too late for regrets now, Cody. Just keep your head down an' shoot as careful as you can when there's a target. If we're careful, we'll make it out of this alive."

Cody wagged his head. "I ain't so sure, Marshal," he said in a hoarse, dry whisper. "When it comes to luck, mine ain't been all that good, usually."

A noise somewhere to the north made Wyatt jump—the sound of a gun. He'd gotten accustomed to the quiet, all the while knowing it wouldn't last much longer. "Maybe the other bunch is comin' out of the Dodge City Savings Bank," he said, risking yet another quick look around the windowframe.

He saw another body lying near a brown mare that was tied in front of the bank owned by David Feagin, and several more horses, two with packsaddles, tied out front.

Maybe Jensen got another one, he thought, wondering if Smoke Jensen could possibly be as deadly as Cody believed he was. Cody was young, impressionable, not the sort to be accurate about any number of things.

"What was it?" Cody asked. "Did they shoot some-body else?"

"There's a body in front of Mr. Feagin's bank,

but it could've been there all along. The gent wasn't movin'."

"No tellin' how many bodies we're gonna find when this is over," Cody whispered, "if we're alive after it's over to make a count. I know Beth's at home, worried to death hearin' all this shootin'. She'll be cryin', figurin' I was the first one to get killed."

"Then she'll be twice as glad to see you when you get home," Wyatt said, wishing Cody would shut the hell up with all his damn worrying.

He wondered about the Indian . . . if it truly was Scar Face Parker, and what would happen when the man ran into the tall cowman from Colorado . . . unless the gunshot they had just heard meant that Jensen was already dead.

Chapter 20

Catlike, moving soundlessly on the balls of his feet, Smoke stepped across to another rooftop, bending low to keep from being seen from the street. Every instinct he had was sharpened, keened by anger over the senseless killing of women, and the boy who was blinded by buckshot. It was not uncommon, for men who had bad intentions, to kill or maim others who could defend themselves in a contest with weapons. But when coldblooded murder occurred, with the victims being women and children—killing for the sake of killing alone—Smoke couldn't bridle his temper, no matter what kind of promise he'd given Sally.

And as he moved farther away from the cafe roof, he was sure someone would be coming after him. Throwing the body down where every bank robber in the gang could see it, was a form of challenge that men who believed they were tough couldn't ignore. And with this in mind, Smoke was certain he had lured one or two more outlaws up on the roofs on the east side of Main Street, men who had been sent to hunt him down and kill him. In the fit of rage he found himself in, he was looking forward to this contest with more anticipation than he had experienced in years. Like in the old days, when killing was little more than a day's work.

He crept to the rear of a roof over a narrow building in between the cafe and a cobbler's shop, looking cautiously into the alley, for it was from the alleyway that manhunters would be most likely to come, like the two before who wound up with a slug through the neck, and another with a shattered skull.

"Come on up, boys," Smoke whispered, mouthing the words silently. He knew he had to be back in a good firing position with a view of Main when the robbers tried to make a getaway with their loot.

While this wasn't Smoke's natural range, being caught inside a town, without mountains or trees or underbrush to give him cover from enemy fire, he knew lawless men well enough. His surroundings would make little difference, like the time he and Preacher tangled with Casey and the TC Riders; that time reminded him of the standoff he was in, with men inside buildings, protected from bullets by walls his guns couldn't penetrate, facing overwhelming odds with no choice but to dig, or lure, or burn his enemies out. . . .

Stopping in a stand of timber a couple of hundred yards from the ranch house, Preacher said, "There she is. Got any plans on yer mind?"

"Start shooting," was all Smoke said in reply.

"The house an' the outbuildin's?"

"Burn 'em to the ground," Smoke answered.

"You a hard young 'un, Smoke."

"I suppose I am." He smiled at Preacher. "But I had a good teacher, didn't I?"

"The best around," the mountain man replied.

The house and bunkhouse were built of logs, with sod roofs. *Burn easy*, Smoke thought. He yelled, "Casey! Get out here!"

"Who're you?" a shout came from the house.

"Smoke Jensen!"

A rifle bullet wanged through the trees. High.

"Lousy shot," Preacher muttered.

The rifle cracked again, the slug humming closer.

"They might git lucky and hit one of the horses," Preacher said.

"You tuck them in that ravine over there," Smoke said, dismounting. "I think I'll ease around to the back, just to see if it looks any easier."

Preacher slid off his mustang. "I'll stay here and worry 'em some. You be careful now."

"Don't worry."

" 'Course not," the old man replied sarcastically. "Why in the world would I do that?" He glanced up at the sky. "Seven, maybe eight hours till dark."

"We'll be through before then." Smoke slipped into an arroyo that half circled the house, ending at the rear of the ranch house.

Fifty yards behind the house, he found cover in a small clump of trees and settled down to pick his targets.

A man got careless inside the house and offered part of his forearm on a sill. Smoke shattered it with one round from his Henry. In front of the house, Preacher found a target and cut loose with his Henry.

From the screams of pain drifting to Smoke, someone had been hit hard.

"You hands!" Smoke called. "You sure you want to die for Casey? A couple of your buddies already bought it a few miles back. One of them wearing a black shirt."

Silence for a few moments. "Your Daddy ride with Mosby?" a voice yelled from the house.

"That's right."

"Your brother named Luke?"

"Yeah. He was shot in the back, and the gold he was guarding got stolen."

"Potter shot him . . . not me! You got no call to do this, so ride out an' forgit it."

Smoke's reply to that was to put several rounds of .44s through the windows of the house.

Wild cursing came from inside.

"Jensen? The name's Barry. I come from Nevada. Didn't have nothin' to do with no war. Never been no further east than the Ladder in Kansas. 'Nother feller here is the same as me. We herd cattle . . . don't git no fightin' wages. You let us ride outa here!"

"Get your horses and clear out!" Smoke cried.

Barry and his partner made it to the center of the backyard before they were shot in the back by someone in the ranch house. One of them died hard, screaming his life away in the dust of southeast Colorado.

"Nice folks in there," Preacher muttered as he crept up to Smoke's firing position, motioning for Smoke to continue his stalking of the men forted up inside the log house.

Smoke followed the arroyo until the bunkhouse

was between him and the main house. In a pile behind
the bunkhouse, he found sticks and rags. In the empty
bunkhouse he found a jar of coal oil.

He tied the rags around a stick, soaked them in
oil, lighted them, then tossed the stick onto the roof
of the ranch house. He waited, Henry at the ready,
watching the house slowly catch on fire.

Shouts and hard coughing came from inside the
ranch house as the logs caught and smoldered, the
rooms filling with smoke and fumes. One man broke
from the cabin, and Preacher cut him down in the
front yard. Another raced from the back door, and
Smoke doubled him over with a .44 slug in the guts.

Only one man still appeared to be shooting from
the house. There were two on the range nearby, at
least two hit in the cabin, and two in the yard. While
he and Preacher had begun that affair badly outnum-
bered, the odds were swinging their way.

"All right, Casey!" he shouted over the crackling
of burning wood. "Burn to death, shot, or hung—
it's up to you!"

Casey waited until the roof was caving in before he
stumbled into the yard, eyes blind from swirls of
smoke inside. He fired wildly as he staggered about,
hitting nothing but earth and air. When his pistol
was empty, Smoke walked up to the man and knocked
him down, tying his hands behind him with rawhide.

"What do you figure on doin' with him?" Preacher
asked as he walked up, shoving fresh loads into his
Henry.

"I intend to take him just outside of town, by that
creek we rode past, and hang him."

"I just can't figure where you got that mean streak,
boy. Seein' as how you was raised . . . partly . . . by a
gentle man like me."

Despite the death he had brought, and the destruction wrought, Smoke had to laugh at that. Preacher was known throughout the West as one of the most dangerous men ever to roam the high country and vast Plains. The mountain man had once spent two years of his life tracking down—and killing, one by one—a group of men who had ambushed and killed a friend of his, taking the man's furs.

" 'Course, you never went on the hunt for anyone yourself?" Smoke asked, dumping the unconscious Casey across a saddled horse before tying him down.

The house was engulfed in flames, black smoke spewing into the endless sky.

"Well . . . mayhaps once or twice," Preacher responded, "but that was years back. I've mellowed some."

"Sure," Smoke said, grinning. Preacher was still as mean as a cornered puma.

They mounted and rode slowly away from the flaming ranch, with black smoke spiraling into a cloudless sky. That had been a time when killing meant nothing to Smoke, something akin to swatting a fly.

Smoke glanced up and down the alley, finding nothing, yet his senses told him someone was there. Two bloodied bodies lay behind the cafe, but that was not the reason for his concern. A voice inside his head warned that someone was coming for him, a man he couldn't see at present.

He walked quietly over to an eave of the building and lay down, resting his Winchester beside him as he drew his Arkansas Toothpick. This was likely to be a job requiring a silent kill, a job for a knife.

Then a shadow moved farther south down the alley,

near the spot where he'd killed the two robbers who tried to come up on the roof after him. A pair of horses still stood ground-hitched near the bodies of both men, a piebald gelding snorted at the scent of blood puddling around one of the corpses.

Smoke's eyes narrowed, fixed on the shape he saw moving a moment before. And there it was—the faint outline of a man in a derby hat staying close to the rear of a building.

Even in the slanted sunlight of early morning, Smoke saw the glint of a knife blade in the man's hand.

So, he thought, reaching for his own Arkansas Toothpick, drawing it slowly out of his boot . . . it was to be a duel of steel and nerves. It suited Smoke, never one to complain about an opponent's choice of weapons. One factor would force the fight to be short and sweet; in minutes, perhaps even now, the gang of bank robbers would be attempting a break with the town's money, tied to packsaddles.

Frozen, evidencing the patience Preacher taught him so long ago, Smoke waited for the shadowy stalker to make his next move. In most any form of combat the one who struck first had a better chance of victory—in particular, when the battle was fought with guns, or in a fistfight, even a war with knives. But when there was a game of cat-and-mouse, a stalker and his prey, it was often best to be patient, waiting for the right opportunity. The man who moved first gave his position away.

Time seemed to stand still. Smoke watched the figure in the alley, remaining motionless. He could see the shape of a feather protruding from the man's hatband.

An Indian, he thought. *He'll be careful.*

The shadow moved again, inching down the back of one building and then another, coming closer to the spot below the roof where Smoke was hidden.

"A little bit more," Smoke breathed. The man in the derby was within easy rifle range, yet the movement of a barrel in sunlight might alert him to the danger.

Out in the street, an angry voice shouted, "We're comin' out, an' we've got prisoners! Women! Any sumbitch shoots, we'll blow these women to pieces!"

Time was running short. Smoke needed to be back facing Main Street with his rifle ready in order to stand any chance of saving the women and Dodge City's money. But there was an Indian to be dealt with first, creeping toward him where shadows hid his progress.

A shotgun blasted somewhere on Main, the first shot to be fired in several minutes.

"I done warned you!" the same thick voice cried. "Just to show you we mean business, we're gonna shoot one of these here women an' shove her out where everybody can see her!"

A pistol shot cracked, followed by a muffled woman's scream and then dry laughter, faint, hard to hear.

"The bastards," Smoke hissed. He'd wasted too much time waiting for the Indian in the derby to make his move.

Slipping his rifle forward until it rested against his left shoulder, the off-side he avoided when firing a rifle, Smoke pulled the hammer back on the Winchester as silently as he knew how.

"You dirty sons of bitches!" a high-pitched voice cried from the roadway behind Smoke. "Any yellow bastard who'd shoot a woman like that oughta be hung!"

"Come try an' hang us!" the first man shouted. "You'll be the next one to die!"

Smoke couldn't wait any longer. Sighting along the barrel of his rifle, he did something he rarely ever allowed—he pulled a trigger on a man first.

The Winchester exploded, rocking hard against Smoke's upper arm and shoulder. The man in the derby jumped, both feet leaving the ground before he fell over on his back, kicking furiously as Smoke pulled back away from the eave.

He ran across the roof, bent over like a man in pain, until he had a view of Main Street. He levered a fresh cartridge into his rifle, certain that the man lying in the alley was out of the fight forever.

Chapter 21

Jack Starr was worried. Three men defending Dodge City had good aim and iron nerves. One was in the Marshal's office with a shotgun. Another was down the street, across from the Dodge City Bank, picking his shots carefully. One more kept moving from rooftop to rooftop, the bastard who threw Homer Suggins down in front of the cafe.

Jack had other concerns. Anderson had been wrong about the amount of resistance they would face in robbing the banks. Someone had known they were coming.

"Take a look outside, Sammy," Jack said, holding his Dance .44 beneath the trembling chin of a woman who was employed by the bank. "We've lost too goddamn many men already. Make damn sure nobody's out there, an' look real close up on them roofs across the street."

Jack couldn't have cared less if cross-eyed Sammy

McCoy got shot peering outside. Claude, his brother, was a far better marksman and his nerves were like ice. And Claude's brain was twice the size of Sammy's.

"Somebody's liable to shoot me," Sammy protested, taking a rifle with him to a spot near a busted front windowpane. "If it's all the same to you, Jack, I'd just as soon not git shot takin' a look outside."

"I'll kill you myself if you don't do like I say," Jack snarled. "You ain't got near the big balls your brother Claude has got."

Sammy swallowed hard. He saw bodies of his friends lying all over the street.

Sammy knew Jack meant what he said, that he would kill him if he didn't follow orders. He wondered which was better—to be shot in the back by a member of his own gang or to die by another man's bullet. Winding up dead was the result, either way. He made up his mind that it did not make all that much difference.

"Do it!" Jack snapped.

Sammy went closer to the windowsill and looked out cautiously. "It sure as hell seems okay to me, only there's two guys in the Marshal's office who fire off shotguns every now an' then. I wish there was some way fer some of us to shut them shotguns up afore we git killed."

Jack's attention was taken away from the window when the man who ran the bank groaned. Scar Face Parker had stuck a knife in the banker's belly when he reached in a desk drawer for a small-caliber pistol. The banker was losing a lot of blood, and the vault was still closed. Jack turned to the woman he held by the back of her navy blue dress. "I'm gonna give you one more chance to open that goddamn safe, bitch," he said. "If you don't do it, I swear I'll kill you."

"No . . . one else knows . . . the combination," she said, blue eyes bulging with fear when she felt a nudge in the soft flesh of her neck from Jack's gun barrel.

"You're lyin'!" Jack cried. "There has to be somebody else who knows the combination, an' I figure that's gotta be you." He jacked back the hammer on his .44. "This is it, you ol' bitch. Open the safe or I'll blow your damn head off."

"I swear I can't do it," she cried.

"Then say your damn prayers, woman. Your body's gonna be fillin' a casket 'less you open that vault right now. There's gonna be a funeral procession in Dodge tomorrow, an' it's gonna be fer you."

"I can try," she whimpered. "I think I remember the first number is ten, after two spins clockwise to clear the lock. Then, I believe the next number is eighteen. . . ."

Jack shoved her over to the safe. "You get just this one chance," he said. "If it don't open, you're the same as dead. You can count on it."

The woman put a shaky hand on the combination dial and spun it clockwise two times. Tears streamed down her slightly wrinkled cheeks. "I can't recall the last number," she said. "It may be twenty. Please don't kill me. When Mr. Herring wakes up he'll tell you what you want to know, if he doesn't bleed to death beforehand."

"He shouldn't've gone fer that gun," Jack said. "He was a damn fool to try that."

"He won't refuse you now. Please give him a chance to tell me what the last number is."

Jack looked over at Tinker Barnes. "Rouse that banker, an' ask him what the last number of the combination is. If he don't give you no answer, then shoot the son of a bitch.''

"Somebody's movin' outside,'' Sammy said from his spot near the window. "He ran across the road just now. Make's two of 'em behind that brick wall in front of the blacksmith's shop, if I got 'em counted right.''

"How come you didn't shoot the son of a bitch?'' Jack wanted to know.

"He was runnin' real fast,'' Sammy answered, "an' I seen he had a rifle.''

"You yellow, gotch-eyed bastard!'' Jack snapped. "If we wasn't already short of men I'd put a hole through you big enough to fit a man's fist.''

"Don't shoot me, Jack,'' Sammy said, tightening his grip on his Winchester. "I'll do whatever you say. I need my share of that money bad as you do.''

"I oughta kill you anyways, Sammy. You ain't showed not one bit of backbone, hidin' behind that window.''

Sweat beaded on Sammy's face and neck. "I'm just wantin' to make sure I live to spend the money, Jack.''

"Where's Scar Face?'' Jack demanded. "He shoulda been back by now.''

"He went after that sumbitch up on the roof,'' Frankie Weaver said. "Bill gave the order hisself.''

Jack wondered what was taking the half-breed so long to get a simple job done. Some local citizen with a rifle had gotten up on top of the cafe, probably catching Homer by surprise. Jack had never completely trusted Homer. He was a suck-ass, shining up to Bill whenever he had the opportunity.

Frankie stepped over to another broken pane of glass. He looked out for a moment. "If we use them pack animals as a kind of shield, we can git cleared out of here with the money without bein' shot all to hell.''

Jack scowled at the woman trying to open the safe. "First thing is to get our hands on the money. If this ol' bitch don't open the door on this here vault, I'm gonna scatter her damn brains all over the front of it."

"Please don't shoot me," the woman begged. "I'm doing the best I can."

"It ain't good enough 'cause it ain't open yet," Jack said bitterly.

Frankie kicked the wounded bank president in the stomach, producing a groan.

"Kick him again," Dave Watkins cried, his face the color of milk. "Like Jack said, we's runnin' out of time."

Frankie obliged, kicking Sheldon Herring in the gut just above his bleeding wound. Herring's eyes fluttered open. He gave the bank lobby a distant stare.

"What's the last number of the combination?" Dave demanded with his boot cocked, ready to deliver another swift kick to the banker's groin.

"Twenty-two," Herring sighed, closing his eyes again with a look of pain wrinkling his face.

"You heard him," Jack snarled to the woman. "Use twenty-two for the last number. If this vault door don't open I'm gonna put a bullet through you."

She gave the lock another spin, trying the sequence of numbers. Tumblers clicked into place, and the door swung open a few inches.

"That'll do it," Jack said, suddenly swinging his pistol barrel down on top of the woman's head, making a dull thud when it landed.

She fell to the floor, unconscious.

Jack pulled the safe door open. Sacks of currency and coins filled almost every shelf. "Start loadin' this stuff on them pack animals, boys," he said. "We're rich as six foot up a bull's ass now. Soon as the money's loaded, we're clearin' out of here."

"What about Bill an' them boys down the street?" Frankie asked.

Jack didn't need much time to think about it. "They're on their own," he said.

Sammy gave him a questioning look. "You mean we's gonna leave 'em?"

"You heard what I said."

"But Bill's gonna be mad as hell."

"Maybe he won't be around to get mad," Jack replied. "Our job is to clean out this here vault. His job is to take care of the other bank. So long as everybody does his own job, we got no problems."

"But Bill's trapped. That bastard up on the roof has got him pinned down," Frankie argued.

Jack aimed a chilly stare in Frankie's direction. "That's Bill's problem now," he said. "We empty this safe like he told us to, an' we'll be followin' his orders."

Sammy hesitated. "He'll kill every damn one of us if'n we ride off an' leave 'em there, Jack."

"A dead man ain't gonna kill nobody," Jack replied.

"That sure as hell is cold," Frankie muttered. "If it was me down there, I'd sure want somebody to help me git out." But as Frankie said it, he headed over to the vault to begin taking out sacks of money.

A thundering shotgun blast rattled the front door of the Cattlemans Bank. It came from across the road.

"We gotta git rid of them bastards holed up inside the Marshal's office," Sammy declared, as he, too, walked over quickly to help Frankie take bags from the safe.

"Wish to hell Scar Face would get back," Jack said, with an eye on the street. "Wonder what's keepin' him?"

"Maybe that jasper up on top of the cafe went an' killed *him* too," Frankie said, pushing bulging sacks of currency into packs they would tie to the animals out front.

"Scar Face Parker ain't gonna be easy to kill," Jack said under his breath, wondering. The half-breed was sneaky, good in a tight spot, always careful.

"Just 'cause a man ain't easy to kill don't mean he's gonna live forever," Frankie added, when one side of a pack was full of bank notes.

"My money's on Scar Face," Jack said, shoving the crying old woman out of the way. "He knows his business, an' his business is killin' folks, when he ain't down off a horse readin' sign for us to follow."

"I sure hope you're right," Dave Watkins remarked, his face near the window. "Our biggest problem's gonna be them two sons of bitches in the Marshal's office. We git past them, an' we've got a chance to git outa here with our skins."

"You're a born worrier, Dave," Jack said.

"I'm still alive," was Dave's only reply, looking the other way down Main Street.

"Hurry up, damn it!" Jack snapped, when it appeared Frankie and Sammy were taking too long loading the second set of packs with money.

"I'm loadin' as fast as I can," Sammy replied.

"Me too," Frankie insisted, although he stuffed a

few more of the bags into a pack pocket hurriedly, forgetting to tie it shut in his haste.

"Let's get ready to ride," Jack said, ambling over to the front doors before he peeked out.

The street was littered with the bodies of men and horses, and women. Blood lay in crimson pools from one end of Main to the other. Flies had begun to gather at the corpses, and the noise made Jack angry. "Hurry the hell up!" he shouted over his shoulder. "Looks like they've got Bill surrounded."

Jack did not really mind leaving Bill Anderson behind with gunmen all around him. Of late, Bill had begun to ramble, and it seemed his mind wandered back to the past, to the war, as if he were still living it.

"We're damn near ready," Frankie said, "only what the hell we gonna do 'bout them two shotguns over at the lawman's office when we run outside?"

"Stay low," Jack told him. It made no difference to him if the shotguns brought Frankie and Sammy down.

"They'll sure be shootin'," Sammy promised. "Every damn time somethin' moves out yonder, one of them shotguns goes off real loud."

Jack grinned, intending no humor. "Are you scared of loud noises, Sammy?"

"I'm sure as hell scared of dyin'."

"You ain't gonna die. Just git that money on the backs of them horses yonder. We're all gonna be filthy rich soon as we git clear of Dodge."

"It's gettin' clear of Dodge that's worryin' me," Frankie said, hoisting a pack over his shoulder.

"Like I said before, you worry too much," Jack answered in a dry voice.

"Somebody cover me," Frankie said as he went over to the front door.

Jack grinned. "I've got you covered, an' who's any better at coverin' a man's ass'n me?"

Chapter 22

Wayland Burke crouched down behind the brick wall across the front of the blacksmith's shop. Jim Bob Watley was sweating, and with shotgun shells lying around his boots, he seemed out of place somehow. He didn't look like a deputy or a man who belonged in a deadly shootout with outlaws.

"I fetched my scattergun," Wayland said, blinking furiously as he gazed across the street at the Cattlemans Bank. "Somebody's gotta help you an' Marshal Earp an' Cody. Don't seem nobody else is willin'."

"We're obliged fer your help," Jim Bob said, "only you gotta remember one thing—the Marshal said to keep our heads down an' only to shoot when we git a chance without gittin' our own heads blowed off. With so darned much lead flyin' all over the place, it ain't been so easy to do what Marshal Earp said."

"I'll be real careful," Wayland told him, wondering. "Who the hell woulda believed so many bank robbers would show up in Dodge at the same time? My wife said I gotta help the Marshal keep our money safe, 'cause nearly everything we've got is over yonder in that vault of Mr. Herring's. Our little store don't make all that much money, but we need every cent of it in order to keep on livin' here.''

Jim Bob watched one of the outlaws peer out a shattered bank window, and with an opportunity like that he knew that Marshal Earp expected him to shoot. Thumbing back the hammer on his Stevens twelve-gauge double barrel, he took quick aim and fired.

The kick of his shotgun drove Jim Bob back a half step at almost the same instant a yell came from the Cattlemans Bank.

The outlaw standing at the windowframe threw both hands to his face and fell out of sight.

"You got him!" Wayland cried, rising up just high enough to take a shot of his own. With nothing to shoot at besides a bare window at the front of the building, he pulled one trigger on his scattergun, the explosion making him wince, shutting both eyes until a cloud of blue smoke cleared. He grinned as soon as he opened his eyelids again, blinking, trying to see if he'd been able to hit one of the robbers himself.

"Git down, Mr. Burke!" Jim Bob shouted. His warning came too late.

The roar of a rifle thundered from the front of the bank. Wayland's head jerked backward, and his best beaver-felt derby hat went flying off his scalp, twirling, wobbling as it fell to the ground behind him, fluttering there like a wounded bird. A dark mass squirted out of the rear of his skull, a twist of his black hair moving just ahead of a thick stream of blood.

Jim Bob cowered behind the brick wall, watching

Wayland make a slow half turn in his direction with an odd expression on his face, a look of surprise. Then Jim Bob noticed a hole below the storekeeper's right eye, a hole the size of a man's thumb.

"Git down, Mr. Burke!" Jim Bob said again, softer when he realized what the hole in Burke's face (and the stream of blood) meant. "Jesus, Mr. Burke! How come you didn't git back down behind this here wall?"

Wayland's lips were moving as if he were trying to answer Jim Bob's question, but no sounds came from his mouth. Pinkish foam began bubbling from his throat, rolling off his tongue as his knees slowly buckled.

His shotgun fell to the dirt, butt first, causing the second barrel to discharge with a tremendous blast. A sizzling load of buckshot tore off Wayland's right arm, sending it into the air with his coat sleeve covering it the way it had when he had put it on that morning. Blood showered over the brick wall where Wayland was standing, and over the brim and crown of Jim Bob's hat, pattering down like red rain all over Jim Bob and the place where he hid behind the wall.

Wayland sank to his knees, the stump of his missing arm pumping blood. He toppled over on his face and lay still until one of his booted feet began to twitch.

"Jesus," Jim Bob said again, turning away from the grisly sight, retching up his breakfast, gagging desperately to breathe. "Oh, dear Jesus. . . ."

From one of the rooftops, a rifle cracked twice, yet Jim Bob was afraid to look over the wall to see if the shots had done any damage. Neither could he force himself to look at Mr. Burke then, thinking only of what he'd unwittingly seen when the rifle shot had torn through Wayland's head, and then when his hunting gun had blown his arm away.

"Take that, you son of a bitch!" a young voice yelled from the roof. Jim Bob recognized it as coming from the young cowboy who rode with Smoke Jensen.

Jim Bob had also seen Jensen stand up on the rooftop of the cafe not long after the fight had begun, throwing a dead man off the building. Jensen had guts—either that, or he was crazy as all hell. Cody claimed Smoke Jensen was an honest-to-goodness gunslick. Maybe he was, after all. He sure had been willing to throw in with the Marshal to help defend the town when it wasn't none of his affair.

Jim Bob risked a quick look over the top of the wall. A shadow moved inside the bank, only an outline because of the slant of the sun. Then a man ran outside carrying canvas bags of money, heading for a packhorse that was tied at the hitchrail directly in front of the bank.

Jim Bob shouldered his shotgun quickly and sent a charge blasting across the road. The outlaw carrying the money staggered and slumped down beside the packhorse just as pellets of stray buckshot struck the horse's rump.

The animal lunged out of the way, fighting the pull of its halter rope, trying to break free. The horse's sudden movement gave Jim Bob another shot at the downed outlaw. He jacked back the second hammer and fired again.

The robber flipped over on his back, screaming with pain as the money sacks fell to the dirt beside him. One of the bags opened, and in gusts of wind sweeping down Main Street, a swirl of paper currency tumbled down the road like giant snowflakes.

A rifle popped as Jim Bob was ducking down to

reload, and he felt something sting the top of his head. His Stetson, still red with Wayland Burke's blood, was swept away before he could make a grab for it.

The stinging sensation became a sharper pain. He touched the spot with his fingertips, feeling something wet in his hair. And there was more he couldn't see . . . his fingers traced a deep gash running from the front of his scalp to the back of his head.

He glanced at his fingertips and found them dripping blood, and then blood ran from his hairline down his forehead into his eyes.

"I'm shot!" he gasped, feeling suddenly dizzy. "Son of a bitch! I'm shot!"

He fell against the bricks, too shocked to think of reloading at the moment. The pain across the top of his skull was worsening. Blood began to pour down his cheeks, staining the front of his shirt.

"No," he whispered, trembling from head to toe, still staring at his bloody fingers. He was sure he would bleed to death unless someone came to help him.

"I'm shot, Marshal Earp!" he yelled at the top of his lungs, overcome by fear of dying. "Somebody come help me afore I bleed to death!"

No one answered him.

"Marshal! Can't you hear me? I'm shot right on top of my head, an' I'm bleedin' somethin' awful!"

Again, no voice answered his plea for assistance.

"Don't leave me here to die! Somebody's gotta come over here an' help me git to the doctor's house!"

He could hear someone groaning near the front of the bank during a moment of quiet. Then suddenly, two shotguns opened up from the marshal's office—four thundering blasts in quick succession.

"I'm gonna die," Jim Bob whispered. Right then, more than anything else, he feared dying alone. And he was thirsty. It seemed an odd time to want water.

"I hope you die real slow!" a voice cried from the bank, a thin voice filled with anger. "You done went an' shot Frankie down, you son of a bitch!"

A strange calm spread over Dodge City. Even though two banks were being robbed, not a sound could be heard from either end of Main Street. Jim Bob wiped blood away from his face, then his gaze happened to fall on Wayland Burke's body. Clouds of dark flies hovered over his corpse, making a noise like swarming bees.

"We're all gonna die," Jim Bob said, swallowing the bitter bile that was rising in his throat. "Every last one of us is gonna die on account of that money." He thought about his mother back in Clay County, Missouri, wishing she could be there with him then before he bled to death.

He hadn't wanted the deputy's job in the first place, but in the absence of any other employment until the big herds came up from Texas, he felt he had no choice. It was becoming a deputy, or cleaning out spittoons and mopping floors at one of the town's saloons. Being a part-time deputy, he earned less than twenty dollars a month.

"I'm gonna die over a twenty-dollar-a-month job," he said to himself, touching the tear in his scalp again. He shuddered when he felt bare skull where his skin was parted, and the pain had intensified. "I shoulda took that damn job down at the livery shovelin' out horse stalls fer ten bucks a month." At least he'd have been alive, and his head wouldn't have hurt like it did then; a pain like someone had put a hot branding iron against the top of his skull.

"We're comin' out!" a deep voice announced from the bank's windows. "Any sumbitch takes a shot at us, we're gonna kill him an' every friend he's got. We'll burn this whole goddamn town plumb to the ground! I hope all you sons of bitches are listenin', 'cause we damn sure mean what we say!"

Buzzing flies around Wayland Burke's body took Jim Bob's attention away from what was being said, but only for a moment, until he heard another voice farther down the street, coming from the savings bank.

"We're comin' out, too! The first gunshot I hear, I'm gonna blow this little woman's head clean off. Her name's Sara Jane Peabody. Any you sons of bitches want Miss Peabody's death on yer conscience, you start shootin'."

Jim Bob closed his eyes. Miss Peabody was about the most gentle woman in Dodge City, she played the foot-pump organ at the First Baptist Church every Sunday morning. For some bank robber to be willing to kill her seemed too cruel for him to think about right then.

A rifle exploded from the other end of Main, and at the moment Jim Bob didn't care. His head was throbbing now, and he couldn't clear his brain of a creeping fog.

"I done warned you!" the man shouted.

A gun went off, booming, followed by a woman's shriek.

"Jesus," Jim Bob mumbled, fighting to stay awake while the stabbing pains inside his head got worse. Someone—one of the bank robbers—had shot Miss Peabody.

It isn't fair, he thought, remembering Smoke Jensen for reasons he couldn't explain—what Cody had

said, about how he was a really dangerous man with
a six-gun. If Jensen was the kind of expert with weapons that Cody had said he was, then what was he
doing to save the town?

"Next sumbitch we's gonna kill is this banker
feller!" the same voice bellowed. "Name's Feagin.
He's the next one to die unless all the shootin' stops!"

Jim Bob was losing consciousness. The gray fog was
creeping closer to him, enveloping him like a blanket,
and no matter how hard he tried, he couldn't keep
his eyes open.

He slid down the brick wall, resting his bleeding
head on the cool surface. His thoughts drifted back
to Clay County and all the troubles in that part of
Missouri after the war.

A gang of mounted Rebels led by a fellow named
Quantrill had come blazing through Missouri and
Kansas, killing Union sympathizers, burning their
homes and barns to the ground. Among them was a
man calling himself Bloody Bill Anderson, and opinions differed as to whether or not Bloody Bill had
been killed right after the war was over. In far western
Kansas Territory, all sorts of reports surfaced about
Anderson and a gang of cutthroats still pillaging carpetbagger holdings. Someone had mentioned the
possibility that Anderson might come to Dodge City
on one of his raids.

Jim Bob's eyes batted shut. He wasn't thinking
about Bill Anderson then. In a type of dream, he saw
himself sitting by the edge of a muddy creek, holding
a fishing pole, until he heard the sound of his mother's voice.

"Time fer supper!"

And then Jim Bob felt hungry as well as thirsty. He

wished for some of his mother's sweet cornbread, covered with butter and a splash of cane syrup.

The rattle of guns brought him back from his dream with a start. The din of gunfire seemed endless.

In a daze he opened his shotgun, fumbling to pull out the spent shells, knowing he was expected to help Marshal Earp and the others to win this fight. But when he tried to put fresh loads into his gun, his fingers felt numb and they wouldn't work right.

The last sound he heard was a scream, and he couldn't be altogether sure it wasn't his own. . . .

Chapter 23

Smoke listened to the young deputy's cries for help. He had no way to go to the man's aid without exposing himself to gunfire on two sides. Many times, the innocent became the most tragic of all victims in duels between men with guns. A gun was no better than the man who used it . . . the amount of savvy he had, knowing when to shoot and when to wait for the odds to change in his favor.

The odds were still long against Smoke and his cowboys, and the lawmen sworn to protect Dodge City, although Smoke had done his part to change things. Leaving three men dead in an alley behind the bank, his latest victim being an Indian with a long knife scar on his face, he made his way to a side street with his rifle, pausing at the corner of a building to listen to a voice that was shouting demands to everyone in town who was in hearing distance, a warning to anyone who shot at the raiders, when they left the bank with the loot, that they would be killed.

The bank robbers were coming out, no doubt with the money from both vaults. Smoke hoped Cal and Pearlie had the good sense to wait for an opportunity. When the gang tried to leave town they would be exposed to riflemen on rooftops, and to Marshal Earp, along with his remaining deputy . . . if the last deputy were still alive and able to shoot.

Looking down the side street, Smoke saw two bodies. Blood had pooled around both raiders, attracting flies. The wind was picking up from the northwest. In a matter of minutes the gang would ride out of Dodge with every cent both banks had, including the money Smoke had come all the way from Sugarloaf to bring back to Sally, the profits from their cross-breeding program. And as he thought about this, he decided he'd be damned if he'd let them do it . . . not without a fight. He'd given them as much fight as he could without risking his life in a careless fashion, but as it became clear that the bank robbers were close to making their escape, it was high time he gave those land pirates a lesson in mountain-man justice.

Bent over, rifle at the ready, Smoke made his way cautiously to Main Street, where he hesitated at a corner of the town's lone barber shop. A red and white barber's pole out front told him what was inside the building.

Okay, boys, he thought, *I'm ready for you to make your move to pull out.* He had seven shells in his Winchester, and a dozen more in a pair of pistols. By making sure of every shot, he had a chance to make them pay dearly for the spoils they hoped to take from Dodge.

Someone was moaning near the front of the Cattlemans Bank, a quiet sound, full of the misery of a serious wound. And on the far side of Main, he could hear one of Earp's deputies crying out for his mother, a not-all-that-uncommon occurrence when men were dying.

Tilting his head, he gave the rooftop where Pearlie lay hidden a glance; then his eyes wandered down to Cal's position before he returned his attention to Main Street.

"Let's go, boys," he whispered, growing more impatient as each minute passed, ready for the killing to begin.

A shuffling noise forced Smoke to take a look around the corner of the barber shop. Two men came out of the bank, laden with sacks of money. It was a shot too good to pass up, and he took it quickly, firing his rifle twice, as fast as he could pull the trigger and work the ejection lever.

A man in a fringed buckskin coat yelped when Smoke's first slug hit him in the ribs. He flung four bags of money over his head and fell off the boardwalk, reaching for his right side with both hands.

Smoke's second bullet struck a slope-shouldered cowboy who was wearing a bandanna over his face, catching him between his shirt pockets while he made an attempt to load bags of money onto a nervous bay. He dropped in the dirt as though he'd been hit on the head with an axe handle.

"I done warned you!" an angry voice shouted from inside the bank. "You jest got yer bank president killed!"

A tall, thin man in a vest and blue suit coat was pushed out on the boardwalk, staggering to maintain his balance just seconds before a shotgun blast caught him between his shoulderblades. He dove off the walkway shrieking with pain, arms outstretched as if he meant to embrace a loved one, with tiny tufts of blue material swirling from the back of his coat where shotgun pellets shredded it. His cry echoed up and down Main until he landed on his face, bouncing limply, and then he was silent, still.

"The yellow bastards," Smoke hissed, jaw muscles working furiously. One of the outlaws had shot another unarmed citizen of Dodge.

He pulled back behind the barber shop, feeling white-hot rage swell in his chest. Without knowing how many more innocent people were held hostage inside either of the banks, shooting at the outlaws would be too costly in human lives. He was sure of what Preacher would have done in the same situation, trying to do battle with men inside a town! He would wait until the robbers rode off with their ill-gotten gains, and then he would go after them in surroundings where the advantage would change on behalf of a man who knew wild country, its secrets, and the ways of stalking men who knew less about staying alive with no buildings to protect them. It wouldn't matter to Preacher if there were no mountains to hide him as he went about seeking revenge. Preacher was a man who had mastered the art of hiding in plain sight, a fact known only briefly to many of his enemies before he took their lives. And this was a gift Preacher had given young Kirby Jensen so many years ago— careful instruction in the stalking of men.

Smoke decided it would save lives to let the raiders leave Dodge in peace. Then, he would go after them, killing them off a few at a time.

He rested his rifle against the building and cupped his hands around his mouth, facing the Marshal's office. "Marshal Earp!" he yelled. "This is Smoke

Jensen! Let 'em ride out with the money! Too much blood's already been spilled!''

No answer came from Earp's office for several seconds, and then a voice shouted back. "Whatever you say, Jensen! My deputy an' me are layin' down our guns!''

Smoke added a message to his cowboys. "Pearlie! Cal! Don't shoot when they come outside! Let 'em go!''

He didn't need an answer from Cal or Pearlie to know they would follow his instructions. For a time he waited, listening to wounded men and women moan and groan in the street, until a harsh voice spoke to everyone in Dodge.

"This better not be no trick! We got us a woman here, an' we'll blow her goddamn head off if anybody shoots at us. We're comin' out!''

Smoke drew back, turning for the alley so he could get back up on the roof. He wanted to see what direction the outlaws went while Cal and Pearlie were fetching his horse.

He raced back up the alleyway, jumping atop the empty flour keg to climb up on the roof of the cafe. He gave the three men he had killed only a passing glance before he started up to the rooftop.

Removing his hat, he peered over the false front of Martha's as several men came cautiously from the front door of the bank, a woman being shoved in front of one gunman who was holding a pistol to the back of her head.

A heavily muscled man with a black beard glanced up at the rooftops holding a rifle while five or six men began loading bags of money onto a horse and a brown mule. Turning to the front of the savings bank, he saw eight or nine men move cautiously out on the boardwalk with guns and more bags of money.

One man in particular stood out, an older gent wearing a Confederate cavalryman's hat and a gray tunic. His pants were stuffed into the stovepipe tops of cavalry boots. His long hair had turned silver with age, and his face had a craggy look about it. He wore a curious yellow Confederate officer's sash around his waist, and below it he carried a pair of low-slung pistols in cutaway holsters.

I reckon that could be Bloody Bill Anderson, Smoke thought, not really caring either way.

"Sooner or later I'm gonna kill him for what he done here," he whispered savagely, passing one quick glance across the bloody bodies of two women and a boy with his face drenched in blood, the kid couldn't have been more than fifteen or sixteen. Farther down the street a storekeeper lay in front of his hat-and-boot shop wearing a blood-soaked apron. And in front of the bank, the bank president lay on his chest with a swarm of blowflies feeding on dozens of tiny, bloody holes in his back. There was so much blood in the street and on various boardwalks, it appeared that someone had meant to paint the town and its main road a dark red color. At some rendezvous point away from Dodge City, Smoke intended to add a splash of the same color to whatever ground happened to be occupied by this outlaw gang—when he caught up to them and began killing them one or two at a time, as many as he could before he moved to another position to start killing again. He could scarcely control his anger then, looking down upon what the raiders had done to unarmed folks. He would make them pay when the time and circumstances were right.

A few outlaws were gathering up loose horses, still wary, keeping their guns at the ready while they went about bringing mounts to the front of each bank. Some of the robbers began to mount up, covering the rooftops and the front of the Marshal's office with shotguns and pistols and rifles.

I hope Marshal Earp and his deputy are smart enough to let them ride out without taking a shot, Smoke thought. Earp would likely send a telegram to the army post at Fort Larned, asking for their help. Smoke's experience with soldiers had convinced him that, in most cases, the cavalry was virtually useless. By the time they got to a particular spot where there had been some trouble, the troublemakers were usually long gone.

But in this instance, another revenge-seeker would take up the outlaws' trail long before a company of cavalrymen could get to Dodge—a man who understood how to exact vengeance.

The last bank robber was in the saddle, and the silver-haired gent in the Confederate uniform gave a signal to the others to start riding, proving he was leader of the bunch, as Smoke had known all along.

The rumble of galloping hooves passed beneath the cafe as Smoke dropped out of sight, then he raised up just enough to get a quick count of the men he would be after.

"Less than fifteen," he said. "Closer to fourteen, maybe a few less." Between Smoke and his men, and Marshal Earp, they had thinned the robber's ranks considerably. Not that it gave Smoke that much satisfaction. He wouldn't be satisfied until the last outlaw was dead, and the money was back in the bank vaults.

* * *

Earp's face was waxy white when he met Smoke in the middle of Main Street. He spoke first. "I sent Cody to the telegraph office to get off a wire to Fort Larned," he said, passing a sad look across the wounded and dead who had been citizens of Dodge. "Cody took a slug in his shoulder. Jim Bob's over yonder unconscious with a wound to his head. We'll need the doc quick as he can get here. What folks are still alive are hurt real bad. Timmy, the boy with blood all over his face, lost both of his eyes when they got him with a shotgun."

Smoke nodded, watching Pearlie and Cal hurry toward him from a side street. "We didn't have no choice, Marshal," he said in a tired voice. "They were killin' too many innocent people."

"The army'll catch 'em sooner or later," Earp said, sounding convinced of it.

Smoke turned his gaze to the south, watching the dust cloud rising above the fleeing outlaws. His eyes slitted. "Not if I get to 'em first," he said, barely raising his voice.

"You aim to go after 'em yourself?" Earp asked. "Why, you ain't got but two men to help you."

"They won't go with me," Smoke replied. "I'm leavin' them to watch over our cow herd."

"You can't be serious," Earp said.

"Dead serious," Smoke told him, never taking his eyes from the dust on the southern horizon.

"There's too many of 'em," Earp stated flatly, like he did not fully believe Smoke's intentions.

"Depends," Smoke said, just as Cal and Pearlie trotted up to him.

"What you want us to do, boss?" Pearlie asked, balancing his rifle in one hand.

"Keep a close eye on our cows. Make damn sure they get lots of hay an' water till I get back."

"I just knowed you was gonna say that," Pearlie exclaimed, with a look toward Cal for agreement. "You aim to track 'em down an' kill 'em."

"That's right," Smoke replied, only a hoarse whisper. "Every last one of 'em, includin' that gent wearing the gray uniform."

"I figure that was Bloody Bill Anderson," Pearlie said.

"I don't give a damn who he is," Smoke told him, then his jaw turned to granite.

"I don't believe this," Marshal Earp said, "that just one man would set out after more'n a dozen armed outlaws. You won't stand a chance."

"Maybe not," Smoke answered quietly, as the dust sign moved farther away. "Won't know till I get there, don't reckon."

Chapter 24

Cal hurried up beside Smoke as he was headed down to the cow pens beside the railroad tracks to saddle his Palouse. Smoke's mind was on something else—tracking the bank robbers wherever they were going—and he hardly noticed the boy walking next to him; not until Cal spoke.

"Wanted to ask you somethin', Mr. Jensen."

"Ask," was all Smoke said.

"Pearlie told me there come a time back when you was a whole lot younger'n me, when Preacher took you off with him to tangle with a bunch of honest-to-goodness bad men."

"I was some younger," Smoke answered, walking past the store where the man in the bloody apron lay on his back, his wife at his side, crying. "It wasn't of my choosing. Things happened. I didn't have much selection when the time came. I reckon you could say it was us or them."

"Then I say it's time you took me with you now," Cal said. "I give you my word I won't git in the way an' that I'll be a help catchin' them crooks."

"Too many of 'em this time," Smoke told the boy gently. "If it wasn't gonna be so one-sided, I might take you along. This ain't exactly the right sort of situation for you to cut your teeth on."

"Don't matter how many there is," Cal argued. "I want to go, an' I know I'm ready. I won't let you down—honest, I won't. I can carry my share of the load, an' I'm a right decent shot with a rifle."

"There's some things about slippin' up on a man you ain't learned yet."

"You can teach me now. Couldn't be no better chance than right now."

"Sally would kill me if something happened to you."

"Ain't nothin' gonna happen. I'll do exactly like you say, an' won't give you no argument."

Smoke gave it some consideration. He hadn't been as old as Cal when he and Preacher and Emmett had tangled with that bunch up in the northwest part of Kansas Territory. But Cal was awkward at times, careless, like when he forgot to look for the hump in the bay colt's back when they left Sugarloaf, and a mistake like that could get him killed.

"It's real clear them outlaws've got plenty of experience under 'em," Smoke said, lengthening his strides, forcing Cal to break into a trot to stay up with him. "This would be the wrong bunch for you to cross trails with."

"I ain't scared, Mr. Jensen."

"Being scared's got nothing to do with it."

"I'm nearly beggin' fer the chance. I shot down one of them robbers when they rode in. Hit a movin' target with this here rifle. That oughta be worth somethin', an' I done swore I'd do just what you said to do.''

They got to the corral fence, where their horses grazed on a mound of prairie hay. Smoke couldn't quite make up his mind about Cal's request. In most respects the boy was old enough to take care of himself in a tight spot, however the spot where they met up with this batch of bad men might get tighter than what was ordinary.

"Pearlie could use your help here," he said, knowing that the excuse sounded weak.

"Pearlie's able to take care of these here cows without no help from me, an' you know it, Mr. Jensen. How come you ain't got no faith I can handle myself?"

He halted and turned to the young cowboy. "I *do* have faith in you, son. That isn't what's eatin' at me. The men we'll be after are seasoned to being hunted . . . especially if it's Bloody Bill Anderson's boys. They've been hounded all over the middle of this country by lawmen and the cavalry. They won't be easy to catch unawares. They'll be expectin' somebody to be close on their heels. This job's gonna take a man who's done this sort of thing before."

Cal looked him straight in the eye. "I can do it," he said, a promise Smoke knew he truly meant. "You just gotta give me a chance to prove myself."

What Cal said struck a chord deep within Smoke. There had been a time when Preacher had given him the chance to prove he was a man—a fighting man. But when Smoke thought about what Sally would say, he hesitated. If anything happened to Cal he would have hell to pay with the woman he loved. Cal had become, in a sense, like the son they never had. If Smoke brought him back to Sugarloaf in a pine box, or with a debilitating injury that left him a cripple for the rest of his life, Sally would never forgive him.

"I figure I've earned the chance," Cal said, standing as tall as he knew how. "I've done everything you an' Miz Jensen ever asked me to do, an' a time or two I've showed I had nerve when it comes to handlin' a gun."

"It won't be nerves you'll need. This is mostly open land to the south of here, till we strike the Nations. You need the know-how when it comes to slippin' up on a man where there ain't enough natural cover."

"You can learn me. I'm willin' to do whatever it takes to learn how." He glanced back at the main street through Dodge City. "I've seen my share of blood. Them poor folks who got shot back yonder deserve some justice. I hadn't wanted to say nothin' about it, but seems like you an' Miz Jensen don't never aim to stop treatin' me like a little kid. I'm darn near fullgrowed. Time I learned a few things 'bout stayin' alive, like when Preacher showed you how."

He stared into Cal's eyes, wondering. "There's no doubt you can learn it, son. You've got plenty of smarts. A time or two you've showed a tendency toward distractions. Like when that bay colt tossed you off."

"That was different. Wasn't no reason to be so all fired careful then."

Smoke's expression turned to a scowl. "That's where you're wrong. There's always a good reason to be careful. A man never knows what's out there lookin' to end his days. You can't use that one on me."

Cal tilted his head a little. "How 'bout the real reason I want to go?" he asked.

"And what's this real reason?" Smoke wondered aloud.

"Makin' them sorry sons of bitches pay. I was lookin' right down on that kid they shot in the face. Marshal Earp said the boy was stone blind on account of it. It sticks in my craw like sand when some owlhoot with a gun shoots a man who ain't armed, an' that was just a youngster."

"Made you mad, did it?"

"Yessir, it did. Makes me wanna take a gun to the rotten bastard who done it. It don't seem right he can just blind that boy an' ride off with sackfuls of money. If we don't catch up to 'em, they'll hide down in Injun Territory, an' won't nobody ever make the bastard who shot that kid's eyeballs out of his head pay."

"Justice is a job for the law, Cal. We don't carry badges or have any legal jurisdiction in this affair."

"You know darned well nobody's gonna catch 'em 'less we do, and we gotta git on their trail damned quick."

Smoke let out a deep sigh. Sally was as much of a concern as the boy's safety. If Sally found out he had taken Cal with him after more than a dozen killers, Smoke could count on sleeping out in the bunkhouse with Pearlie all the next winter, and maybe well into the next spring. But there was something about the way Cal said what was on his mind that touched an inner part of Smoke's soul. He understood as well as any man, what it was like to want justice for folks who couldn't defend themselves.

"Please let me go, Mr. Jensen," Cal begged. "It's somethin' I just gotta do. . . ."

"All right, Cal. Get your horse saddled and bring our gear and our saddlebags down from the hotel.

Make sure we've got some coffee an' fatback. We could be on the trail of these robbers for a week or more.''

Cal's entire face lit up with a grin. "I'll be back afore you knowed I was gone," he said, breaking into a run toward the hotel. He glanced back over his shoulder. "I'll tell Pearlie what we aim to do."

Smoke turned back to the corral fence, hoping he'd made the right choice. *Boys have to come of age sometime,* he thought, realizing that some of them did it earlier than others. But if Cal got himself in trouble during this manhunt, Smoke knew he would never be able to forgive himself. And a little woman up in Colorado Territory would be even less likely to overlook what he'd done, no matter what reasons or explanations he gave her. She had taken to Cal almost from the first day he went to Sugarloaf, and she mothered him like her own child.

Pearlie gave him a wary look. "You ain't really gonna let that young 'un go with you, is you?"

Cal was across the corral saddling the stud and his bay gelding. "He sorta begged me into it, Pearlie. I reckon he's old enough."

"What he ain't got enough of is good sense," Pearlie exclaimed. "He ain't smart enough to pour his own water outta his boot."

Behind them, the town of Dodge City was attending to its dead and wounded, and the sounds of sobbing and groaning reached Smoke's ears before he replied. "He was smart enough to put a cocklebur in *your* boot, Pearlie."

"You know danged well that's different, boss. Cal ain't hardly more'n out of diapers."

"He's old enough. High time he learned how to survive when he's up against tough situations."

Pearlie made a disgusted face, and Smoke knew it was because he cared for the boy. "This is a helluva lot more'n a tough situation. Them's some genuine bad hombres, an' they proved it here today."

Smoke disagreed, although he knew the robbers were hard types. "They didn't show me much. Yellow bastards shot down unarmed women an' kids an' the banker, besides that old man who came out with his goose gun. Don't take a lot of courage or savvy with a firearm to do what they did. They're just a bunch of greedy men who had an advantage. Leastways, that's what they figured. I aim to show 'em just how wrong they were."

Pearlie watched Cal leading both horses through a corral gate toward them. "I won't sleep a damn wink the whole time you two is gone," he grumbled.

Smoke was sticking by his decision, even if he did have some reservations. "I doubt we'll get a helluva lot of sleep ourselves, Pearlie. Those boys are gonna be hard to catch in this open country without them knowin' we're back there."

Pearlie lowered his voice, like what he was about to say embarrassed him. "Just watch out fer that young 'un best you can, Smoke. Only, don't tell him I said so."

"Showing you've got a soft side, Pearlie?" he asked with a grin.

"Hell no. Just worried 'bout what Miz Jensen's gonna say if'n he don't come back in one piece."

"He has to grow up one of these days. I'm hoping Sally'll understand."

"She ain't got no understandin' when it comes to that there young 'un. She quit fixin' me bearclaws fer a whole damn month one time after I got on him fer leavin' that south pasture gate open so them weaned calves got back with the cows. Never was so hungry in all my borned days."

Cal walked up, leading the Palouse stud and his bay. He had his rifle booted, with their saddlebags tied behind the cantles of their saddles.

"Ready to ride," Cal said, handing Smoke his reins.

Pearlie wagged his head like he was disgusted. "You's ready to ride into a mess," he said. "You ain't plumb dry behind them ears yet. I'm against what you're doin', only it don't make one damn bit of difference to me if'n you're hardheaded enough to want to do it anyhow."

Cal glanced at Smoke. "I'm doin' it anyhow," he said, as he put a boot in his left stirrup to mount.

Smoke booted his Winchester and climbed aboard the stud with a final glance at the crowds on Main Street. "Take good care of our steers, Pearlie," he said. "We'll be back quick as we can get this job done."

Pearlie looked down at his boots a moment. "Sure do hope the two of you can git it done."

"We'll manage," Smoke answered, reining his Palouse toward the south. "Tell Marshal Earp we'll be back with the town's money, soon as we find the right spot to take it back from those yellow bastards."

"I'll tell him what you said," Pearlie remarked, scuffing one boot toe in the dirt, unable to look directly at Cal when the boy swung his leg over the colt.

Smoke led Cal away from the cattle pens, across two sets of railroad tracks, heading due south. They urged their horses to a gallop.

"Pearlie sure did act strange just now," Cal said above the rattle of iron horseshoes across flinty soil.

"He was just worried," Smoke replied.

"Worried 'bout what?" Cal asked. "He don't think I can take care of myself?"

"That wasn't it," Smoke said. "Pearlie's just a born worrier, is all it was."

Chapter 25

Marshal Earp came down the street toward Pearlie, watching Smoke and Cal ride off. Pearlie heard his footsteps and turned around.

"I was aimin' to tell Mr. Jensen we couldn't get that wire through to Fort Larned. Somebody must've cut the telegraph line some place east of here. Clifford Barnes at the telegraph office has been tryin' to put a message through ever since those outlaws came to town."

"Don't take no real deep thinker to figure who it was," Pearlie said. "Them bank robbers done it. Accordin' to the way Smoke feels 'bout the cavalry, wouldn't've done no helluva lot of good nohow."

Earp watched the silhouettes of Jensen and his cowboy ride toward the southern horizon. "I ain't got much faith in the army neither," he said. "That leaves Mr. Jensen and your pardner to handle things by themselves. No offense to Mr. Jensen intended, but I ain't got much faith in them two havin' a chance against so many shootists. Your bossman an' your pardner are liable to get killed."

Pearlie shook his head. "Won't worry Smoke none at all, Marshal. Fact is, he'd rather do the job all by his lonesome, anyways. A cavalry outfit would only git in his way."

Earp slitted his eyelids against dust that was borne on a gust of wind, and coming at his face. "Is Jensen really that tough a customer?" he asked.

"Toughest I ever knowed. An' he was worse 'bout killin' men back when he was younger, afore he settled down."

"Looks like he killed three men back in that alley behind the cafe, and I saw him shoot down several more. Then there was that pair he got while he was on them roofs. It don't seem all that natural, how just one man can be so all-fired good at killin' folks. I'm sure this robbery was the doings of Bloody Bill Anderson, an' he's got one helluva bad reputation for killin' folks himself. If them two meet up south of here, even as tough as you say Smoke Jensen is, he won't stand a snowball's chance in hell against so many hard-nosed killers as them."

"You could be eatin' them words," Pearlie told him as he saw Smoke and Cal disappear over a rolling hill. "My money's on Smoke an' the boy, only I sure do hope that young 'un don't jump in front of no bullet when Smoke ain't around to see after him like he oughta."

"The boy did look a bit green," Earp agreed.

"He's young yet, only he's got the best teacher he could have."

Earp wheeled like he was headed back to town, then took a moment's pause. "Even if Jensen is every bit as good as you say, there's too many of Anderson's men. Hope this won't be the last time I set eyes on your bossman. He's taken on one helluva big bite this time."

"He can chew it," Pearlie replied. "I've seen him come out of worse messes than this one without a scratch. It may take him some time, but he'll be back with the town's money sure as snuff makes spit."

"I'll try to form up a posse, only I don't figure there's many who'll ride with me. Most folks who live here are businessmen or out-of-work cowboys, waitin' for the herds to come up the Chisholm. Not many who can shoot straight. One of my deputies is hurt bad, an' the other's got a notch in his arm that won't let him sit a horse. That don't leave me too many choices."

"I'd go," Pearlie said, "only Smoke told me to stay with the herd. One thing I ain't gonna do is go against none of Smoke's orders. Sorry, Marshal, but I'd sooner tangle with a grizzly as face Smoke Jensen if I didn't do like he told me to."

"I understand," Earp said, starting off toward Main Street. "Maybe Clifford can find where that wire's been cut. Right now I'd better see to helpin' the wounded over to the doc's place. That boy Timmy is blind as a bat, an' there's others bad hurt. No tellin' how many are dead. Hadn't had time to start a count yet."

Pearlie knew that the death toll would be high. It was small consolation, but there was also a goodly number of Anderson's gang decorating the streets and alleys across Dodge. Bloody Bill had paid a high price to empty out two bank vaults, but he was about to pay the highest price of all, in Pearlie's estimation, for making the mistake of pulling a raid on Dodge City's banks while Smoke was in town.

Chapter 26

Jack Starr was waiting for an opportunity, although he knew Bill would be expecting something from any one of his men. As they pushed their horses south, Jack counted thirteen survivors of the raid, a damned unlucky number for a man who was superstitious. But two of Bill's most loyal followers died in the fight that day, and that would be a help. Homer Suggins and Scar Face had been killed trying to bring down the big cowboy who kept moving around on Dodge City's rooftops. Jack wondered who the guy was, and how come he was so damned hard to kill. Somebody calling himself Smoke Jensen had yelled across the street to the City Marshal, telling him to stop shooting. If Jensen was the man who had killed Homer and Scar Face Parker, it was a name Jack didn't recognize.

One or two more steadfast supporters of Bloody Bill remained alive, riding on either flank. It would be hard to shoot Bill in the back with both of them underlings around, so close to Bill, but killing Bill was a chore that needed to be done. Bill had been losing his mind the last year or two, getting badly drunk, rambling on about the old days, the war. His plan to escape into the Nations was a stupid move, and it meant they'd be living on beans and fry bread for months, instead of heading out to California or some place where they could enjoy the money they'd just stolen. Bill was living in the past, believing that all they needed to do was hide from the army and the law. But the law had gotten a helluva lot smarter lately, and there were telegraph wires and railroad lines running all over the place now. With their ranks so dangerously thin, they couldn't fight off a big company of cavalry or a posse of any size. It was time to take Bill out of the picture, so his damned foolish hardheadedness wouldn't get all of them killed or caught.

Joe Lucas rode off to Bill's right. Lucas was dangerous, a man with eyes in the back of his head. Shorty Russel was the type who'd kill a man in his sleep if Bill gave the order, and he was on Bill's left as Bill led the gang and four pack animals loaded with money toward the Kansas line.

What Jack needed most was an ally, someone he could trust when he shot Bill and Lucas and Russel off their horses, a man who would watch his backside while he told the rest of the gang what his plan was—to cut up the money in equal shares and split up, making them that much harder to track down. But Jack wasn't quite sure who to trust among the survivors. He rode at the rear with big Buster Young and was a quiet man whom nobody knew much about, yet he had been with them for several years and never once shirked a job or his responsibility. If Jack remembered right, Buster was from Texas.

He decided to take Buster into his confidence. Leaning out of the saddle, he spoke to Buster in a hushed voice, ready to kill him if he made like he meant to warn Anderson of his plan.

"The army's gonna come after us hard, Buster," he said as their horses trotted over a rocky knob fifty yards behind the others. "We ain't got enough men left to put up much of a fight if they catch us. I've tried to talk Bill into splittin' up the money an' splittin' up the gang fer a spell. He won't listen to a word I say."

Buster glanced over his shoulder, the same shoulder where he carried a sawed-off Greener shotgun on a leather strap. He wore a Colt pistol in a cross-pull holster. "We all damn near got killed back yonder," Buster said. "That son of a bitch shootin' down from that little cafe damn near got me 'fore I could git in the bank with Bill. Bill was talkin' plumb crazy inside there. He shot Lee Wollard hisself when Lee hit that banker too hard over the head. Said he didn't have no use fer a man without good sense. I got to thinkin', maybe Bill aimed to kill us all. His eyes got this funny look to 'em."

"Bill ain't right in the head no more," Jack said. "He's liable to turn on every one of us an' shoot us down for our shares of the money. Lucas an' Russel will back his play if he decides he wants a bigger share. I been keepin' my eyes on Bill since we rode out of town. He don't act right."

"He damn sure don't," Buster agreed.

Jack let a silence pass. "One thing *we* could do is make sure Bill don't shoot us."

"How'd we do that?" Buster asked.

Jack spoke very softly. "We could shoot him down

first, afore he kills us. Most of the rest of the boys would go along with cuttin' up the money now an' ridin' different directions, maybe in pairs. You an' me could take our shares an' head out to California, or maybe to Texas an' cross over the Mexican border where the law can't touch us."

Buster frowned. "Maybe that ain't such a bad idea, Jack, only we'd best be damn sure we done it right. Bill an' Joe an' Shorty'll kill both of us quicker'n we can sneeze if we don't git 'em first. Mexico would be the safest place to hide. We'd have enough money to live like kings down there."

Jack hoped he could trust Buster to keep up his end of the bargain. "We'd better do it quick," he said, taking the hammer thong off his Dance revolver for an easy, quick pull. "We'll ride up behind 'em like we need to talk about somethin'. I'll shoot Bill soon as I'm close enough. You take Shorty with that scattergun, an' I'll go for Lucas whilst you cover everybody else with your second barrel an' pistol. Then I'll explain what we's aimin' to do. We'll find us a low spot so nobody can skyline us an' we'll count the money an' cut it up ten ways, 'less we have to shoot one or two more."

Buster swelled, rubbing beard stubble and his square jaw. "It's gonna be risky as hell, but I'll go along with it. You ride up behind Bill, 'cause he's gonna be the most dangerous. I can stay off to one side an' blow Shorty plumb outta his saddle 'fore I wheel around an' cover the rest. But watch out Lucas don't git you. He's fast as hell, an' he's got a nose fer trouble when it's behind him."

"Let's do it," Jack said, urging his horse to a faster gait, with his heart pumping. Bill Anderson would be wary, but then he trusted Jack and he wasn't likely to suspect anything was wrong until it was too late.

Jogging past the other raiders and the heavily laden pack animals, Jack kept his hand away from his gun. He wouldn't reach for his Dance until he was close . . . very close.

He noticed that Sammy McCoy was sobbing quietly, and he knew it was over his brother Claude. A lot of good men had died back in Dodge that day—some better than others. Jack hadn't known that Bill had gunned Lee Wollard down until Buster told him. It was just one more reason to kill Bill before his mind left him completely.

He came within twenty or thirty feet of Bill's back before Bill and Joe Lucas both glanced backward. Jack grinned and gave them both a nod. From the corner of his eye he saw Buster riding a little bit behind and to his right.

Bill and Joe turned their gazes toward Buster, and then Bill gave a silent nod. The gesture bewildered Jack, taking him by surprise.

Jack heard the dull metallic click of a shotgun being cocked, and he looked quickly over at Buster. Buster had his Greener aimed directly at *him.*

The blast swept Jack out of his saddle like a hurricane-force wind, a fiery, hot wind that made his face and chest and belly burn. He felt himself sailing toward the ground as his horse spooked, galloping out of the way.

Jack landed on his side in the dirt, opening his mouth to yell, when several of his teeth fell out, rolling off his tongue. He tried to move, to escape the most awful pain he'd ever known, but he found he was paralyzed.

"He was gonna shoot you in the back, Bill," he

heard Buster say, "just like you said he was plannin' to do. He wanted me to help him do it."

"You'll get half of his share along with yours, Buster," he heard Bill growl. "I never did trust the sumbitch. Just leave him there to die. Fetch his horse an' let's keep pushin'."

Jack's last conscious thought was one of anger, because he'd been double-crossed by Buster Young. If he'd been able, Jack would have gotten up and killed them all, the rotten bastards.

His eyes closed.

Chapter 27

Their trail was easy to follow—shod horses crossing barren ground, tracks spread some distance apart, indicating that the outlaws were pushing their horses as hard as they could. Smoke kept an eye on the horizon. Far to the south, when they rode higher hills, he could see scattered trees in the distance. Near the Kansas border they would come to the Cimarron River, and beyond it they would be in Indian Territory. Anderson was running for the most lawless stretch of land he could find, where a handful of Federal Marshals tried to keep peace in lands given to various Indian tribes after the big treaty at Medicine Lodge.

Cal was studying the hoofprints. "They been keepin' their horses in a long trot, Mr. Jensen. Won't be long 'til they have to stop an' rest 'em."

"They'll pick a low place where they'll be harder

to see," he told Cal. "We'll have to be careful we don't ride up on 'em unawares."

"I got it figured they'll keep rear guards posted, 'cause they know somebody'll come after 'em."

"That's a fact," he said. "Might give us a chance to take a few of 'em on, that rear guard you called it. If they stray too far from the main bunch, I might be able to slip up behind 'em."

"But there ain't no cover," Cal protested, giving Smoke a look.

"There's plenty of cover out here," he replied, "if a man knows how to use it."

Cal gave their surroundings another examination. "Just some brush an' tumbleweeds."

"It's enough."

"Then you'll slip up on 'em on foot?" the boy asked.

"Be the easiest way, if they're far enough from the rest of the gang so I can get behind 'em."

Cal shook his head. "Don't seem like nearly enough places to hide to me."

Smoke knew that the youngster wanted an explanation. "It's what some Indian tribes use, son. A white man, unless he's been shown a few tricks, is lookin' for the shape of a man on a horse, or a man walking upright. Most men are lookin' for what they expect to see, and they aren't ready for somethin' else."

"You aim to crawl on your belly?"

"Depends," Smoke said. "I'll have to wait an' see what they give me."

"If they're smart they won't give you much."

"Most men aren't as smart as they think. You learn to use any kind of cover there is, cover that'll hide a man."

"That's some of what Preacher taught you?"

"Some. There's a whole lot more to it. You've got to learn it a little bit at a time. Takes some practice to get it right an' not make any fatal mistakes."

Cal still seemed puzzled. "Even a man crawlin' on his belly in this brush won't be hid from a pair of good eyes, seems like to me."

"That's because you know what I'm aimin' to do, son. These boys we're after expect a posse, or the cavalry, to come ridin' hell for leather on their tracks. They won't be lookin' for one man on foot who understands how a pair of eyes can play tricks on the one doin' the lookin'."

"I'm not real sure I understand, Mr. Jensen, but I'll pay real close attention . . . so I can learn."

"That's the reason I brought you along, Cal. If my wife had any idea what I was doin' she'd yell so loud we'd hear her all the way from Sugarloaf to Kansas."

They rode up on the body, warned by circling buzzards that something dead awaited them—a fresh kill of some kind. When Smoke saw the corpse, he recognized him as one of the bank robbers.

"Appears they've already had some kind of disagreement," he said, halting the stud a few yards from blood-soaked ground where a bearded man lay sprawled on his back, his upper body riddled by buckshot.

Cal's cheeks weren't as dark as they had been. He gazed down at the dead man a few moments. "Shot at real close range," he finally said. "Tore the hell outta his face. Why would they shoot one of their own, Mr. Jensen?"

"Can't say for sure, but maybe this one got greedy. Wanted a bigger share."

Cal swallowed. "A shotgun makes one helluva mess, don't it?"

"It's good for close-quarters fighting, but it don't have much range."

"You hardly ever use one," Cal continued, unable to take his eyes off the body, "but you git real close to the men you're after, sometimes, an' then it seems like you always use a knife on 'em."

"A knife's quieter. Kinda depends on how many of 'em there is."

"You gonna use a knife on them rear guards when we find 'em?" he asked.

With his eyes, Smoke followed the tracks made by more than a dozen horses. "The situation will tell me what to use. If I can, I'll do it quiet. If I can't, I'll do it anyway I can and change positions real quick."

"Change positions? That's so the rest of the gang won't come to the sound of your gun?"

He took a deep breath and collected his reins to ride off along the tracks. "Most times. But once in a while you *want to* draw somebody else to the sounds you make . . . only you gotta be ready for 'em when they show up."

Cal was reading Smoke's face. "How come you don't ever act scared, Mr. Jensen? Don't seem like you show no fear, even when you go up against a big bunch of killers."

Smoke nudged his stud with his boot heels. They rode away from the corpse side by side.

"Fear's a funny thing, Cal. It can do a feller some good if he understands what fear is. It's a warning. So long as you don't let it get the best of you, it can be a help."

"A help? Tell me how bein' afraid can help when it makes a feller nervous."

"You pay more attention to little things . . . the sounds around you—the smells, the way a bird flys, or the way a good range-bred horse behaves when it smells somethin' unfamiliar. It's nature's way of tellin' you to be careful."

Cal frowned, chewing his bottom lip. "I think I understand, Mr. Jensen, only sometimes, when I git scared of somethin', it gives me the shivers. All I can think about is gettin' the hell away from wherever I'm at."

"Most often," Smoke told him in a soft voice, "that's the smartest thing to do. It takes a few years before you know when to run and when to hold your ground."

"Yonder they are," Cal whispered, lying on his belly in a clump of sagebrush, overlooking a dry streambed that wound its way from east to west. "Looks like they's passin' around bottles of whiskey."

Smoke was intent upon what he saw below the hilltop, and he didn't answer for a spell. "All the better," he said. "Whiskey robs a man of the best edges on his senses. A man who's half drunk don't hear or see nearly so good."

"I still can't see no rear guard, like you figured they'd have," Cal continued.

"There's two of 'em," Smoke said. "Back this way about a quarter mile."

Cal focused all his attention on the land between the hill and the dry creek. "I still don't see a damn thing, Mr. Jensen. Not a single thing nowhere."

"Look to the left of that big rock," Smoke whispered. "See how the brush in back of it is layin' down? That's where a pair of careless men walked up to that rock to keep an eye on things while the main bunch rested their horses an' had a little drink or two."

Cal narrowed his eyes in an afternoon sun. "I see what looks like a trail of some kind leadin' up to that rock, but I can't see nobody. Nary a soul."

"That's because they've hid behind the rock," Smoke said as he pushed back on his belly off the crest of the hill. "All you can see is the trail they left behind while they got to that spot on foot."

Smoke straightened up when he was out of sight behind the hill. He walked down to the Palouse and hung his stetson on his saddlehorn.

"Are you goin' after 'em?" Cal asked, watching Smoke take off his boots to put on a pair of Pawnee moccasins he removed from his saddlebags.

"I'll see if I can slip up on 'em before they move," he said, taking his Arkansas Toothpick from the sheath inside his right boot. "You stay here an' hold the horses. Don't look over that hilltop, no matter what you hear. Don't matter what happens, you stay put. You hear?"

"Yessir. I'll be right here, waitin' on you."

He stared into the young cowboy's eyes a moment, thinking of Sally and the closeness both of them felt toward Cal. "If you hear a gunshot, climb on this bay an' head back to Dodge just as fast as these horses can travel."

"I won't leave you if'n yer in trouble, no matter what," he answered.

"I admire that in you, son, but this is one time when you do exactly what I tell you to do. If you hear a gun, it'll mean they saw me before I got to them. Don't give me no argument. You get up on that horse and ride."

Cal wouldn't look at him. "Yessir," was all he said

as Smoke wheeled around on soundless feet to walk toward low ground east of the hillside.

Dewey Hyde tipped back the bottle of whiskey and took a thirsty pull. Sammy McCoy was awaiting his turn with the jug as they sat behind a boulder, watching the amber fluid drain down Dewey's throat.

"Buster sure did blow ol' Jack in half," Sammy said, his crossed eyes fixed on Dewey's face. "How did Bill know Jack was aimin' to double-cross him like that?"

Dewey ran his sleeve across his lips before he gave the bottle to Sammy. "It was easy, I reckon. Jack kept talkin' about going west to California . . . how much he didn't like the notion we'd hide in the Nations fer a spell. Bill put two an' two together. I heard Bill tell Buster to keep an' eye on Jack for him. Bill said the same thing to Homer Suggins, only that crazy sumbitch on top of the cafe got to Homer first, afore Buster did."

"Bill don't hardly trust nobody."

Dewey took a look over the rim of the boulder. "I reckon that's how come he's still alive, Sammy. He don't sleep like most men do. I swear, he keeps one eye open all night."

Sammy took the bottle and drank deeply. He let out a breath and belched. "There's three of us who'd do damn near anything Bill told 'em to."

"That'd be Shorty an' Joe an' Buster."

"Right," Sammy said, taking another swallow. "Buster don't worry me all that much, not the way Jack Starr did. But with him bein' dead now, I'd keep an eye on Joe Lucas. He kinda scares me sometimes."

"Bill Anderson scares me all the time," Dewey said,

pulling back when he saw nothing behind them.
"Shorty's a bad ass with a blade, all right, but Joe's
the one to watch. If Bill thinks you're fixin' to double-
cross him, he'll have Joe put a bullet plumb through
your heart."

Sammy thought about it, drinking again. "Shorty
would kill a man in his bedroll. Joe'd do it whilst you
was lookin' at him square in the eye."

A soft noise distracted both men. Dewey reached
for his pistol, although he kept it holstered. "What
was that yonder?" he asked.

"It made a little rattlin' sound," Sammy replied.
"Maybe it was a rattlesnake."

"Didn't sound like no goddamn rattler," Dewey
growled, his eyes locked on a cluster of brush to the
west, where a setting sun made things harder to see.
"Damn near sounded like somebody took a little rock
an' chunked it off in them bushes."

"You're hearin' things, Dewey," Sammy said. "It
was a snake."

They were looking toward a late-day sun, at brush
close to the rock where they were hidden, when a
razor-sharp steel blade slashed across Dewey's windpipe. Sammy heard a noise, a gurgle when Dewey's
blood spilled down the front of his shirt.

Sammy whirled, clawing for his Colt, staring up at
a huge figure crouched behind him. "Who the hell're
you?" he blurted out, jerking his pistol free of its
leather berth, intent upon shooting the stranger.

A bowie knife plunged into his heart with tremendous force, and he felt bones crack inside him—a
pain that was so intense he could not breathe, pinned
him to the ground.

" 'Afternoon, gents," a soft voice whispered, and
then the blade made a sucking sound when the

stranger pulled it out, dripping wet with Sammy's blood.

Dewey made strangling noises; coughing, choking when he fell over on his face. Sammy wasn't listening. His head dropped back, and he saw the sky for a moment, until a cloud above him began to look fuzzy, indistinct, like a swirling bowl of cotton.

Chapter 28

Joe Lucas stared down at the bodies. His horse snorted when it became edgy over standing so close to the scent of death. Joe turned in the saddle to speak to Bill Anderson. Bill's face was tight with anger.

"Whoever done it had to be slick." He gave the brushlands a sweeping glance, his rifle butt resting on his thigh. "This is damn hard country to slip up on a man. The sumbitch has to be part Indian."

Bill grunted. "If we had the time, I'd have everybody fan out an' hunt him down," he said bitterly. "He's got a horse hid somewheres. Can't be far. I'll hand him one more thing—he's a gutsy bastard, gettin' close enough to use a knife so's the rest of us wouldn't hear him."

Shorty Russel spat tobacco juice off one side of his red sorrel gelding. "Hell, I ain't worried. Means two more shares fer the rest of us. Dewey was dumber'n a rock, if you ask me, an' Sammy was damn near an idiot, with them gotch eyes. We ain't no worse off without 'em.''

Bill was looking north. "I think I know who it is. That big son of a bitch who throwed Homer off that roof done this. I got this feelin' he's the one."

Lucas gave the skyline his own inspection. "He ain't got no posse with him, or they'd be ridin' down on us. Havin' just one sumbitch behind us proves he's crazy, whoever he is. Prob'ly some goddamn pig farmer who lost all his money when we robbed the banks . . . gonna be a hero an' try to git everybody's money back."

"We can't afford the time to look fer him," Bill said, after another look at Dewey and Sammy. "He'll come back. He won't give up, not after he got this done so easy. Sammy an' Dewey was drunk, or this couldn't've happened. Ain't no place to hide in this miserable country. The thing to worry 'bout is if he's got a Sharps so he can shoot us from long range, a few at a time. We ain't got no long guns with us."

"I'll ride back an' track him down," Lucas said, levering a cartridge into the firing chamber of his Winchester. "The rest of you keep headin' south. I'll catch up soon as I've killed this sneaky bastard."

"Maybe I oughta go too," Russel said, " 'case there's more'n just one."

Bill gave it some thought. Wind whipped around their horses in gusts, swirling the animals' manes and tails, causing the brim of Bill's cavalry hat to flutter. "I reckon that's a good idea," he said after a bit. "Two'd be better 'n one lookin' fer him. I owe the son of a bitch, if it's the same feller who killed Homer an' Sikes."

"I figure he got Scar Face Parker likewise," Russel said around a ball of chewing tobacco.

"We got proof he ain't no tinhorn," Lucas agreed. "All the same, he can't outrun no bullet. He ain't gonna git close enough to use no knife on me. Won't be the same as slippin' up on Dewey an' Sammy."

"Find him," Bill snarled, "and kill him. Bring me his goddamm head so I can tie it to my saddlehorn. Homer'd been ridin' with me since the war. I don't take it lightly when somebody kills my friends."

"We'll find him," Lucas said, reining his horse around the bodies. "Just make sure the boys save me an' Shorty some of that whiskey."

Shorty Russel hurried his sorrel up beside Lucas's yellow dun as Bill turned back to rejoin the others. They rode toward the crest of a hill, with rifles ready.

A moment later, Russel glanced over his shoulder to make sure Bill was out of earshot before he spoke to Lucas. "How come you volunteered us fer this job, Joe? Looks like me an' you oughta be playin' it safe so we can live to spend our share of that money."

"I figure this *is* safer," he said, scanning the brush as they rode at a slow walk. "It's gonna be dark in a few hours. If this sneaky son of a bitch is as good as he appears to be, he'll come fer us after sundown. But if we find him first an' kill him, won't be no reason to worry 'bout the dark."

"I don't figure he's really all that good," Russel said. "Sammy McCoy's eyes was so bad crossed he couldn't see a buffalo bull chargin' straight at him. Dewey Hyde was just plain dumb. Homer was gittin' old hisself, an' Sikes never struck me as near careful enough. That breed, on the other hand, woulda been hard to kill fer might' near anybody. If this same feller got Scar Face, we could have our hands full bringin' him down."

"Bill's worried," Lucas remarked, as they neared

the top of a rise. "He had robbin' them banks figured as bein' easy, only we lost damn near half of them that come with us."

"Bill wasn't helpin' things none, shootin' Lee like he did. Bill's temper's been real bad lately. He don't act quite right sometimes."

"He's still smarter'n most an' dangerous as hell too. He knowed Jack was gonna try an' double-cross him. He sent Buster back to keep an eye on Jack. Bill can smell a rat, same as he always could. I'll grant you, he ain't the same as he was, but I'd have to give it a helluva lot of thought 'fore I tried to cross him."

"Me too," Russel agreed, stopping his horse when they could see what lay beyond the rise—more of the same empty hills. "I did think about it once, that night he shot my pardner Curly Boyd whilst we was plannin' this job. Curly an' me went back a few years. Wasn't no call to gun Curly down when all he done was ask a question."

Lucas nodded and urged his horse forward again. "We've both been with Bill a long time, Shorty, an' we know how crazy mean he can git at times. After we git our shares of the money, maybe you an' me oughta light outta here . . . head fer Arizona or some other place. After pullin' a job big as this, the lawdogs an' the cavalry are gonna be turnin' over every rock lookin' fer us. There'll be plenty of 'em out to hang us, fer sure."

"I ain't lookin' to stretch no rope. That's a good idea, Joe, to head west when we collect our money."

"I've sure been thinkin' on it aplenty," Lucas said, guiding his dun into a shallow ravine.

* * *

Lucas jerked his horse to a halt in a clump of sagebrush and broomweed. He pointed to something with the barrel of his rifle. "Yonder he is, Shorty."

Russel stopped his sorrel, stood in his stirrups, and grinned wide. "I'll be damned," he said. "The fool's just sittin' out yonder on his horse, leading a spare, one of them spotted Palouse Indian ponies from up in Idaho country. The dumb sumbitch ain't even tryin' to run fer it now that he sees us. He's just sittin' there like he was froze or somethin'."

"Don't seem quite right," Lucas wondered aloud. "Spread out an' we'll rush him. Shoot both them horses if we can, so he'll be afoot. Let's ride!"

Lucas and Russel spurred their horses into a hard gallop toward the lone rider, who was leading an extra horse. Lucas was puzzled when the horseman made no move to turn and run, sitting motionless while they came charging at him. Russel rode off to the left, bringing his rifle to his shoulder, waiting for the right range. Wind gusted through the broomweed and brush, creating waves across the prairie hills that surrounded a cowboy with two horses, who simply sat there, waiting for them.

In the back of Joe Lucas's mind, a warning sounded that something was wrong.

Smoke drew a bead on a lanky gunman who was wearing a black cowboy hat and racing toward Cal with a rifle at his shoulder. It was a calculated risk that neither man would be able to get off a shot at Cal before Smoke killed them. But a man on a running horse had more difficulty steadying a pistol or a rifle. A man lying on his belly, peering through a tangle of broomweed, resting his elbows on the ground, had a distinct advantage—better still, when that rifleman understood guns and the nature of a rifle slug's drop at greater distances.

He feathered the Winchester's trigger very gently and did not wait to see the result of his shot before he levered another round into the chamber, the crack of his gun carried away on the winds.

The man in the black hat appeared to run into an invisible rope or a wire while his dun was at full speed. The gunman's head was jerked backward, and the rest of him went along off the rump of his charging mount. He sailed through the air, flinging his rifle away, clawing wildly for his throat as he began to tumble downward.

Smoke fired again, feeling the hard jolt of the rifle butt against his shoulder. A stocky gunman atop a bounding sorrel did a circus flip out of his saddle, folded over, knees tucked under his chin. He appeared to be suspended there while his horse ran off without him.

He landed in curious fashion, on the back of his neck with his butt sticking straight up, while his legs flopped over his head. Somehow he'd managed to hang on to his rifle, and it discharged the moment he fell, a muffled pop from a distance of at least two hundred and fifty yards, a difficult target for even the best marksman at that range.

Smoke came slowly to his feet as his second empty cartridge flew from the rifle's chamber. He had to make sure both gunmen were dead. When he saw Cal start riding off the hill to investigate for himself, Smoke waved him back, unwilling to take any form of chance with the boy's life.

He walked up on the first man he shot, and what he saw left him satisfied. A slack-jawed man in his middle thirties with deep brown hair lay on his back with his throat torn open where a slug had gone through. He was still breathing shallowly, blood pumping from the gaping hole in his throat to form a spreading, red stain around his head and shoulders. His eyes, as black as coal, filled with a mixture of pain, surprise, and hatred, turned on Smoke when Smoke's shadow fell across his face.

"If you see Anderson again, which ain't likely," Smoke said tonelessly, "tell him his men make real good target practice. I heard Bloody Bill Anderson rode with some of the toughest gunmen west of the Mississippi. You can tell him for me it just ain't so. I haven't met up with a tough one yet."

"Bastard . . . ," the dying man croaked through a torn windpipe, his empty hands making claws in the dirt.

"That's a real bad reflection on my mother," Smoke told him without a trace of inflection in his voice. "Under damn near any other circumstances, I'd make you sorry you said that. But it looks like I'd be wastin' my time showin' you the error of your ways. You'll be dead in a minute or two."

Smoke walked away to find the other bank robber, with his rifle cocked, ready. Remembering the way the shorter gunman had fallen on his neck, it wasn't likely he would need a gun.

The man lay in an odd pose, with his butt up, feet over his head, as if he'd meant to land that way.

"This one's dead," Smoke muttered, turning to Cal, beckoning to him, lowering the hammer on his Winchester. Like he'd set out to do, he was making Bill Anderson and his killers pay for what they'd done to unarmed citizens of Dodge, and for emptying both banks of their money.

Cal came galloping up, leading the Palouse. He reined to a halt a few yards from the gunman.

"Right unusual way to die," Cal said, staring at the body, the blood from a chest wound around it.

Smoke took the stud's reins and mounted quickly. "Let's get clear of this spot," he said, swinging southwest. "No tellin' if there's some comin' behind these two."

"Beats anything I ever saw, Mr. Jensen," Cal said as they hit a steady trot away from the scene, "how you killed two men afore they ever fired a shot. They didn't even know you was there."

"We baited 'em, son," Smoke said, booting his rifle. "Like putting a worm on a fishin' hook."

"How's that?" Cal asked.

"It's simple enough. I hope you'll remember it. They saw you on that hill where I told you to wait. That drew 'em to you like a bear comes to honey. They weren't expectin' anybody else to be there, figurin' you had to be the one who got them others with a knife. They didn't do a helluva lotta thinkin' just now. They thought they saw what they expected to see. That can be a man's biggest weakness when he goes lookin' for somethin' special because he believes it's gonna be there. Learn from it, Cal. Never trust yer eyes without makin' sure of everything around you."

"You said we was gonna trick 'em, only you didn't explain how. I understand, Mr. Jensen. They didn't look close enough at little things, like when I saw sunlight shine off your rifle barrel just a second or two afore you shot 'em. On top of that, they should have done even more thinkin'. I was sittin' up there with a spare horse, but it was also wearin' a saddle. A man don't take two saddles when he rides cross-country with a fresh mount. No need for but one saddle if it's just one man.''

"You've got the idea,'' Smoke told him as they circled a knob to ride into an arroyo. "It's the little things that often make the difference between livin' and dyin'. It's better to be sure of things before you make your play.''

Cal was gazing south. "You sure showed 'em,'' he said in a low voice. "Hasn't been but a couple of hours, an' you've already killed four of 'em. If they've got a lick of sense, the rest'll be worried by now.''

"We'll send them a little message,'' Smoke said, halting his stud, pointing to the gunmen's riderless horses, which were grazing farther down the ravine. "Go fetch up those two geldings and hand me your lariat rope. You just gave me an idea. . . .''

Chapter 29

Bill stood on a rock ledge just before dusk, watching their backtrail with his field glasses. He and Buster Young talked as Bill studied the horizon from the highest point they could find, while the men waited in a draw, resting and drinking whiskey to pass time or dress a few minor flesh wounds that three of his gang had taken during the robbery. It had been a hard push to cover so much ground—hard on horses as well as on men. And there was a problem of another sort—a man, or several men, who kept following them, killing Dewey and Sammy with a knife in a spot where they should have been able to see someone stalking them. Bill had watched closely for dust sign to the rear, and he'd seen nothing all day—not so much as a wisp of trail dust. What was happening didn't make a hell of a lot of sense. He'd been running from lawmen and Union cavalry for so many years, he was sure he knew all the tricks of the game. Until then. And for reasons he couldn't explain, he felt it was the work of just one man, and that was even more puzzling. Who would go alone after a gang the size of his? Only a madman, or one crazy son of a bitch.

"Joe an' Shorty ain't comin," Buster said. "The guy who got Dewey an' Sammy got them, too."

"Not Joe Lucas," Bill answered. "He's too damn careful to get bushwhacked. It's just takin' 'em more time than they had it figgered."

"This gent's slippery," Buster argued. "He could even be the feller who got Scar Face. Maybe he's got some others with him . . . a posse. That'd explain why it's takin' Joe an' Shorty so long to git back. They coulda run into a whole bunch of guns back yonder."

"We'd've seen some dust if it was a posse," Bill said, passing his glasses along the crests of hills, then along the low places between them. "It's that sumbitch who flung Homer off the roof who's responsible. I've got this feelin' about it, about how it's him."

"It can't be no good feelin', if it's just one man," Buster told him, frowning. "It just don't figger why some tough son of a bitch would be in Dodge this time of year. The gent who got Homer wasn't no lawman. Big feller . . . real tall, from what I seen of him. I remember one more thing. He yelled real loud when he throwed Homer's body, like he wanted us to know it was him an' that he was up there. Damn near like he was darin' somebody to shoot at him. Could be he's crazy."

"Crazy like a fox," Bill replied angrily, still reading the horizon through his lenses. "A genuine crazy man woulda showed hisself by now. I seen a few crazies durin' the war, when they seen too much blood, too much dyin'. They'd come runnin' at our lines like they was bullet proof, screamin' their damn fool heads off 'til a bullet shot 'em down. Some of 'em would get right back up an' come chargin' at us again whilst they was dyin'. It was a helluva sight to see. But this bastard who's followin' us ain't that kind of crazy. Somehow, he's able to sneak up on us without showin' hisself ... which is damn hard to do in this open country. But I still don't figger he got Joe. Shorty, maybe, but not Joe Lucas."

"Ain't no man bulletproof, not even Joe," Buster said after a pause.

Bill's glasses found movement on a distant hill. A pair of horses came trotting into view. Bill let out a sigh. "Yonder they come. Both of 'em," he told Buster. "I can see both their horses—a sorrel an' Joe's big buckskin."

"Let's hope they killed the sumbitch," Buster remarked. "If they did, we can quit worryin'."

Bill watched the horses a little longer, because something about them seemed wrong, and yet he couldn't put a finger on just what it was. Dusky darkness made it hard to see detail. Long black shadows fell away from the hills in places, preventing him from seeing Joe and Shorty clearly.

He waited while the horses came closer, holding a slow trot along a trail of horse droppings and hoofprints his gang had left in their wake. Bill was in too much of a hurry to make the alabaster caves west of old Fort Supply, where they could hide out, and there wasn't time to be careful about leaving a trail to follow until they crossed over the Kansas line at the Cimarron River. In the river, they could ride downstream in the shallows and lose any possemen or cavalry when the current washed out their horse tracks.

"I can see 'em now," Buster said, squinting. "Two horses, only they sure as hell are comin' real slow.

Looks like they'd be in a hurry to bring good news. Maybe they couldn't find the sneaky son of a bitch."

The pair of horses rounded a low hill, and Bill could see them plainly enough. His jaw muscles went taut when his teeth were gritted in anger. "Damn!" he said, taking one last look before he lowered his field glasses, hands gripping them so tightly his knuckles were white.

"What the hell's wrong, Bill?" Buster asked, unable to see all of what Bill had seen, without magnification.

"He got 'em," Bill snapped.

"What the hell're you talkin' about?" Buster wanted to know, glancing back to the horses that were approaching the ledge where they stood. "Yonder they come. That's Joe's yeller dun, an' that's Shorty's sorrel, ain't it?"

Bill's rage almost prevented him from answering Buster. A moment passed before he could control himself. "It's the right horses," he growled. "Shorty an' Joe are tied across their saddles. Means they're dead."

"Dead? Why would the bastard take the time to tie Shorty an' Joe to their saddles?"

"He's sendin' us a warning," was all Bill could say right then, fuming.

Buster frowned at the horses a third time. "Son of a bitch," he said softly, unconsciously touching the butt of his pistol when he said it. "They *are* dead. I can see their arms danglin' loose." He turned to Bill. "What kind of crazy son of a bitch would do that?"

Bill tried to cool his anger long enough to think. "A man who don't give up easy. He aims to dog our trail all the way to the Nations. Can't figure why, only it's real clear he ain't in no mood to give up."

"I ain't so sure it's one man, Bill. One man

couldn't've handled Joe an' Shorty so quick. I say there's a bunch of 'em back yonder. Damn near has to be."

"I've got this feelin' you're wrong," Bill said, swinging off the ledge, taking long, purposeful strides down to the spot where his men rested. "But there's eleven of us left, an' we'll be more careful from here on," he added.

"We've lost some of our best shooters," Buster reminded, when he saw the men waiting for them in the draw.

Bill was in the wrong humor to discuss it. "Send a couple of men out to fetch Joe an' Shorty back here. Their horses're comin' too slow, followin' the scent of these others. I'll have everybody get mounted. Maybe we can lose that bastard when we come to the river."

Pete Woods and Stormy Sommers led the horses, with bodies lashed to saddles, over to Bill. Stormy's face wasn't the right color.

"Joe's got a hole blowed plumb through his neck," Pete said while jerking a thumb in Joe Lucas's direction. "Shorty caught one in the chest right near his heart."

Bill paid no attention to the swarm of blowflies that were clinging to both bodies, wondering how anyone could have taken Joe Lucas by surprise. "Cut 'em down an' leave 'em here. We'll use their horses for fresh mounts. See if there's any money in their pants pockets. Don't leave nothin' valuable behind."

"Whew, but they sure do stink!" Pete said, climbing down to cut pieces of rope that were holding the corpses in place. Shorty's body fell limply to the dirt.

Joe slid out of his blood-soaked saddle to the ground with a sickening thump. "Goddamn flies been eatin' on 'em, on the blood."

Bill didn't care to hear about the smell. "Search their pockets like I told you," he said. "Time we cleared outa here quick. Been here too long. We oughta hit the river close to midnight."

"Who you reckon done this?" Charlie Waller asked, fingering his rifle in a nervous way.

"A crazy man," Buster answered, when Bill said nothing. "He has to be outta his goddamn mind."

Bill wheeled his horse, heading south onto a darkening prairie, leading ten men and four pack animals loaded with bags of money toward the Cimarron.

In the back of his mind he wondered what kind of man was following them. Unlike Buster, Bill wasn't quite so sure the stalker was crazy. *Deadly* might be a better word.

And to make matters worse, the man on their trail seemed to be enjoying himself, in a way. Why else would he have sent the bodies back, unless he wanted fear to cause Bill and his gang to make another careless mistake?

Smoke led Cal down a series of winding dry washes, staying off the hilltops, where they might be seen. It took longer to travel this way, yet time was unimportant to Smoke. Facing far superior numbers, caution was his best weapon.

Cal rode up beside him, peering into the dark. "How come you don't act worried they'll ambush us, now that there ain't no light?" he asked.

"This Palouse'll warn us. A tribe of Indians up in the far northwest bred an' raised the Palouse for special reasons. First off, they're tough. Got more stamina than any other breed of horse. On top of that, they've got real unusual noses an' the best ears ever attached to horseflesh. They can smell a man or another horse from half a mile away, if the wind's right, an' the slightest sound'll make this stud's ears prick up."

"How come everybody don't ride a Palouse?" Cal asked. "Do most folks know how they're special?"

"Ain't many of 'em left, son. When the army captured Chief Joseph an' the rest of the Nez Perce tribe, they killed off most of their spotted ponies."

"That's mighty coldblooded, to kill horses fer what a tribe of Indians done."

"Another reason I've got damn little respect for the army. An outfit that kills horses for no reason other than they're better than most is the act of cowards."

"I always wondered why you favored that stud an' his colts so much."

"I want the best animal I can find between my knees when I strap a saddle on."

Cal glanced up at a cloudless, moonless sky. "Them bank robbers'll be more careful now. How do you aim to git the rest of 'em?"

"They'll give me my chances."

"You sound mighty sure of it, Mr. Jensen."

"It's the nature of men on the run. When they feel somebody close, they make mistakes. Get in too big a hurry."

Cal nodded. "I've been payin' real close attention to most everythin' you do. So I can learn from it. You ride low country, an' you always keep your eyes movin'. You don't never look at one spot fer long."

"Old habit, I reckon."

Cal seemed to be pondering something. "Does it ever bother you that you've killed a bunch of men?"

"I used to think about it some, until I met Sally. Since we got married, I've tried to live peaceful, only there's been times when my past catches up to me."

"Old enemies, from before you hitched up with Miz Jensen?"

"Mostly. I still have trouble passin' up a one-sided fight where someone who's in the right is facing men who mean to do them wrong."

"Like the folks who live in Dodge City, maybe," Cal said, thinking. "If you hadn't been there, more of 'em would have died tryin' to save their money."

"I told Marshal Earp it was time to let 'em ride out of town with what they came for. This way's better. It's just us and them. Nobody else gets hurt or killed."

"I reckon I hadn't oughta tell you this, but I was scared when all that shootin' was goin' on. I stayed hid behind the front of that roof most of the time. Couldn't hardly make myself rise up an' shoot nearly as regular as I shoulda."

"You played it smart. No need to apologize for it. You did a right decent job of shootin' when you had the chance, and that's all anyone can expect from you."

"Didn't do as much shootin' as you or Pearlie. I was just too scared."

"Fear can be a good thing," Smoke explained. "Until you know a little more about fighting, it's better to take it slow and easy. You'll learn as you get older. Experience is the best teacher. I suppose that's why I brought you along, but I don't want you to take any big chances. Leave that to me."

"One of these days I aim to be as good as you when

it comes to fightin'," he said. "I'm real determined to learn it."

"There's a lot better things for a young man your age to spend his time learning. Like the cow business, and horses. Leave the fightin' to them that have a knack for it."

"Like you, Mr. Jensen."

Smoke couldn't offer much argument, even though it hadn't been his choice to learn how to kill.

Chapter 30

The clatter of horseshoes on rock announced their arrival at the Cimarron River. Beyond the sluggishy, late-fall current, trees grew in abundance, which suited Bill Anderson just fine. More places to hide in the all-but-total darkness of a night without a moon.

Buster rode up next to him while they halted on the riverbank to look things over.

"Seems quiet enough," Buster observed.

Bill wasn't satisfied. He gave the far bank a close look, listening.

"You act real edgy, Bill," Buster said. "That bastard can't get ahead of us, hard as we been pushin' these horses. I say we get across quick."

Bill had been thinking about what had happened to Joe, Shorty, Dewey, and Sammy, for the last few hours. "I've done give up on tryin' to predict what he'll do. But once we get in the river, we're gonna ride down it maybe a mile or two. It'll make it harder for him to find where we came out. We'll look for a stretch of rock north of them alabaster caves to ride out. Can't no man track a horse on them hard rocks.''

"This ain't like you, Bill, to act worried 'bout one or two men, however many there is. We used to ride off like we was in a damn parade every time we pulled a job. Seems like we're runnin' with our tails between our legs now, an' all on account of one or two gents chasin' us.''

Bill scowled at the forests beyond the Cimarron. "Things have started to change, Buster. This land ain't empty like it was before. An' the sumbitch behind us—maybe it is two or three—has proved to be pretty damn good.''

"That ol' fort is abandoned. We could ride for it hard an' be there by daylight. No matter who's behind us, we can stand 'em off there real easy.''

"It's gettin' across this river that's got me playin' things safe. Send a couple of men down to the water ahead of us. If nobody shoots at 'em, we'll bring the money down.''

Buster turned back in the saddle, picking out less-experienced men. "Floyd, you an' Chuck ride down to the river, an' keep your rifles handy.''

Two younger members of the gang spurred their trail-weary horses past the others to ride down a rocky embankment to the water's edge. Both men approached cautiously, slowing their mounts to a walk.

Bill waited until no shots were fired at his men. "Let's go,'' he said, sending his horse downslope.

Floyd Devers turned to Chuck Mabry. Beads of sweat glistened on Floyd's face. "Looks safe enough,'' he said to his cousin from Fort Smith.

As Chuck was about to speak, a rifle cracked from

the opposite bank, accompanied by a blossom of white light from a muzzle flash.

Mabry, at the tender age of nineteen, the newest member of Bill Anderson's gang, fell off his horse like he'd been poleaxed. Floyd's horse bolted away from the shallows when it was spooked by the explosion.

Floyd was clinging to his saddlehorn when a bullet struck him in the right hip. "Yee-oow!" he cried, letting his rifle slip from his fingers. Pain like nothing he'd ever known before raced down his leg, causing him to let go of the saddle and to slide slowly off to one side.

Floyd landed in the water with a splash, thrashing about, making a terrible racket, yelling his head off about the pain.

From Bill Anderson's men, half-a-dozen guns opened up on the muzzle flash. The banging of guns rattled for several seconds more, until the shooting slowed, then stopped.

Bill turned his horse quickly to ride back behind the bank of the river, out of the line of fire.

"Goddamn!" Buster yelled, trying to calm his plunging, rearing horse. "How'd that bastard get across ahead of us?" he wondered at the top of his voice.

Bill was furious. He knew he should have sent an advance scouting party ahead to get the lay of things at the river, but with fatigue tugging at his eyelids, he'd forgotten to do it until it was too late.

He could hear Floyd thrashing about in the water, making all manner of noise. The kid, Chuck, fell down like he was dead the moment the bullet hit him.

"This don't make no sense," Bill said, when Buster

got his horse stilled. "We've been ridin' as hard as these damn horses could carry us an' he still beat us to the river."

"Give me two men," Buster said, "an' I'll ride upstream an' cross over so we can get behind him. He won't be expectin' that from us."

Bill knew men as well as he knew anything on earth. "This son of a bitch, whoever he is, has got us outguessed with every move we make."

"We can't just sit here all night, Bill."

"Wasn't aimin' to," Bill replied. "We'll swing to the east and ride hard as we can. Let's test his horse, see if he can stay up."

"He sure as hell ain't had no trouble so far," Buster said before he reined his mount around.

"Make sure you stay close to the money," Bill added in a quiet voice. "If one of our own decides to get rich while all this is goin' on, shoot him."

"I'll stand by you, Bill. Always have. But this gent we got shootin' us a few at a time is smart. You'll have to hand him that. We need to stay together. It's when we split up that he cuts some of us down."

"Numbers don't appear to make no difference to this son of a bitch," Bill answered. "Just do like I say. Stay close to the packhorses. We'll ride the riverbank for a ways an' see what he does next."

"We need to make it over to them trees, Bill," Buster told him. "Out here in the open, he's got a clear shot at us damn near every time. We'll be a helluva lot safer on the other side. We keep on this way, he's gonna bushwhack us all."

"I've got eyes, Buster, an' I don't need no help countin' the men he's killed. Start ridin'."

"Hold on a minute, Bill!" Pete Woods cried, pointing down to the river. "Listen to Floyd yonder. He's hurt real bad, an' he needs somebody to go an' fetch him outta that water."

Bill aimed a hard-eyed look at Pete. "You go fetch him out, if you want," he said. "I ain't gonna make no target out of myself. Floyd can figure his own way out."

"He's just shot in the leg!" Pete protested.

Bill had grown tired of the useless banter. "You could get shot in the head if you run down there, Pete. This was a chance every one of us took when we decided to rob them banks. Men get bullet holes in 'em sometimes when they take what ain't theirs. But if you're so damn softhearted, you ride right on down to that river an' lend Floyd a hand."

"Sure seems hard," Pete said, quieter.

"Robbin' folks of their money ain't no church picnic," Bill said.

Pete lowered his head, unwilling to challenge Bill over it any longer.

Bill rode off in the lead, and beyond the lip of the riverbank he could hear Floyd crying out for help. It reminded him of the war, when no one had been there to save all the brave soldiers from Missouri or Tennessee when they begged for assistance.

Someone near the loaded pack animals began to gag, and Bill knew it was the kid, Stormy Sommers. He ignored the sound and spoke to Buster. "High time some of the little boys learned a thing or two about robbery. If it was easy, every son of a bitch who owned a gun would take up the profession."

Buster sounded a touch worried. "Don't leave us with but nine men, Bill."

"Nine?" Bill asked, his voice rising. "You don't think nine men stack up right?"

"Whoever's doin' the shootin' at us has been real good, or real lucky today," Buster answered.

"Luck is all it is," Bill said.

Another rifle shot boomed from across the river, and Bill pulled his horse to a stop, turning his head to listen. He heard another painful cry coming from the Cimarron.

"Damn! Damn!"

It was Pete Woods's voice.

"Pete was dumb to ride down there so soon," Buster said with his head turned toward the sound. "He shoulda waited for a spell to see if things was clear."

"We don't need no careless men," Bill anounced to the men around him. "Pete wasn't thinkin' straight, or he'd've knowed to wait, like Buster said."

Stormy continued to gag, gripping his sides. Bill's nerves were on edge, and he had to do something to calm them. "Shut the hell up, Stormy, or I'll kill you myself. If you ain't got the stomach for robbin' banks, then ride the hell away from here an' do it now!" Bill's right hand was on the grips of one revolver when he said it.

"We're all gonna die," Stormy whimpered. "That feller who's follerin' us ain't no ordinary man."

Bill didn't want Stormy's fear to infect the others. He took out his Colt .44, cocked it, and fired directly at Stormy's head.

Stormy's horse bolted away from the banging noise as he went off one side of it. He landed with a grunt, falling on his back, staring up at the stars.

"Anybody else don't like the way I'm runnin' things?" Bill asked defiantly.

When not another word was said, he reined his horse to ride east, spurring his horse to a trot. He hadn't wanted to kill any more of his own men, like he'd had to do when Lee Wollard pulled that damn fool stunt inside the bank, hitting the banker so hard it knocked him out. But there were important things for men to learn if they aimed to stay outside the law, and one was when to take orders and follow them to the letter. A leader couldn't run a military outfit any other way.

Keeping his men and their precious cargo well out of rifle range from the far side of the Cimarron, Bill led his men east at a gallop, determined to make a crossing into the Nations as soon as he felt it was safe.

Smoke and Cal rode across the river, finding it shallow that time of year, until they reached the wounded outlaw, who was holding his bleeding leg on a flat rock, moaning softly. When the robber saw them coming, he threw up his hands.

"Don't shoot me no more!" he begged, showing that his hands were empty. "I give up! I swear, I do! My leg's killin' me, an' I gotta git to a doctor real soon, or I'm gonna bleed to death."

Smoke swung down beside him, holstering the Colt he held in his right hand. "It's high, your wound is," he said. "If we tie a rag around it real tight an' catch one of these loose horses, you can sit a saddle back to Dodge. Give yourself up to Marshal Wyatt Earp, an' he'll see to it you get medical attention."

"You gonna trust me like that, mister?"

"If you aren't in Dodge when we get back, I'll come lookin' for you."

"Sweet Jesus, but my leg hurts. I'll do like you say. Don't want no more of Bloody Bill or this bank robbin' business anyhow. I'm done with it for good."

Smoke glanced at the other three motionless bodies before he knelt next to the raider. He was hardly more than a kid, nearly Cal's age. "What's your name, son?" he asked, taking a faded, blue bandanna from his neck to tie around the wound.

"Floyd. Floyd Devers. I been ridin' with Bloody Bill fer a couple of years, only there never was nothin' like this. We never shot no unarmed folks, nor no women an' kids before. Made me belly sick."

"Where is Anderson headed with the money?" Smoke asked as he tied the cloth tight over Floyd's bullet wound.

"It's near this abandoned fort named Fort Supply. The army give it up years ago. There's these deep caves where we hid our horses when the law came lookin' fer us. The big one is where a fork comes in a dry riverbed. But watch out, mister, 'cause he'll have guards all 'round."

"We'll be careful," Smoke said, finishing the knot in the dark, doing it by feel. He turned to Cal. "Catch one of them horses, an' we'll put this boy on it."

Cal rode off toward a black gelding that was grazing upriver a few hundred yards. Smoke helped the young outlaw to his feet.

"You got Bloody Bill mighty worried," Floyd said, wincing when he put weight on his bad leg. "He can't figure out who'd be slick enough to slip up on us a few at a time like you two've been doin'. He figures there's just one of you. You're the same feller who tossed Homer Suggins off that roof, ain't you?"

"Never did know the dead man's name," Smoke replied.

Floyd nodded once. "I tol' my pardner Chuck we oughta cut out before we got our own selves killed. That's Chuck layin' over yonder."

"Who's the other man?" Smoke asked. "I only fired at three of you."

"That's Stormy Sommers. I saw Bill shoot him down 'cause he wouldn't stop actin' scared. Makes two of us Bill went an' killed. He shot Lee inside the bank 'cause he hit that banker too hard an' knocked him cold. Bill's been actin' crazy as hell lately."

"We'll find him and get the money back," Smoke said as Cal came up, leading the horse.

"I'll turn myself in to the Marshal just like you said, only I can't tell the Marshal who it was ordered me to do it 'less you give me your name."

"Tell him Smoke Jensen sent you, an' that I said to take you to the doctor. Just make damn sure you show up in Dodge, or I'll track you down."

"Yes, sir, Mr. Jensen. You got no worries 'bout that," Floyd said as Smoke helped him climb in the saddle seat.

Chapter 31

Four men sat huddled around a small fire, deep within a rock cavern with curious, glistening walls of solid alabaster. Bill was chewing a mouthful of jerky, washing it down with whiskey. Deeper into the cave, their horses and pack animals were hobbled and fed what little grain the gang had left in towsacks. Bags of money lay near the fire, and piles of currency, along with gleaming gold and silver coins, were stacked in neat rows. Bill watched Walter Blackwell count the money.

"More'n forty thousand so far, Bill," said Walter, a quiet, retiring man who was a remarkably good shot with a pistol.

"We're rich," Bill said, cocking an ear toward the entrance into the cavern where Buster, Billy Riley, and Cletus Miller were standing guard. "Best of all, we gave that sneaky bastard the slip, so our troubles're over. He'll never find us here. Hell, the cavalry an' dozens of U.S. Marshals from Fort Smith've been ridin' past these caves for years. Hardly nobody knows they're here. We lay low for a little while, maybe five or six weeks, an' then we ride out free as birds.'' He gave Walter a stare. "Keep on countin'. You ain't hardly more'n half done. There's gonna be sixty thousand dollars, the way I figure.''

Tad Younger, a cousin to Cole and his famous outlaw bunch, was frowning. "Sure do hope whoever's been behind us don't show up. He's made a habit out of showin' up when he ain't supposed to.''

Bill wagged his head. "We lost him. Can't no Indian or white man find a horse's tracks where we just rode. Slabs of rock don't leave no horse sign.''

"Here's ten thousand more," Walter said, adding a stack of banknotes to the counted money.

Bill grinned. "Maybe there's gonna be seventy thousand after all. . . .'' He abruptly ended his remark when a series of loud explosions came from the mouth of the cave.

Bill leapt to his feet, clawing both six-guns from his holsters, shattering the bottle of whiskey he'd been holding.

A scream of agony came from the tunnel, followed by a much louder bellowing string of cusswords that was Buster Young's voice.

Bill took off in a run for the entrance, leveling his pistols in front of him, almost tripping in the dark. Then two more heavy gun blasts sounded, and he recognized Cletus Miller's cry of pain.

Racing up to the opening, caught in a wild fury beyond his control when he knew the man who'd been tracking them had showed up at the cave in spite of all his precautions, he stopped when he saw three dark shapes lying behind a pile of boulders where his guards had been hiding. Big Buster Young was writhing back and forth, holding his belly, gasping for air, his face twisted in a grimace.

Billy Riley lay face down on the rocks in a pool of blood, and he wasn't moving. Cletus sat against a big stone, a shotgun resting in his lap, arms dangling limply at his sides while his mouth hung open, drooling blood on his shirt.

And when Bill saw this—all three of his men dead or dying from three well-placed shots—he tasted fear for the first time in his life. Gazing out at the darkness, where only dim light from the stars showed any detail of his surroundings, something inside him stirred— a knot of terror forming in his chest that had never been there before. And he noticed that the hands holding his pistols were shaking so badly that he knew his aim would be way off target . . . if he could find anything to shoot at.

"Come on out, Anderson!" a deep voice shouted. "Got you cornered! There ain't gonna be no escape!"

Bill crouched down. In spite of the night chill, sweat poured from his hatband into his eyes. "You're gonna have to kill us!" he yelled back. "You ain't takin' none of us alive!"

"Suits the hell outta me!" the voice answered.

Bill heard soft footsteps coming up behind him. He didn't bother to turn around to see who it was. "Get your rifles," he said in whisper. "We'll gather up the money an' shoot our way out of here."

"He'll kill us!" Walter Blackwell said.

"Like hell he will," Bill snapped. "Just do like I say, an' get rifles ready. Tell the others to saddle our horses an' put the money on them packsaddles."

Walter, always soft-spoken, said, "I've never disobeyed an order from you, Bill. But this is different.

It'll be like we killed ourselves if we try to ride out. Whoever that feller is, he don't miss."

Bill's fear turned to anger. "Shut the hell up, Walter, an' do what I ordered!"

"I won't do it," Walter said very quietly.

Bill turned an angry glance over his shoulder, staring up at Walter's dark shape standing right behind him. "You what?" he demanded.

Bill heard a soft click while Walter spoke. "I won't let you get the rest of us killed," he whispered.

The sudden realization of what Walter meant to do struck Bill Anderson a split second before the hammer fell on a Mason Colt .44/.40 conversion. A roar filled the cave mouth, and Bill's ears, when it felt like a sledgehammer had hit him squarely in the middle of his forehead.

He was slammed against a cavern wall, with his ears ringing, until the noise made by the gunshot died away. Then he heard Walter shout from the entrance.

"I just shot Bloody Bill! Don't shoot at us no more! We give up! You can have the money, only don't kill no more of us! We're done runnin' from you!"

Bill saw two more dim shapes walk outside the cave behind Walter. All three had their hands in the air. Someone else, a voice he didn't recognize, said, "Please don't shoot. We ain't carryin' guns, an' Bill Anderson's dead!"

Bill wondered if he could be dying. He couldn't move his arms to touch the painful place in the center of his head. A growing weakness rendered him helpless, yet he was still listening when he heard Walter ask, "We sure have been curious 'bout who you was, mister. Never had nobody on our trail so hot an' heavy before this."

"Smoke Jensen," a coarse voice said from farther

away. "I don't see how names make any difference now. . . ."

Bill's eyelids fluttered shut. He found a dream creeping up on him, a recollection of the war, back when he was with the best of them all, William Quantrill. Quantrill and his soldiers were invincible then. Nobody ever rode them down.

He saw burning farmhouses and heard women and children screaming when the flames consumed them. He heard the pop of cap and ball pistols and the louder crack of muskets when they led a raid on an unprotected farm.

Then he saw another scene, the terrible, stinking trenches at Franklin, Tennessee, when the Army of Tennessee was being commanded by General John Bell Hood from Texas, one of the bravest men ever to lead a battle charge. Eight thousand Confederates died at Franklin, with twice that many wounded who would die later from gangrene, dysentery, and infection. Death always seemed to ride with the Confederate Army, and Bill Anderson had been proud to be one who had lived through it all.

But an inner voice told him he was dying, although he had some satisfaction: He was dying a rich man.

A black thought struck him, as he recalled what had happened as the shooting had started in front of the cave. Walter, one of his own men, had refused a direct order and betrayed him with a bullet to the head. He never would have guessed it from Walter.

He felt sleepy, yet he still wondered about this man named Smoke Jensen. Just who the hell was he? And how could he be so clever as a manhunter?

Bill wished that Smoke Jensen had been riding with them when they had hit the banks in Dodge. That was the reason this robbery failed—because he couldn't trust his own men to get the job done.

At last, he slipped away into a dreamless sleep.

"Tie their hands real good," Smoke told Cal, keeping a Colt aimed at the three survivors of the Dodge City raid. "Then we'll go in the cave an' fetch the money out."

Cal was busy tying knots with cut strips of Smoke's lariat rope. "Sure was unusual that one of his own men went an' shot him for us," Cal said.

One man spoke. "We got tired of followin' stupid orders. I shot him. Can't say as I'm one bit sorry."

"Maybe the judge'll go light on you at your trial," Smoke said.

"I'm hopin' he will."

Another outlaw asked a question. "Where'd you learn to track a man like you been doin' all day an' tonight?"

"From an old mountain man up in the High Lonesome of Colorado Territory."

"Never saw nothin' like it before, mister. You killed some mighty tough men since we came to Dodge."

"Sometimes being tough isn't enough," Smoke told him as Cal finished the last knot on an outlaw's wrists. "Now walk in front of me, boys, while we go down for that money. Don't reckon I have to warn none of you that if you try anything, I'll kill you so quick, you won't have time to blink."

"You won't git no more trouble out of us," one man said as they turned for the mouth of the cavern with their hands tied.

As Smoke walked past Bloody Bill Anderson, he gave the old Confederate a passing glance. Anderson had met his end at the hands of a Judas, and somehow it seemed fitting.

"What about these here bodies?" Cal asked as they went down into a dark tunnel. "We gonna bury 'em?"

"Leave 'em," Smoke replied. "The buzzards an' coyotes'll scatter their remains. I'd give an honest man a decent burial, but I never was inclined to dig graves for them that don't have it coming."

When Smoke and the others were out of sight, Bill Anderson's eyes blinked open briefly.

Their return to Dodge City with three prisoners and four pack animals loaded with money ended a long funeral procession on its way out to the city cemetery. Marshal Earp and Pearlie rode out on the prairie south of town at a gallop to meet them.

Earp looked at the three packhorses and the mule first, a surprised expression on his face. "You got all the money back?" he asked. "Where's Anderson and the rest of his gang?"

"Had to kill a few," Smoke replied.

"One of Anderson's own men shot him," Cal said. "We had 'em trapped inside this cave, an' there wasn't no way out. Anderson still wanted a fight, until this feller over on the left settled it hisself by shootin' Bloody Bill in the head."

"One of 'em came to town with a hole in his leg to give himself up," Earp said. "He told us a little about what had happened on their way to the river." Earp shook his head and gave Smoke a one-sided grin. "You're every bit as good with a gun as we heard you were, Mr. Jensen. Hard to believe you came back with our money . . . just the two of you."

Pearlie was giving Cal a close inspection. "I reckon

this young 'un ain't got no scratches on him that'll upset Miz Jensen when we git back.''

"Cal was a big help," Smoke said, before his mate could speak. "He showed a lot of nerve."

"It wasn't his nerves I was worried 'bout," Pearlie said, and then his face turned red when he realized he had admitted to worrying about Cal. "Not that I was really all *that* worried 'bout him."

"Let's get this money back in the vaults," Smoke said to Earp. "Then me an' Cal need a few hours of shut-eye before I finish that cattle deal with Mr. Crawford Long. It's high time we got back to our home range, where things are quieter."

Chapter 32

Bill awakened slowly. He found Buster Young sitting beside him. Buster's belly was leaking blood, and despite his great size, he seemed small, childlike, and afraid.

"I'm dyin', Bill," Buster said.

It required a moment for Bill's head to clear. He gave big Buster a vacant stare.

"You hear me, Bill?"

"I . . . hear . . . you."

"I'm gutshot. Worst way to die there is."

"What . . . happened to . . . my head?"

"Walter shot you, only the slug grazed across the top of your skull. Looks like you're gonna live, only you're bleedin' bad as I am."

Bill raised an arm and touched his scalp tenderly. A slice of skin and hair went all the way to the bone. "I don't remember much."

"There ain't but one horse," Buster whispered,

twisting his face with pain. "If I can git to a doctor. . . ."

"One horse?"

"Down yonder, grazin' on short grass."

"I need it," Bill said.

"So do I, Bill. I'm gonna die 'less some sawbones can stop this blood."

"One horse can't . . . carry the both of us."

Buster appeared to be near passing out. Bill tried to focus his eyes. A sorrel wearing a saddle, trailing its reins, grazed a few hundred yards from the cave.

"I can go fetch help," Bill said.

Buster's head wagged. "You won't come back for me, Bill. I know you."

Bill's hand moved to a pistol that was lying on the rock near his left leg. His choice seemed easy, crystal clear. "Then I'm gonna have to take the horse," he said, wrapping his palm around the butt of the Colt.

Buster looked up at him. "You'd leave me here to die?"

"No choice," Bill told him, lifting the .44, cocking it with a trembling thumb. "Sorry, Buster. Wish it didn't have to be this way."

The sharp report of a gun echoed up and down the dry riverbed. Buster's head was driven back against the rock where he was sitting. A crimson splash spread across the alabaster stone like a ball of fire.

Buster relaxed his grip on his belly. His thick arms fell to his sides.

Bill sleeved blood from his eyes, his head throbbing with unimaginable pain, then he came unsteadily to his feet while his head cleared.

"To hell with you, Buster," he said, hoarse, strangled. "I got to get to a doctor myself."

Staggering, almost falling, he made his way slowly to the red sorrel gelding and caught its reins.

After a moment of rest he managed to pull himself across the saddle.

He rode off, leaving a trail of blood spots on the rock at the bottom of the dry river.

Chapter 33

Gray clouds cloaked the mountaintops. Spits of light snow came sweeping down mountain valleys. Bundled in their coats, Smoke, Cal, and Pearlie sighted the ranch house, and when they did, Cal let out a yell.

"Yahoo! Sure feels good to be home."

Pearlie gave the sky a look. "We's just gittin' here ahead of a powerful storm. My ol' bunk sure is gonna feel nice an' warm tonight."

Smoke couldn't suppress a grin when he saw the house—the barns and corrals, all the product of his own labors, his and Sally's. And he couldn't remember when he had longed to see Sally so badly. This trip had been about the worst when it came to missing her.

He noticed that Johnny North had put plenty of hay out in the pens for cattle and horses. Everything looked like it was in order.

"It does feel good to set eyes on this place again," Smoke said, when the stud's strides lengthened to a faster trot. It was ready to be back in its own stall after weeks of hard miles and wet saddle blankets.

A figure came out on the porch of the ranch house, and Smoke recognized Sally at once. He touched his heels to the Palouse's ribs and said, "I've got a kiss or two to deliver to that woman yonder, not to mention a saddlebag full of money. See you boys at the supper table."

He let the stud strike a gallop toward the front porch, and even from a distance, he saw the smile on Sally's face.

Smoke pulled the stud to a halt at the porch rail and swung down with his saddlebags, a grin crinkling his sun-weathered face before he reached the porch steps.

"Howdy, stranger," Sally said, beaming, opening her arms to him.

He went into her embrace, dropping the saddle-bags on the floor. Then he wrapped his arms around her and bent down to give her a lingering kiss, feeling the warmth of her body come through the front of his shirt where his mackinaw was unbuttoned.

"Damn, but it's good to see you, woman," he said, staring into her eyes.

"I've missed you so much, Smoke."

"You wouldn't believe me if I told you how much I've missed you. This time it was different, for some reason or other. I got a bad case of lonely while I was gone."

"We can make up for lost time tonight," she said, smiling coyly, and he knew what she meant.

"Howdy, Miz Jensen!" Cal shouted as he rode past the house toward the barns at a steady trot.

"Howdy-do, Miz Jensen," Pearlie cried, tipping his battered, felt hat politely.

"Hello, boys," she said. "As soon as you've put your horses away I've got two apple pies on the kitchen table. I made them yesterday. I'll be warming them up for you."

"Lordy, Lordy!" Pearlie exclaimed, grinning from ear to ear. "Did you hear that, young 'un? Two apple pies. One's fer me, an' you gotta share the other with the bossman."

"Like heck I do!" Cal replied, wearing his own wide grin. "I always git my very own pie. Just ask Miz Jensen if that ain't so."

Pearlie bent down when he rode up to the stud, gathering the Palouse's reins. "I'll feed him good an' rub him down, boss, only don't let that boy with the tapeworm git too much apple pie afore I git there."

"I'll make sure we save you plenty," Sally said, turning back to Smoke. "Now tell me how the steers did, and if you had any difficulties along the way. Come inside. I've got coffee on the stove."

He followed her through the front door, to a warm, familiar room and a fireplace full of flaming wood, which was throwing off wonderful heat. "The steers trailed better than I ever expected," he said as she led him into the kitchen. "And they fetched a price I'd never've dreamed they'd bring." He placed the saddlebags on the kitchen table, pointing to them. "There's better'n six thousand dollars. A buyer came early, and he paid my price quick as I could ask it."

"Why, that's almost twenty dollars a head," Sally exclaimed as she poured him coffee.

"That's exactly what it was ... twenty a head for

three hundred and seven steers. Just over six thousand dollars for a crossbred yearling calf crop. I'd say we had a mighty good year this year."

She gave him his coffee and kissed his cheek, still beaming after she heard the cow price. "It'll get better every year from now on, Smoke," she said. "This spring's calves already look heavier. We'll be showin' a nice profit next fall, too."

"I knew you'd be happy," he said, warming his insides with the contents of his cup before he sweetened it with brown sugar. "You were right about a Hereford making a good cross with our longhorns, but then you claim to be right about everything."

She sat down beside him and took one of his callused hands in her own. "I was right about you, wasn't I? How many women would have taken a chance by marrying a gunfighter like the man you were when we met?"

He sipped more coffee, grinning behind the lip of his cup. "I knew it when I met my match. Only a fool takes on a contest he knows he can't win."

Her face darkened a little. "Was there any difficulty on the way? Any trouble?"

Smoke knew he couldn't lie to her—she could read his mind any time she wanted. "We ran across a few renegade Osages on the way to Dodge."

She searched his eyes. "There's more, isn't there?"

"A little. Both banks got robbed while we were in town, and I lent the City Marshal a hand gettin' the money back, seein' as some of it was our money, money for our steers."

"You got in a gunfight, didn't you?"

He shrugged. "Some might call it that."

"Oh, Smoke. When will you ever stop?"

"I didn't have a choice, Sally. Several innocent citizens of Dodge City were wounded or killed, including women and kids. You know I can't turn my back on that sort of thing."

She let out a sigh. "I suppose not. I don't suppose you ever will."

He thought about it. "This time, I really didn't have a way out."

"And you killed some men," she said—a statement and not a question.

"A few. What's in a number anyway?"

"I suppose I don't really want to know, do I?"

"It'd be better if you didn't. Now, open those saddlebags and take a look at all that pretty money. The only thing on this earth that's any prettier right now is you."

Sally smiled, unbuckling a strap over one of the saddlebags. She pulled out a canvas bag with The Cattlemans Bank printed on it.

When she opened the sack, her eyes rounded. "This is an awful lot of money!" she said. "It'll buy everything we need, with plenty to spare." She pulled bundles of wrapped currency out of the bag and placed them in front of her on the tabletop.

But then she ignored the money to look at him, and he knew that look on her face. "I wouldn't trade all the money in the world for you, Smoke Jensen. That's why I keep hopin' that one of these days, when you leave the ranch, you'll leave yer guns at home."

"Maybe that time ain't far off," he said. "Things are changin' in this part of the West. But until they do, I'll keep on carryin' my guns. I won't let anybody take what's rightfully ours. We worked hard to build this ranch an' stock it with the best animals we could find. What we make is ours to keep."

"I know," she said softly, squeezing his hand. "And I know I can't change that part of you that won't let you pass up a wrong. Maybe that's a part of why I love you, only I can't help it if I worry."

They were interrupted when Cal and Pearlie came stomping through the back door. Cal was first to eye the pair of apple pies, and he promptly licked his lips.

"Prettiest sight I ever saw, one of your apple pies," he said. "That one on the left's mine, Miz Jensen, if you've got no objections."

"Ain't fair," Pearlie complained, hanging his hat on a peg near the door. "One cowboy don't git a whole pie to eat all by hisself."

Sally got up to bring plates to the table. "Cal's a growing boy, Pearlie," she said, smiling. Let him eat as much as he wants. I've got bearclaws under that linen over on the drainboard. There's plenty to go around."

Pearlie gave Cal a satisfied smirk. "See there, young 'un. Miz Jensen made them bearclaws fer me. Go ahead an' stuff yerself with pie, so you'll grow. I hope you bust wide open at the belly, so we have to haul you to town in the wagon to see the doctor. I think you'd look good with stitches across yer middle. Maybe the doc can put one of them newfangle zippers in yer belly so's we can open you up afore you bust open every time you sit down to eat."

Smoke accepted his slice of pie with a nod, sipping coffee, thinking how lucky he was to have Sally and good men like Cal and Pearlie and Johnny around him. Things hadn't always been this good for Kirby

Jensen—not in the beginning, not until he changed his ways.

Then he reckoned he hadn't played much part in the changes. Sally deserved the credit. He found himself looking forward to sundown, when he could crawl into bed beside her and forget about the bloodshed in Kansas.

WILLIAM W. JOHNSTONE
THE PREACHER SERIES

THE FIRST MOUNTAIN MAN   (0-8217-5510-2, $4.99/$6.50)
In the savage wilderness of America's untamed West, a wagon train
on the Oregon trail must survive thieving renegades and savage Indians. A legend known as Preacher is the only mountain man with
enough skills to get these pilgrims through safely.

BLOOD ON THE DIVIDE (#2)   (0-8217-5511-0, $4.99/$6.50)
Stranded on the Continental Divide, Preacher and his wagon train
seem eaasy targets to the vicious Pardee brothers and the savage Utes,
but it is Preacher who waits to strike.

ABSAROKA AMBUSH (#3)   (0-8217-5538-2, $4.99/$6.50)
Preacher goes up against scavenger Vic Bedell and his gang of cutthroats to save a hundred and fifty ladies from captivity.

FORTY GUNS WEST (#4)   (0-8217-5509-9, $4.99/$6.50)
A family reunion leads Preacher back to his homestead . . . and drops
a price on his head. Now he must defend himself from headhunters
who want to use him for target practice.

CHEYENNE CHALLENGE (#5)   (0-8217-5607-9, $4.99/$6.50)
Preacher dealt with gun-crazed Ezra Pease ten years ago, but Pease
is back for a final confrontation, this time leading Preacher and some
old friends into an all-out Indian war.

PREACHER AND THE
MOUNTAIN CAESAR (#6)   (0-8217-5636-2, $4.99/$6.50)
Preacher thought he had seen it all, until he was opposite Nova Roma
and the oddest, most dangerous army. With only a small band of
mountain men to survive, his skills are put to the test.

BLACKFOOT MESSIAH (#7)   (0-8217-5232-4, $4.99/$6.50)
Promised victory by their prophet, Blackfoot Indians rage war against
the white man. Preacher, with a loyal Cheyenne as his guide, must
unmask the Messiah to win this war.

*Available wherever paperbacks are sold, or order direct from the
Publisher. Send cover price plus 50¢ per copy for mailing and
handling to Kensington Publishing Corp., Consumer Orders,
or call (toll free) 888-345-BOOK, to place your order using
Mastercard or Visa. Residents of New York and Tennessee
must include sales tax. DO NOT SEND CASH.*

WILLIAM W. JOHNSTONE
THE ASHES SERIES

WILLIAM W. JOHNSTONE
THE BLOOD BOND SERIES

BLOOD BOND   (0-8217-2724-0, $3.95/$4.95)

BLOOD BOND: BROTHERHOOD OF THE GUN (#2)
           (0-8217-3044-4, $3.95/$4.95)

BLOOD BOND: SAN ANGELO SHOWDOWN (#7)
           (0-8217-4466-6, $3.99/$4.99)

WILLIAM W. JOHNSTONE
THE EAGLE SERIES

EYES OF EAGLES (#1)   (0-8217-4285-X, $4.99/$5.99)
Raised by the Shawnee Indians, Jamie Ian MacCallister made
the perfect scout for Santa Ana's Mexican army, which was
fighting against rebel Texans. What lay ahead was the Alamo.

DREAMS OF EAGLES (#2)   (0-8217-4619-7, $4.99/$5.99)
MacCallister joins up with famed frontiersman Kit Carson on
the first U.S. expedition from Missouri to the wide Pacific.

TALONS OF EAGLES (#3)   (0-7860-0249-2, $5.99/$6.99)
With his sons on opposing sides in the Civil War, MacCallister
fights two battles—North against South and father against
son—as he leads the Confederate Marauders from Georgia to
Tennessee (Bull Run to Shiloh).

SCREAM OF EAGLES (#4)   (0-7860-0447-9, $5.99/$7.50)
His wife has been brutally murdered at the hands of the wild
Miles Nelson gang. Out for revenge, MacCallister's search for
justice leads him to Little Big Horn.

RAGE OF EAGLES (#5)   (0-7860-0507-6, $5.99/$7.50)
Falcon MacCallister roams the West searching for the man who
ambushed his father. The pursuit of his father's killers takes
him from Wyoming's Johnson County War to Montana.

*Available wherever paperbacks are sold, or order direct from the
Publisher. Send cover price plus 50¢ per copy for mailing and
handling to Kensington Publishing Corp., Consumer Orders,
or call (toll free) 888-345-BOOK, to place your order using
Mastercard or Visa. Residents of New York and Tennessee
must include sales tax. DO NOT SEND CASH.*

FICTION BY WILLIAM W. JOHNSTONE